ALSO BY GEOFF NICHOLSON

FICTION

Gravity's Volkswagen

The Hollywood Dodo

Bedlam Burning

Female Ruins

Flesh Guitar

Bleeding London

Footsucker

Everything and More

Still Life with Volkswagens

The Errol Flynn Novel

The Food Chain

Hunters and Gatherers

What We Did on Our Holidays

A Knot Garden

Street Sleeper

NONFICTION

Big Noises

Walking in Ruins

The Lost Art of Walking

Sex Collectors

Day Trips to the Desert

THE CITY UNDER THE SKIN

THE CITY UNDER THE SKIN

GEOFF NICHOLSON

FARRAR, STRAUS AND GIROUX   NEW YORK

Farrar, Straus and Giroux
18 West 18th Street, New York 10011

Library of Congress Cataloging-in-Publication Data
Nicholson, Geoff, 1953–
    The city under the skin : a novel / Geoff Nicholson.
        pages   cm
    ISBN 978-0-374-16904-6 (hardback) — ISBN 978-1-4299-5485-3 (ebook)
    1. Kidnapping—Fiction.   I. Title.

PR6064.I225 C58 2014
823'.914—dc23

                                                              2013038778

Designed by Jonathan D. Lippincott

Farrar, Straus and Giroux books may be purchased for educational, business,
or promotional use. For information on bulk purchases, please contact the
Macmillan Corporate and Premium Sales Department at 1-800-221-7945,
extension 5442, or write to specialmarkets@macmillan.com.

www.fsgbooks.com
www.twitter.com/fsgbooks · www.facebook.com/fsgbooks

1   3   5   7   9   10   8   6   4   2

"Now when I was a little chap I had a passion for maps . . . At that time there were many blank spaces on the earth, and when I saw one that looked particularly inviting on a map (but they all look that) I would put my finger on it and say, When I grow up I will go there."　　　　　—Joseph Conrad, *Heart of Darkness*

THE CITY
UNDER
THE SKIN

1. UNDERGROUND

The old man was walking to his car. He was dapper, sedate, serious, wearing a dark navy blazer, a plume of silver handkerchief rising from his breast pocket. His hair, similarly silver, glinted in the lights of the underground parking lot. There was only the slightest hesitancy in his step, and although he carried a walking cane—lacquered mahogany with a silver head in the shape of a globe—it might well have been just for show.

Another man stood in the shadow of a broad concrete pillar. He was a big man, but there was something compacted about him, so that his considerable size and weight didn't suggest fatness but a concentration of flesh and energy. His face was flat, and carved into frown lines. His eyes were grave and sly. His name was Wrobleski. He watched the old man as he approached his car and produced the key. Wrobleski smoothed down his jacket. Some guys liked to put on special gear when they worked; wraparound shades, scarves, black kid gloves, but Wrobleski was not "some guy." He preferred to wear a good suit—though not too good, given the task ahead.

The old man matched his vehicle: it was Wrobleski's experience that they always did. They both looked sleek, polished, well-appointed, but maybe a little sluggish. Wrobleski stepped out of the shadow, hands by his sides, his face heavy but open, and he walked over to the old man.

"Nice ride," he said, nodding toward the car.

The old man looked just a little surprised to find someone suddenly standing so close to him. He'd assumed he was alone. Even so, he was unruffled. He nodded back in agreement. Yes, it was a nice ride.

"What kind of mileage do you get from this thing?"

"I have no idea," the old man said suavely, demonstrating that he didn't have to care about such things.

"Right," said Wrobleski, "you're my kind of guy."

"I doubt that," said the old man; and then, "Do I know you?"

"My name's Wrobleski."

The old man did his best not to react, though that wasn't easy. A slight stiffening of his bottom lip was all that showed.

"Really?" he said. "Wrobleski?"

"You've heard of me."

"Yes, but I thought you were just an ugly rumor."

"If only."

"And you're here to kill me?"

"Very good. It's easier if we both know what's going on."

"I don't think so," the old man said calmly. "I think you've made a mistake."

"I really don't make mistakes."

The old man's eyes skimmed around him, from recessed shadow to bright burns of artificial light. Both men knew there was nothing to be seen, no escape routes, no panic buttons, no Good Samaritans. The security cameras had been put out of commission.

"Why exactly?" the old man said.

"Because I'm being paid to."

"That's no answer."

It would have to do. Wrobleski wondered if the old man was going to make a run for it: some of these old guys prided themselves on being fit. He also wondered if he might have a gun on him: some of them liked to think they could defend themselves. They were always wrong about that. But by then Wrobleski had his own gun in his hand and he fired it into the old man's right leg. The draped flannel of the pants and the flesh beneath splashed open and the victim sank to one knee.

"Oh good God," the old man said quietly, and he grabbed his injured leg with one hand, his chest with the other. Wrobleski wondered if he might be having a heart attack. Well, wouldn't that be a joke?

The old man didn't have the strength to remain kneeling: he fell over onto his side, gasping for air.

"Couldn't you do it 'execution style'?" he sneered gamely.

"But where's the sport in that?" said Wrobleski.

He fired again, into the other leg. The impact straightened the old man out, left him lying horizontally, legs apart, both arms now clutched to his torso. His car key was lying on the ground a couple of feet away, and Wrobleski picked it up and unlocked the car. He reached inside, popped open the trunk, then scooped up the wounded man and folded him into the trunk, as if he were a ventriloquist's dummy. It was easy: there was plenty of room in there. It could have been designed for it. He slammed the lid shut.

"You all right in there?" Wrobleski yelled.

The voice from inside said something that answered the question, however unintelligibly. Wrobleski only needed to know that the old man was still breathing, still able to feel.

He got in the driver's seat, started the car, revved the engine just a little, selected reverse, then floored the accelerator, so that the vehicle shot backward at speed, across to the wall on the other side of the parking lot. The trunk slammed into the pale, rubber-streaked concrete. Wrobleski was pretty sure that once would be enough, but he did it again anyway, just to be sure. Then he got out, surveyed the damage, the crushing and crumpling of the car's bodywork, which indicated similar damage to the old man.

Wrobleski gave no signal, made no phone call, but precisely as arranged and scheduled, a tow truck lurched down the ramp from the parking level above and positioned itself in front of the damaged car. A young, long-limbed black man in indigo overalls levered himself out of the cab and walked languidly to the back of the truck, where he began hooking up the old man's car.

"Thank you, Akim," Wrobleski said to the driver with exaggerated formality; then added, "It's good to see a man who believes in the dignity of labor."

Wrobleski scrutinized the area where he'd driven the car into the wall. There were various liquids smeared across the concrete floor, pools and rivulets, forming a pattern, a not quite random design, that to a certain kind of eye might look like the map of some undiscovered country. Satisfied that none of the liquids were blood, he allowed himself a small flicker of pride at a job well done.

2. WHAT THE SOCIAL WORKER SAID

She said, "This is a rather unconventional living arrangement you have here, Mr. Moore."

"Thanks," said Billy Moore, and he gave her a smile that he knew in most circumstances would be read as charming. He understood that he had a good face: trustworthy to a degree; pale, strong, hard-edged; the face of a tough guy but a decent one. He was also wearing an unfamiliar, uncharacteristic, brand-new white shirt, so fresh out of the pack that the folds still showed. The scarlet tie he wore with it felt like a noose. He wondered if the woman was trained to notice things like that, if she could tell he was a man who normally wore a beautifully scuffed leather jacket.

"I didn't necessarily mean it as a compliment," said the social worker.

"I didn't really take it as one," said Billy. "I was being flippant."

The social worker, Mrs. Janet Marcus ("Call me Jan"), was a large, well-padded woman on the lower slopes of middle age. She seemed, worked hard at seeming, warm, sympathetic, perhaps even motherly, but she sounded less than warm or sympathetic when she said, "It's probably better not to be flippant in the current circumstances, Mr. Moore."

"Right. I guess I'm nervous."

"There's no need to be."

"Isn't there? You're here to check on my parenting skills. You've got the power to take my daughter away from me. That makes me nervous."

"All right, I can understand that. So let's discuss this unconventional living arrangement."

They were standing in a parking lot on the edge of downtown, at the corner of Hope Street and Tenth. In front of them was a long, low trailer, a mobile home, old, a minor classic, humped rather than streamlined, its outer walls paneled in eye-popping blue and yellow, with a striped aluminum awning overhanging its porthole-shaped windows.

"You're living in a trailer in a parking lot, Mr. Moore."

"Well, I do own the parking lot."

"You do?"

"Sure. This is what I do. I'm in the parking business now."

"That's your job?"

"My career. My passion, Mrs. Marcus. My old life's behind me. I'm here to serve the people who need somewhere to park."

He said it jauntily, though it wasn't entirely a joke. The social worker nodded noncommittally but not dismissively.

"And the trailer?"

"It's not just a trailer," Billy Moore said. "It's a Lofgren Colonist."

"Is that good?"

"Well, it's not as good as an Airstream, but it has its fans. Come on in, take a look around."

Dutifully she followed him up a couple of steps, through the low doorway, into a brightly colored though dimly lit blob of space.

"This is the living room, the famous Lofgren Luxury-Look interior," said Billy. "This is the dinette, the step-saving kitchen, the patented Thermograce windows. The full-size bathroom is through there."

"It seems a little poky."

"Feels like the wide-open spaces to me."

"And there are two bedrooms?"

"Sure."

"One for you, one for your daughter?"

"Oh no," said Billy, "she has her own place."

"Excuse me?"

Billy Moore pulled back the bamboo-patterned drape from a Thermograce window to reveal a view of another trailer, just a few yards behind this one, similar in most respects but scaled down, only half its length.

"Your daughter has her own trailer?"

"It's a Lofgren Scamp," said Billy. "The budget model. Carla's in there right now."

"Let's go see her," said the social worker.

"Sure."

Billy Moore opened the rear door and took the few steps necessary to get from one trailer to the other. With some ceremony he tapped on the glass of the small trailer's window, and a moment later Carla Moore, Billy's twelve-year-old daughter, appeared. She was wearing a school uniform, had her long black hair in a ponytail, glasses perched uncertainly on the end of her nose. She was holding a weighty math textbook, her thumb lodged inside to keep her place.

"Come on in," said Carla brightly.

Billy let the social worker go first. She stepped inside, looked around at the fold-down desk with the laptop, at the well-stocked bookshelf, at a vase of flowers, some fringed scatter cushions, at a large cuddly koala bear perched on top of the mini refrigerator. There was a plate of oatmeal cookies and some freshly made peppermint tea, and classical music played in the background, its volume pitched perfectly between the audible and the unobtrusive.

"That's Bach," the social worker said.

"Yes, it is," said Carla. "Are you a fan?"

Mrs. Marcus surveyed the space again, more slowly this time.

"This," she said, "this is quite lovely."

"Isn't it?" said Carla.

The social worker sat down carefully, helped herself to tea and cookies: that occupied her for a while. At last she turned to Billy, crumbs still dusting the corners of her mouth, and inquired, "So how is Carla's . . . condition? You'll have to remind me of the name, I'm afraid."

Carla was quite capable of describing her own condition. "Dermatographia," she said.

Carla had already pushed her right sleeve up and was drawing on her bare arm with the end of a key. She drew a heart and a peace symbol. On healthy skin a brief white impression would have been left behind, fading and disappearing within seconds. On Carla's arm, however, the marks showed red, and a few seconds later cherry-colored wheals appeared in the exact shape of the lines she'd drawn.

"Dermatographia," she repeated. "It's exactly what it sounds like. 'Derma' means skin. 'Graphia' means writing: skin writing. The classic medical photographs always show a patient who's had someone 'write' on them with the wrong end of a pencil, so that the word 'dermatographia' appears."

Mrs. Marcus looked at the girl's arm, tried to appear sympathetic and understanding, though she feared she might be gawking inappropriately.

Carla continued, "The skin cells become oversensitive to what they call 'minor trauma,' like scratching," she explained. "When you touch the skin, the cells release chemicals called histamines. They're what cause the redness. But really, it's no big deal."

"Does it hurt?" the social worker asked.

"No. It itches sometimes, but it's not really painful. And it never lasts very long, and in any case, the doctor says I'll probably grow out of it."

"It must be a bit of a problem at school, yes?" said Mrs. Marcus.

Carla shrugged. "One of them," she said.

"I hear there are worse problems in schools," Billy Moore said, hoping he sounded intelligent. "There are worse problems everywhere."

Half an hour later he was able to escort a satisfied Mrs. Marcus off the premises. She told him she was impressed by what she'd seen. If standards were maintained, if there were no "issues," as long as Carla's "condition" didn't deteriorate, and as long as he didn't break the terms of his probation, she saw no reason why his daughter shouldn't continue to live with him, at least until his ex-wife was out of rehab, when the situation might have to be reassessed. For his part, Billy Moore told her that if she ever needed some good, secure downtown parking, there would always be a spot waiting for her.

He waved her off and returned to Carla's Lofgren Scamp, by which time his daughter had torn off the school uniform, thrown aside the nonfunctional glasses, and turned off the music. She had already opened a can of beer for her dad, which she now handed to him.

"The Bach was going a bit far," said Billy.

"What?" said Carla. "You think subtlety's going to get us anywhere in this world?"

"Okay, probably not."

"Just as well she didn't see my other arm," said Carla.

She pushed up her left sleeve to reveal, on her skin, a hastily drawn, and now faded but quite distinct, skull and crossbones.

"Aren't I a pistol?" said Carla.

"That's one of the things you are," said Billy.

"And as a matter of fact," Carla added, "I thought the shirt and tie looked pretty sharp."

3. OVER

Something is over: something has stopped. Not the pain, that's still completely with her, but for now there are no new shocks to the flesh. The process is finished, the damage has been done, though she can't tell the extent or even the precise nature of what has just happened to her.

She was walking home, and yes, it was late, and yes, she'd been at a party, and no, she wasn't completely clean and sober, and she was wearing heels, and she certainly knew the risks in this, or any other, part of the city. Perhaps she was trying to test herself, prove something about her toughness, her self-reliance, her ability to shrug off the all too obvious dangers, but when the moment came, toughness and self-reliance had nothing to do with it.

She had no sense that anything bad was about to happen. He was on her before she knew it. He came at her silently from behind and she never saw him, but she had the sense of a man who was strong rather than big, fiercely purposeful but not frenzied. He knocked her to the ground, pressed her down. She started to scream, not so much because she was afraid (though she was), but because she thought *he* might be and the screaming would scare him off, but it didn't, and already there was something being placed over her head, a bag, a fetish hood made of leather, no openings for eyes or mouth, but with a small rubber valve to breathe through. Apparently he wanted her alive, at least for the time being. The smell of cowhide and somebody else's sweat and saliva filled her nostrils.

She squirmed, tried to roll away, kicking as she moved, but he was ready for that too. He seemed skilled, practiced, keeping her immobile as he tied her wrists and ankles. He didn't speak, didn't threaten her, didn't press a weapon to her head or throat, didn't need to.

She assumed the obvious, that this was the prelude to humiliation, violation, rape at the very least, though since her ankles were tied and her face covered, she already had an inkling that he might have something specialized in mind. But first there was a journey. She was lifted up, then placed in the back of a vehicle, a van. The way he handled her wasn't exactly careful, but he didn't throw her around, expended no unnecessary energy. The doors slammed, and in due course the van began to move. The journey seemed a long one, and even though she wanted it to be over, she also knew that what came next would surely be worse.

The van stopped. He hauled her out. She was aware, briefly, of being in the open air and then inside a building and then being maneuvered awkwardly, half-carried, half-dragged, down a set of stairs into a basement. There she was lifted up again, set facedown on a metal bench, maybe an examination table, and belts or cords were strapped around her to hold her in place.

It hardly came as a surprise when her clothes were pushed aside, but they were not ripped, not pulled off; instead, they were carefully raised and folded back. She remained some way from being naked, but her back and buttocks were laid bare. She steeled herself for the touch of his hands, but it seemed some preparation was required. She could hear drawers and cabinets being opened and closed. Some kind of equipment was being set up. She wondered if he was going to play doctor and patient.

Then it started. She heard a drone, like a high-pitched dentist's drill, and then she felt something in her back, a precise line of pain. Was that a knife, a needle? A syringe? Was that the feel of drugs or chemicals entering her body? No, that wasn't it. It wasn't an injection, nothing so limited or clearly defined. Rather, something seemed to slice through her, repetitive, broad but not deep. She thought of a sewing machine, as if she were being stitched and patched. She considered several other possibilities before she thought of a tattooing machine, but then she knew that's what it had to be. She was being marked, inked, tagged.

It hurt, of course, but it was hard to separate the specific pain of the tattooing from the more general pain and degradation that went with being kidnapped, bound, hooded, bared, penetrated. The needles going into her flesh might have been bearable in themselves, no more than a long series of nasty stings, but not knowing how long it would go on and when, if ever, it would stop: that was excruciating.

She knew next to nothing about tattooing, but even so, she'd heard that sooner or later endorphins were supposed to kick in, that the pain became a kind of pleasure. But she didn't let it happen. She wasn't going to allow herself to experience relief, much less pleasure. Her back felt hot and cold, alternately then simultaneously. She knew her skin was wet, with sweat and blood and maybe ink and some liquid that he kept swabbing her with. She had no idea what design he could possibly be making. She tried to make sense of it, tried to envisage what the clusters and lines of pain might add up to, what private imagery they were mapping: cracked madonnas, orange-eyed felines, devil women, galleons with their black sails on fire. She knew she was close to hallucinating.

She had no idea exactly how long it went on. It seemed like hours, but it could have been much less, and as with the journey in the van, she didn't know what would come at the end. If he wanted to kill her, then there'd be no stopping him. She was his. Nobody was coming to save her, and she certainly wasn't going to be able to save herself.

At last the tattoo machine stopped. There was a silence and a stillness that seemed the most delicious she had ever known, a tide going out, a reprieve, even though her back and buttocks felt as if they'd been mashed into raw hamburger. Then there was the sound of the equipment being cleaned and stashed, drawers closing, water running, something being washed away. She felt her clothes being straightened and put back into place. The straps that held her to the table were removed.

Her hands and feet were still tied, and the leather hood remained in place as she was made to stand up. She could just about keep herself upright, but her legs felt elastic and newborn, and the ground seemed very far away. She was led up the stairs, back out onto the street, and again into the van. The anticipation of what might or might not come next was its own torture. The drive seemed shorter this time, the journey less urgent, until the van stopped and she was being hauled out, dumped on the sidewalk. The ties at her hands and feet were loosened though not removed. The hood was taken from her head, and she was pushed facedown onto the ground again so she couldn't see her assailant. Somehow the cold, abrasive surface of the street felt reassuring and solid, and there was air, not good air, not fresh air, but something wonderfully different from the inside of that hood. Before she could even sit up, she heard the van driving away, and it was gone before she could turn around and try to get a sighting of it.

She realized that with just a little effort she could untie herself. She still didn't know if this was a beginning or an end. And as she looked around her she realized he had delivered her to exactly the place he had picked her up, not far from where she lived. That indicated a fastidiousness, a kind of consideration that was deeply menacing.

She stood up. She was in one piece. She was herself. She hadn't even been robbed. Her keys, money, and cell phone were still in her pockets. She walked the short distance home, convinced that nothing worse could happen to her. She went inside, through the outer gate, up via the big, unstable elevator, into her own space. She sat on the bed, too hurt to cry, and at last, because she knew, however unbearable, it would have to be done, she went into the bathroom, stripped off the clothes that she knew she'd have to burn. She steadied herself, took a deep breath, and turned her back to the mirror so she could look over her shoulder and see what had been done to her.

4. HOW BILLY MOORE FIRST MET "MR." WROBLESKI

A hulking, matte-black SUV stood at the center of the courtyard, customized to express deep aggression and luxury. The
courtyard, a broad, wet, scuffed square of tarmac, was enclosed
on three sides by several levels of solid, workaday buildings, a
series of former workshops, offices, storage units, all linked by
open metal staircases, decks, and catwalks. There were many
doors, all of them shut, and all the windows were covered, in
some cases barred. It was impossible to tell what went on here
now, but certainly nothing explicitly industrial. A few guys in
overalls who looked as if they might have jobs to do were standing around, conspicuously not doing them.

But one guy was working, which was why the tarmac was
wet. A young black man, wearing shimmering orange shorts and
nothing else, was cleaning the SUV, resentment oozing from
his every pore. Above him, on a second-story deck, his boss,
Wrobleski, was watching him intently. This car, these buildings,
this whole compound, belonged to Wrobleski. This was the place
he did a lot of business, and it was also where he lived. If you
looked up to the rooftop, you'd see that along one side of the
structure was an extra level, a lavish, hard-edged architectural
addition. In a way this new part looked just as industrial as the
buildings below, with metal girders, glass walls, exposed ducting;
but it was an apartment, a penthouse. The girders were painted

bright red, the walls of glass curved symmetrically, the ducting had a polished gleam to it. The corner of a domed conservatory was visible nearby on the flat roof.

Wrobleski could hear the sound of a car idling outside the solid, gray steel gate that separated the compound from the rest of the world. Charlie, a lean, rigid, sunburned old man, with impeccably disreputable credentials, had been employed by Wrobleski solely to open and close the gate, and now he performed his job with quiet, solemn efficiency, and saluted, not quite seriously, not quite playfully, at the car that entered the courtyard. It was a metallic-blue Cadillac, a good thirty years old, sagging, battered, with a scratch or dent on every panel. The car parked alongside the SUV as Charlie slid the gate shut. Billy Moore got out of the Cadillac, adjusted his leather jacket, as battered as the car, and readied himself.

He didn't especially want to be here. This whole part of the city was alien territory as far as he was concerned. He had got here only by obeying the instructions of his GPS, a bit of modern gadgetry his daughter had insisted he buy. He was glad he hadn't had to think his way here, through the old meatpacking districts and between the abandoned factories and the gravel pits. He didn't belong here at the edge of things, where the city was all but exhausted, close to the docks, in sight of power stations and rail yards, near dumps, landfills, and recycling facilities that used to call themselves junkyards. He couldn't imagine anybody wanting to live here, although he knew that these days, in this city, people lived in all kinds of postindustrial wastelands and considered themselves very fancy indeed.

Certainly Wrobleski's place was close to fast roads that might take you to bridges and tunnels, to airports and ferry terminals, a good place to be when you needed to be somewhere else in a hurry. But Wrobleski didn't look as if he needed to be anywhere else, and he definitely didn't look like a man you could hurry. Today he was wearing one of his better suits, charcoal-gray mohair with a bright blue pinstripe, single-breasted, single-buttoned, single-vented, all the edges scalpel-sharp, but he was wearing it for his own pleasure, certainly not in anticipation of meeting Billy Moore. Wrobleski eyed the battered Cadillac, and disapproval registered briefly on his face, but the look was gone before Billy Moore had crossed the courtyard. Billy raised his eyes toward Wrobleski, and Wrobleski beckoned him up to the open second-floor deck.

This was not in the strictest sense a first meeting, and Billy had heard plenty about Wrobleski long before he saw him in person. He was quite a legend in some of the dubious worlds into which Billy had occasionally strayed, considered to be a mad dog, way out of Billy's league, in a league Billy did not aspire to join.

Their actual first encounter had taken place at a real estate auction. Billy Moore was there to buy a piece of land suitable for turning into a parking lot and home for a couple of trailers. Originally he'd had his eye on a plot out by the shuttered women's reformatory—there was talk of turning that place into a boutique hotel or maybe live/work spaces—and he'd registered his interest with the auction house, but right before the bidding was due to start, one of the auctioneer's flunkies asked him to step aside for a "private word."

The flunky was tall and lean to the point of chemical imbalance. In a low-ceilinged, institutional-yellow corridor outside the main auction room, as people pushed and milled around them, the flunky said, "This is slightly delicate. One of our special clients has his eye on the same plot as yourself. We think it would be better if you didn't bid against him."

"What?"

"In exchange he won't bid against you on the lot at the corner of Hope Street and Tenth."

"I'll bid on what I want."

"Of course, but if you bid on the reformatory lot, you'll only drive up the price, and in the end you still won't get it. And if you then try to buy the Hope and Tenth lot, our client will most likely bid against you and ensure that you don't get that either."

"Who is this jerk?"

"I'd rather not say."

"And why do you care?" said Billy. "Don't you want the price as high as possible?"

"Sometimes there are other considerations."

"Why don't you tell this special client to go fuck himself?"

The flunky winced, and something he saw over Billy's shoulder caused him to cast his eyes down. Under his breath he said to Billy, "The other bidder, the special client."

A voice behind Billy said, "Who's telling who to go fuck himself?"

Billy turned and looked at a man he'd never seen before, large but compact, serious, dangerous-looking.

"Who are you?" said Billy.

"My name's Wrobleski," said the man.

"Okay," said Billy calmly, cautiously, as several important things clicked into place. "Well, only a damn fool would tell the great Mr. Wrobleski to go fuck himself."

"So you're not a damn fool," said Wrobleski, and if he was the kind of man who smiled, he might have done it then.

They took up seats on opposite sides of the auction room. The bidding went fast. Wrobleski got what he wanted, and Billy got the lot at the corner of Hope Street and Tenth, and he did get it cheap. In the end there was nothing to feel bad about. The thing that surprised him most was that a guy like Wrobleski was involved in anything so small-time as buying pieces of land. The Wrobleski of his imagination inhabited a quite separate world, one of speedboats, limos, assignations in foreign hot spots. He was even more surprised when word came through, sometime later, that Wrobleski wanted to see him. A part of him was flattered, and in any case, there was no way he could have refused to go, even if he'd wanted to. Wrobleski was a man very few people got to meet, and certainly there were quite a few who never met him more than once. Even so, as Billy climbed the metal staircase that led to the second-floor deck of the compound, where Wrobleski was waiting for him, he thought it unlikely that this meeting was going to be either pleasurable or straightforward.

Billy put out his hand for the expected handshake, but Wrobleski declined it. "Billy Moore," he said quietly. It wasn't quite a greeting, more a simple acknowledgment that Billy Moore existed. If the president and first lady had turned up at his gate, Wrobleski would have addressed them in the same easy, gruff tone of voice.

"Do you want my man Akim to clean your car for you?" Wrobleski asked.

Billy had a feeling that something might depend on his answer, that with Wrobleski there would never be anything so simple as a direct yes or no, and simultaneously he realized he might be overthinking this whole business.

"He's very good," Wrobleski added.

Billy said, "Okay then, sure."

Wrobleski peered down into the courtyard where Akim was already moving sullenly toward the Cadillac, bucket, hose, and chamois at the ready. Without saying more, Wrobleski turned and walked away along the deck, and Billy could only follow.

The layout of the place was confusing, walkways and staircases running up and down and across, some open to the elements, some enclosed, leading into inscrutable hallways and landings, and everywhere more blank doors and windows. Wrobleski opened one of the doors, at random, as it seemed to Billy, and they went into an unexpectedly welcoming space, not so industrial after all, carpeted, carefully lit, with groupings of leather chairs and couches. It looked like a waiting room, though Billy couldn't imagine who'd be waiting here or for what, and he didn't have much time to think about it before he was distracted by what was on the walls: a multitude of framed maps, and of course Billy had seen framed maps before, in hotels and in certain kinds of bar, but he hadn't seen any quite like these.

Some of them were conventional enough, though sufficiently antique that the shapes of countries and continents didn't quite resemble those on contemporary maps. Others were more modern, but there was something off-kilter about them. There was a symbolic map of a railway line passing through cities named Sacrifice, Enlightenment, Hubris, and False Friendship. There was a map of an imaginary country in the shape of a woman's head, another was a tapestry with a map of the Hindu Kush woven into it. There were maps of desert islands, diagrams of caves and cavern systems. Few looked like maps of places anyone could ever set foot.

Wrobleski turned to see what was interesting Billy. "This stuff's okay," he said. "But one day I'll show you some really good stuff," and he waved a vague hand, to indicate that those closed doors outside gave access to a storehouse of real cartographic treasures, not that Billy Moore had any idea what a real cartographic treasure would look like.

Billy saw now that at one end of the room was a small elevator, and he and Wrobleski stepped inside and went up to the top of the building. The doors opened onto the roof terrace. Billy could see

Wrobleski's penthouse with its glass walls and metal girders, and he got a brief impression of high ceilings, ancient polished hardwood, violently colored rugs, and many, many more framed maps. But he and Wrobleski weren't going there. Wrobleski wasn't inviting him into the place where he lived. They were heading for the domed conservatory at the other corner of the roof.

They entered, through angular glass doors, to be enveloped by bone-dry heat. Billy saw that there were very few plants. Stands and low tables arranged around the edges of the space supported just a small number of cacti and succulents, some small, a few very large, a ghost euphorbia, agaves, barrel cacti, opuntias: the overall effect was of a sparse skyline of spikes, columns, spheres, paddles, flailing arms. The arrangement seemed appropriate enough: Billy wouldn't have expected Wrobleski to be growing petunias.

Something more surprising was in the center of the conservatory: a horizontal, glass-topped display case that took up a good amount of the space. At first Billy thought it was a model village, something a kid might have played with, but a second look showed it was something more serious than that. It looked as if it belonged in a museum: detailed and carefully constructed. And he saw now that it wasn't a village but a whole island, shaped like a leg of lamb, surrounded by a blue resin sea.

Wrobleski's explanation—"It's a raised relief map of Iwo Jima"—didn't help, but Billy said nothing, and things got no clearer when he saw there was a woman in the conservatory, draped diagonally across a rattan sofa, reading a thick, unwieldy fashion magazine. She looked young, and her heavy makeup and overelaborate hair didn't make her appear any older. A tiger-print dress and some discarded stripper shoes only emphasized the sense that she was playing dress-up. There was a bright pink cocktail on a low table beside her.

"This is Laurel," said Wrobleski. "Some people might say she's a filthy, gold-digging slut. But I'd never say a thing like that."

The young woman didn't look up, but she giggled quietly to herself, and Billy Moore still did and said nothing, since he couldn't imagine what was the right thing to do or say.

"So how's the parking business?" Wrobleski asked.

"It's okay," said Billy.

"Made your first million yet?"

"No."

"Made anything?"

"Sure, but expenses run high. You wouldn't believe what you have to pay to get a competent parking lot attendant, and—"

"I don't need details," said Wrobleski. "I'm just establishing that you might be interested in a little freelance work to help your cash flow. Consider this your job interview."

"I'm trying to stay out of trouble," said Billy.

"Aren't we all?"

"Yes," said Billy, "but I think your idea of trouble is a bit grander than mine."

"Really?" said Wrobleski. "Look, I know you must have heard a lot about me. But only half of it's true."

"Which half?" Billy asked, and Wrobleski looked pleased with the question.

"Even I don't know that," Wrobleski said. "But the fact is, having people say terrible things about you is never bad for business."

Billy nodded; he didn't intend to argue, but surely it all depended on what business you were in.

"And obviously, since our encounter at the auction, I've asked around about you," said Wrobleski. "And I've heard good things."

"And you believed it?"

"Well, half of it."

Wrobleski stared out through the glass wall of the conservatory. There was something out there, invisible but palpable, that didn't make him happy.

"The word is, you've got a brain," said Wrobleski. "And I can use some extra brainpower right now."

Billy grunted. He was not foolish enough to imagine that Wrobleski wanted him for his brain.

"And they say you're a tough guy," Wrobleski added.

"I don't go around thinking what a tough guy I am," said Billy, and they both knew that was the right answer.

"How old are you?" Wrobleski asked.

"Thirty."

"You're divorced, right?"

"Right."

"And you've got a twelve-year-old daughter."

"Yes," said Billy.

It was true, of course, and hardly a secret, and Billy Moore wasn't surprised that Wrobleski had done his homework, but it still made him uneasy to be discussing his daughter here and now, in these circumstances, with this man.

"She lives with you?" Wrobleski asked.

"For now," Billy said. "That's why I have to stay out of trouble."

"Kids: they're a liability, aren't they?" said Wrobleski.

"I'll say."

Billy suspected that Wrobleski didn't know or care much about children, but he was quite right about the liability.

"Hey, Laurel," Wrobleski said, all thoughts of children now gone, "get up, take your top off."

She did as she was told, stood, eased her shoulders out of the straps of her dress, let it fall forward and pool around her waist. Her eyes met Billy's for only a moment, then she turned away. It seemed unexpectedly modest, but it had nothing to do with modesty. She was turning so that she could show Billy her back. It was tattooed roughly, crudely, with intersecting lines in red, black, and blue, some rough cross-hatchings, squares, circles, symbols, a line of arrows. It was an ugly mess, done hastily and ham-fistedly.

"What do you make of that?" Wrobleski asked.

"What am I supposed to make of it?" said Billy.

"What if I told you it was a map?"

"Then I guess I'd have to believe you."

Billy looked again. If these markings really constituted a map, it was more inscrutable than any of the others he'd seen elsewhere in the building.

"Confusing, yeah?" said Wrobleski.

Billy nodded in agreement.

"It confuses me too," said Wrobleski. "And I don't like to be confused."

There was a fat golden barrel cactus, the size of a basketball, in a black enameled planter positioned next to the sofa. Wrobleski absentmindedly pressed his index finger against one of the hooked spikes, as if he were trying to draw his own blood.

"Knowledge is power, right?" Wrobleski said. "But there are two kinds of power, as I see it. There's one kind where you can make other people do what you want. That's what most civilians think of as power. But there's another kind, where nobody can make you do anything you don't want to do. That's better, if you ask me. But right now I haven't got either."

Billy Moore was surprised by this admission. It suggested that Wrobleski wasn't quite the swirl of deranged impulses and killer instincts he was reputed to be. That he was prepared to admit to a degree of weakness and powerlessness only made him stronger in Billy's opinion, though he was well aware that his opinion counted for absolutely nothing.

"I've got a job for you, Billy," Wrobleski said. "Or for someone like you."

"What's the job?" Billy asked.

Wrobleski offered a deep sigh as his first attempt at a job description.

"It seems that Laurel here isn't the only one with these tattoos. And okay, I know every slut in the world's got tattoos nowadays, but not like these."

Billy stopped himself from asking, "Like what?" He couldn't tell what the tattoos' defining characteristics were, but maybe that wasn't his business. Instead, he said, "How many women are we talking about?"

"You ask all the right questions, Billy. And I wish I knew the answers. The job is open-ended for now. But if I give it to you, it'll happen like this. You'll get a phone call from my man Akim. He'll tell you there's a tattooed woman who needs to be brought in. He'll tell you where she is. He'll have found her. He's good at finding things. You'll go get her and bring her to me. I'll do the rest."

"It sounds too easy."

"Yeah, doesn't it?"

"Will these women want to come?"

"Not necessarily," said Wrobleski. "That's where it might get less easy."

He looked away again, out through the glass of the conservatory, at a soft, broad, fading indigo sky, and at the city beneath, at an office block in the process of being demolished, at an Erector Set skyscraper rising stealthily beside it. Billy looked in the same direction and tried not to jump to conclusions.

"Is something bad going to happen to these women?" Billy asked.

"Something bad has already happened to these women."

Billy was mystified. He knew he was supposed to be mystified.

"Look," said Wrobleski, "unless you're a complete maniac, killing people really takes it out of you."

He said it carefully, as though it were something he'd discovered only recently and hadn't completely understood as yet. He got up, walked out of the conservatory onto the roof terrace. Billy followed. He didn't want to be left alone with Laurel and the cacti and the relief map of Iwo Jima.

"I hear you're not a complete maniac, Billy, and neither am I, despite what you might have heard. Trust me. Or don't. It's all the same, really."

Wrobleski fell into silence.

"So what happens next?"

"You go away," said Wrobleski, "and if I decide you're the right man, then you'll get a phone call, and if you want the job you'll say, 'Yes, I'd love to work for Mr. Wrobleski.' And if you don't want the job you'll say, 'I'm going to have to turn down Mr. Wrobleski's kind offer.' But I don't think you'll turn me down, Billy. Any more questions?"

"Money?" said Billy.

"Money won't be a problem," said Wrobleski.

"And why me?" Billy said.

Wrobleski didn't quite have an answer to that.

"Maybe I like the cut of your jib," he said dismissively. "Or maybe you remind me of me. Isn't that the kind of shit people say in interviews?"

"Sure," said Billy. "People will say anything in interviews."

And then it was over. Wrobleski had no more to say, and he led Billy Moore down to the courtyard where his Cadillac was waiting for him. It had obviously been given some attention, since it was still wet and there was water on the ground surrounding it, and yet as Billy looked at the car, it didn't appear to be any cleaner than before: if anything, it looked dirtier. Was that possible? Was it intentional? Meanwhile, the SUV was so clean, so densely black, it seemed to suck in the light.

"Nice ride, I know," said Wrobleski. "I've got a lot of nice things. I was serious about showing you my map collection sometime."

"Great," said Billy, and he hoped he managed to disguise his lack of interest. Maps: who cared? He got in his car, ready to drive back to where he belonged. He knew Wrobleski would offer him the job, and he knew he'd accept it, because he needed the money, and he already recognized that this might force him to accept much more as well. He also realized this might not be everybody's idea of staying out of trouble.

5. ZAK WEBSTER PUTS HIMSELF ON THE MAP

It was 6:30 on one of those long, restless city summer evenings, a time when Zak Webster could justifiably have closed up the store. Chances were there'd be no more customers today; there were few enough at the best of times. In fact, he could have opened and closed pretty much whenever he liked. Nobody was breathing down his neck. Ray McKinley, his boss, the owner of the business, and of much else besides, prided himself on a hands-off management style. He trusted Zak, which was perhaps only to say that he was well aware of Zak's overdeveloped sense of responsibility; and since the sign on the door said the opening hours were 10:00 till 7:00, those were the hours Zak kept.

The store was named Utopiates, a name that by no means said it all. It was an oblique reference to an Oscar Wilde quotation: "A map of the world that does not include Utopia is not worth even glancing at, for it leaves out the one country at which Humanity is always landing." But as Zak would tell anybody who'd listen, there were in fact a great many maps of Utopia, starting with the version in the 1516 edition of Thomas More's book, as well as any number of later engravings, woodcuts, prints, and so on.

That was the business Utopiates was in: selling cartographic antiques—maps, atlases, globes, navigation charts, the occasional mapmaking instrument, folding pillar compasses, snake-eye dividers. Some were no more than decorative curiosities, but the best of them were rare, exquisite, expensive, perhaps "important," maybe even "museum quality." It was a specialist market, perhaps too special by half, it sometimes seemed to Zak.

The store was a small, brown, oaky, two-roomed space with a basement for storage, in a quiet backwater of what was now known as the Arts and Crafts Zone, previously the red-light district, but transformed by population shifts, property development, and marginal gentrification. Neighboring businesses included an outsider-art gallery, a seller of French horns, a designer of one-off wedding dresses. None of these enterprises were conspicuously thriving, and neither was Utopiates.

For the time being, that was okay with Ray McKinley, who regularly made it clear to Zak that the store was the most minor and most trivial of his many, many business ventures. He had a mild enthusiasm for maps and antiques, so he'd bought the store on a whim, when he'd seen how desperate the previous owner was and how much he'd lowered the asking price. The deal included the premises, the stock, and Zak, the store's single, poorly paid employee; though Zak had no idea how long the current arrangement would last. For now the store remained open, but Ray McKinley insisted the value was in the site not the business. Before long the area's gentrification would peak, then he'd sell up and make a killing. Exactly where this would leave Zak had never been discussed, but the chances were that he'd be left jobless, and homeless too.

Zak lived above the store, in a small apartment made smaller by the excess stock kept there. This was the stuff that wasn't remotely collectible or important—mostly things they'd got stuck with while acquiring genuinely desirable items. There were boxes of out-of-date road maps, a job lot of school atlases, a few dozen cheap and cheerful illuminated globes. Zak made the best of living with the store's leftovers.

Having to find another job and another apartment would hardly be a novel experience for him, but he was tired of it, and in many ways this was the best job he'd ever had, probably the best he could hope for. He wasn't enjoying precisely the life or career he'd imagined for himself, but then he'd never been over-burdened with ambition or specific goals. His education had been a patchwork of only marginally related courses: anthropology, nineteenth-century history, avant-garde film, museum studies, ar-chival management, and, of course, cartography in various forms, including historical, critical, planetary, and radical.

It was hard to see what this had, or could have, prepared him for. Despite a certain scholarly manner, he wasn't any kind of academic; his interests were way too eccentric and personal for that—Leon Battista Alberti, eighteenth-century "dissected maps," the debates surrounding "information primitives." He wasn't go-ing to study for a Ph.D. or write a book, and he was certainly never going to teach. And although there were days when he imagined himself as curator or custodian of some magnificent, highly specialized, and possibly clandestine map collection, he also realized this was pure fantasy. Most days he was content to think of himself as a map nerd, and map nerds ended up working in map stores—if they were lucky.

Now he sat at his desk and stared out the window into the street, his gaze as idle as a gaze ever gets, and when he saw what looked like a bundle of rags moving along the sidewalk, he needed a moment to realize what he was looking at. Naturally he knew the bundle wasn't moving under its own steam, that there must be somebody inside it, crawling along. There was still a small population of tattered street people in the area, but that didn't seem to be quite what he was looking at here. For one thing, these rags had obviously started out as fine fabrics, perhaps as a cape or velvet curtains. They were dirty and matted now, but they still had an air of ruined luxury.

The bundle came to a halt, was still for a moment, and then began to rise, as the person inside stood up. A head emerged, a woman's head, the face young but not youthful, drawn, with long hair the color of wet newspaper: she might have been beautiful once, but not recently. Her eyes looked up at the UTOPIATES sign and saw something hopeful there. She hugged the rags to her and walked toward the store.

Instinctively Zak got up from his desk. His first thought was to block the entrance, to keep out an undesirable, but he opened the door just a little, so he could speak to the woman, tell her—with as much emphasis as was required—to keep walking. But as he looked her in the eye, something small and compassionate stirred in him, and he felt he ought to do just a little more than that: give her some money, for instance.

The woman stared back at him hesitantly, suspiciously, but then she detected something benign and trustworthy in his face, and said, in a clotted, deliberate voice, "Would you help me? Can you?"

Zak assumed she too was thinking about money, and he felt around in his pockets, only to discover that he had an insultingly small amount of change.

She spoke again. "What is this? A clinic?"

"No," he said. "It's a store."

She looked horribly disappointed, though not surprised, as though this was only the latest in an endless series of disappointments. In fact, there was an emergency room not far away, and Zak was about to give her directions, but he never got that far.

The rags were evidently in place only because she clutched them to herself. The news that Utopiates wasn't a medical facility caused her to slacken her grip, and they fell all the way to the ground. Zak suddenly had a naked woman standing on his doorstep. She had a lean, pale body, grubby at the edges, the ribs prominent, the skin loose, but Zak hardly had time to take in the sight before the woman swiveled, turning her back to him.

Her back looked less naked than the rest of her. It was marked with tattoos: wild, incomprehensible lines and symbols that Zak first read as a meaningless accumulation of ink, a savage scribbling, and yet there was something compelling about it, something that suggested it wasn't entirely haphazard. He wasn't sure, but he thought it might just possibly be a kind of wild, ramshackle map, but the glimpse was brief, and then the woman turned again to face him, quickly pulling the rags up over herself. She'd allowed him a glimpse of something precious and secret, and that was as much as he was entitled to.

Unsure of what he'd seen, and why he'd been shown it, and to a large extent wishing he hadn't seen it at all, Zak stuttered that he could close up the store and take her to the emergency room if that was what she really wanted. She said nothing, but shook her head sadly.

Zak had no idea what to do next. He feared the two of them might stay like that for the rest of the night, perhaps for all eternity, without words or volition, but then he noticed a battered metallic-blue Cadillac parked a little way down the street: perhaps it had been there the whole time. Now it moved, traveling a hundred yards or so until it pulled up directly in front of the store.

The driver, a man in a beat-up leather jacket, pushed open the two front doors of the car before he got out. Zak watched him move swiftly and determinedly toward the woman, place one hand firmly on her arm, the other on her waist, and push her inside the car. It wasn't violent, it wasn't even rough, but it seemed irresistible. Certainly the woman didn't try to resist. Once she was inside, the driver slammed the passenger door shut after her, then looked up for a second and caught sight of Zak staring at him. Zak turned away, avoided eye contact, pretended lamely that he was checking something in the window of the store. He didn't dare watch as the man got into the Cadillac and drove away.

Zak remained in the doorway, poised among various kinds of uncertainty and inertia. The incident had been so brief, so self-contained. What had he actually seen? Was that really a map on the woman's back? Had she really been showing it to him? And if so, why? The mental image was already fading, and he felt that was probably no bad thing. And who was the guy in the car? The woman's keeper? Boyfriend? Kidnapper? He looked in the direction the car had gone, curious and intrigued, but equally aware that there was nothing more to see, no conclusion to be drawn. It was a little while before he realized there was somebody standing beside him.

It was a woman about his own age, maybe a little younger. She was tall, a little gawky, fit-looking, with something steely yet quizzical in her face. She was wearing thrift store clothes, a man's jacket that was too big for her, baggy pants, combat boots, and her big dark eyes looked out through ornate tortoiseshell glasses. Something about the image didn't quite suit her, as if she was trying to appear more bookish and hipsterish than she really was. She straddled a bike that was either an old wreck or some-thing very cool and retro—Zak couldn't tell which—and there was a serious-looking camera slung over her shoulder.

"Did you just see what I just saw?" she said to Zak.

"I'm not sure what I saw," Zak said, honestly enough.

"Sure. But the woman and the stuff on her back. You saw that, right?"

"Yes," said Zak: how could he not have seen it?

The woman looked at the window of the store with detached curiosity.

"How long has this place been here?" she asked.

"Quite a while," he said.

"Strange, I never noticed it before."

He didn't think that it was all that strange. If you weren't interested in antique cartography you'd have no reason to be aware of Utopiates' existence.

"Come in if you like," he said. "Take a look around."

He wasn't exactly sure why he said that. She certainly didn't look like a potential customer, a fact that was confirmed when she took half a step toward the front door, hesitated, peered into the interior of the store, then gave a mild but distinct shudder.

"No, I don't think so," she said. "The place kind of gives me the creeps."

As he watched her get on her bike and pedal away, he couldn't understand quite why he found her remark so hurtful.

At last Zak closed up the store and went for a walk around the neighborhood. He did a lot of that. The city was a big mess these days: in the process of being simultaneously built and unbuilt, reshaped and made formless. Well, perhaps all cities are like that, but here special conditions applied: big changes were being made in the name of regeneration and renewal, a civic master plan, public and private initiatives, a cultural and commercial renaissance. Yeah right. At the same time, nothing ever quite got finished. Projects were constantly stalling, running out of money or coming up against planning "snags." Buildings sat half-built, while others sat half-demolished; the whole city seemed to be suffering from completion anxiety.

And so wherever Zak walked he encountered detours, blocked sidewalks, metal plates covering the street, giant trucks making impossible turns. Roads were closed or made one-way. The fabric of the city was being torn wide open, both above- and belowground. One of the more glittering prestige projects involved extending the subway system, creating the new Platinum Line to connect downtown with the slums on the northern edge of the city, a connection that not everybody thought was such a great idea. Work on the subway created occasional deep, subterranean rumblings as new tunnels were blasted through some particularly unyielding section of the earth below—a trembling, an unsettling that Zak sometimes chose to see as symbolic.

As he drifted, he kept trying to make sense of what he'd just seen, unsure whether there was any "sense" to be made. It was puzzling, but hardly one of the world's great mysteries. Strange women got into strange cars with strange men at any time of the day or night, every day, every night. People had all kinds of weird stuff tattooed on their backs. People lived incomprehensible and desperate lives. It probably meant nothing: things only meant what you decided they meant. He would probably forget all about it in a day or two. But he kept thinking about the woman in the tortoiseshell glasses; he knew he wouldn't forget about her quite that soon.

6. BILLY MOORE'S FIRST JOB

The first one was easy, so easy that Billy Moore couldn't understand why Wrobleski even needed him. Any idiot could have done it. But maybe that was to be expected. It was a chance for him to prove he was not less than an idiot. He knew that the real tests, the real complications, would come later.

There had been a phone call, and a thick, deep, somehow affected voice that he didn't recognize said, "I'm calling on behalf of Mr. Wrobleski. He'd like to offer you that job."

And as predicted Billy Moore didn't say, "Tell Mr. Wrobleski I've found alternative employment." Instead, he said, "Can't Wrobleski make his own phone calls?"

And the voice said, "He can, but he doesn't need to."

"So who am I talking to now?" said Billy.

"The name's Akim."

"Right. Are you the one who washes cars?"

"That's one of my more minor responsibilities."

Billy Moore reckoned there was no point telling him he'd done a lousy job on the Cadillac: he must know that already.

"And you have others?"

"Clearly. Which is why I'm calling you. This is to tell you the time and the place where you will locate a certain woman and bring her to Mr. Wrobleski."

"Okay," said Billy. "Then I guess that's what I'll do."

Beforehand he wondered if he'd have any trouble recognizing the woman, but that proved to be the least of his concerns. He'd been told she was living rough, and that she had a tattoo similar to the one he'd seen on Laurel, but he never thought that finding her would be so simple. He certainly didn't imagine she'd be naked in the street. And once he saw the state of her, he wasn't so happy about having her in his car. The Cadillac may have been beat up on the outside, but the interior was his territory. Those rags of hers were filthy and they'd surely stink. She looked as though she might throw up or bleed or piss on his leather upholstery. He also wondered how eager she'd be to get in the car, whether he'd have to drag her in kicking and screaming, whether he'd have to slap her. But again, it wasn't a problem. He just maneuvered her toward the car and in she got. Yeah, it was all far too easy.

Once inside, she slumped in the passenger seat, maybe exhausted, maybe a bit mad, and she closed her eyes and seemed quite content, maybe relieved to be anywhere other than the street. She looked as if she was falling asleep, which was fine by Billy. They drove in silence, but he knew it wouldn't last. Before long the woman opened her eyes, stirred herself, and if she didn't exactly seem alert, at least she took an interest in her surroundings. She looked around the inside of the car and approved of what she saw.

"Elegant," she said; then, "Where are we going?"

Nobody had told Billy what he was and wasn't allowed to say, but his inclination was to be cryptic. "A friend's place," he said.

"A friend of yours or a friend of mine?" the woman asked.

"Both, I expect."

That satisfied her for the moment. She peered out through the side window of the car, her eyes drooping, sliding in and out of focus. Then a new thought occurred to her.

"How am I going to get back?"

Billy didn't know the answer to that, so he said, "On the bus."

"I go out in a Cadillac; I come back on the bus."

"That's about the size of it."

"Okay."

She seemed to find that a perfectly reasonable state of affairs, and then another thought arrived.

"And what's going to happen to me when I get to your friend's place?"

Billy had even less idea of the answer to that.

"That'll be a surprise," he said.

She let that one float away.

"My name's Genevieve," the woman said.

"You don't look like a Genevieve," said Billy.

"I used to."

"Maybe you will again."

"You think?"

They approached Wrobleski's compound, and Charlie, the efficient old gatekeeper, opened up the gate as the Cadillac arrived. Wrobleski and Akim were waiting in the courtyard, standing by the SUV, which seemed not to have moved since Billy's last visit. He stopped his car, left the engine running, then got out and went around to the passenger side to let the woman out. He knew he was behaving like a chauffeur, yet it seemed the decent thing to do, to show the woman some respect. Genevieve got out, hugged the velvet rags to her, and stood swaying gently, moving to some distant music only she could hear.

"Nobody saw you, right?" Wrobleski said to Billy.

It was the kind of question that allowed only one answer.

"Nobody saw me," Billy lied.

"If somebody sees you, then you'll have to do something about that."

"Understood," said Billy.

Akim took charge of the woman. He put an arm around her shoulders, seeming rather happier doing that than washing cars. He gave her something to drink, and he had something in his hand that looked like a syringe. Billy didn't ask what was going to happen to her. It wasn't his business, and he already knew you didn't ask Wrobleski questions like that.

As Billy Moore drove away from Wrobleski's compound, it started to rain: big thick globs of water stippling the Cadillac's windshield. He waited as long as he could before turning on the wipers and watched the world become marbled. He drove with the window half-open so he could feel the spray on the side of his face, and at last he snapped the wipers into life, blurring, smoothing, eventually clearing his field of vision.

Beside him on the passenger seat was an envelope of money Wrobleski had given him for his work. He decided it was time to open it. He pulled over, stopped the car in front of a shuttered halal supermarket, and unsealed the envelope. There was too much money inside. Billy could find a good use for all the cash that came his way—there was some upgrading to be done on the parking lot, and Carla was always begging for a new cell phone— but this was far more than you'd expect to be paid just for acting as driver to some homeless woman. Wrobleski was being generous, and that was flattering and worrying in equal proportions. Billy tried not to think about what was happening to Genevieve inside Wrobleski's compound, but he couldn't quite manage that.

Carla was awake and waiting for him when he got back. She was in her trailer, at her desk, an image of a lion on the screen of her laptop.

"Have a good night out?" she asked.

"I was working," said Billy.

"This parking business takes up a lot of time, doesn't it?"

"It sure does. What have *you* been doing?"

Carla said, "I've been thinking about lions."

Billy looked at the screen and said, "So I see."

"Yeah," said Carla. "And about *The Wizard of Oz*. They talk about the Cowardly Lion like that's something out of the ordinary, but it's not, is it? All lions are cowardly. I mean, when they attack a herd of antelope, they always pick off the stragglers, the weak ones at the back, don't they? It's not like they go and fight the biggest, toughest antelope they can find, just to show how brave they are."

"Are there any big, tough antelopes?" said Billy.

"Some of them have got to be bigger and tougher than others."

"I suppose so. Is that all you've been doing? Thinking about lions?"

"Sure."

"How's your skin?"

"The same."

"Let's have a look."

"No."

"Come on, roll your sleeve up."

"I don't want to."

"What are you trying to hide?"

She wouldn't admit that she was trying to hide anything, so she pushed up her sleeve to reveal her right arm. At first all Billy could see was a red, inflamed rash.

"You've been playing with it."

"It helps pass the time."

"You weren't happy with the skull and crossbones?"

She shrugged. "Change is good," she said.

When Billy looked more closely, he saw there was a pattern in among the disorder. By constantly pressing and drawing on her skin she'd made a word appear, a livid, blotched, temporary tattoo that read DAD.

"That's a very weird thing to do," Billy Moore said. "Kind of sweet and touching, but also very weird."

Without being asked, Carla pushed up the other sleeve and revealed on her left arm the word MOM.

"Even more touching," he said, though he was touched in a very different way by this.

"Don't worry," Carla said. "They'll fade eventually."

7. NIGHT UNDER GLASS

Rain stippled the roof of Wrobleski's domed conservatory, and inside it, a few scattered candles burned among the cacti, their flames reflected in the glass between the spines and paddles, reinforcing the wet darkness beyond. Shadows flicked over the relief map of Iwo Jima. Laurel was there, lolling, angled across the sofa, awake but drunk or stoned or exhausted, her head just a few inches away from the blue-black point of an agave leaf, her attention a million miles away. Wrobleski and the improbably named Genevieve sat in rattan chairs facing each other. He had poured two glasses of wine, and Genevieve was holding hers tightly in both hands, as if it might fly away.

"How are you?" Wrobleski asked, sounding, or at least trying to sound, concerned.

Genevieve blinked a couple of times, looked not quite at him, and said, unconvincingly, "I'm good."

"Great," he said. "I'm glad you could come."

If she found this an odd way of putting it—and how could she not?—she gave no indication. Perhaps she was no longer capable of being surprised.

"You're a train wreck, aren't you?" Wrobleski said.

She shrugged: it made no difference.

"I didn't ask for this date," she said.

"No, you didn't," Wrobleski agreed. "What's that thing you've got wrapped around you, anyway?"

"It's a curtain," she said, and that was all the explanation she thought necessary, or was prepared to give.

"And you're naked under there?"

"We're all naked under our clothes," she said.

"Very profound," Wrobleski said quietly. "Let me see."

She hesitated only long enough to take a gulp from her drink, set it on the floor, and then she stood up slowly, regally, so that the velvet curtain—if that's what it really was—remained behind her on the chair. She stood naked, about to place her dirty fingertips on the edge of the case containing the relief map, for support, but Wrobleski raised his hand to indicate she wasn't allowed to do that. She took a step back and looked sideways at her own bare, milky, phantom reflection in the glass of the conservatory, and then she faced Wrobleski with an unconcerned calmness.

"I need you to turn around," he said.

"Of course you do," she said.

She did what he asked, as if she were being examined by a doctor, or posed by the instructor of a life drawing class. Wrobleski got up from his chair and moved very close to her. Yes, there was an odor rising from the body, onion and tired sweat, but Wrobleski didn't care about that. He was staring very closely at the tattoos on the woman's back.

"When did you have this done?" he asked.

"I didn't have it done. It was done to me."

"Who by?"

"I don't know. I never saw his face. Could have been anybody. Could have been you."

Wrobleski declined to respond to that.

She continued, "I was tied down, on a metal table. I don't know where I was, a basement, I think. I'm not sure. Doesn't matter much where it happened, does it?"

"And you've been on the street since then?"

"I was already on the street," she said.

"And do you know what the tattoo means?" he asked.

"What do you mean by 'means'?"

"You really are a philosopher," said Wrobleski. "I mean that the tattoo is a map, right?"

"You're smart," she said. "It took me a while to realize that's what it was."

"So don't you ever wonder what it's a map of?"

"I used to. Then I stopped wondering. Wherever it's a map of, I don't want to go there."

"Maybe it's somewhere you've already been," Wrobleski said, and he continued to stare, squinting in the flickering light, the explorer in the cave, confounded by the writing on the wall. He moved even closer and stretched out a hand as though to touch the woman, but his fingertips stopped an inch or so away from the surface of the skin, as if touching it might burn him, or worse.

"You ever think of getting it removed?" he asked.

"Never quite had the budget for that."

"Or you could have something tattooed over it, something better, maybe something Japanese."

"Could I?"

"Unless you think it's too late for that."

It sounded like a threat. Genevieve said, "What are you going to do to me?"

He looked at her with some sympathy. He accepted that was a fair question.

"I don't know," he said plainly. "I haven't decided yet."

"What are the options?"

"I haven't decided that either."

"My glass is empty," Genevieve said.

He filled it for her.

"Look, Genevieve," he said, "you're going to have to stay here for a little while. Out of harm's way. Till I work out what's best."

"Best for who?"

"Who do you think, Genevieve?"

She looked across at Laurel, who was staring at her, offering what might have been a smile of welcome.

"You're starting a harem?" said Genevieve.

"No. I'm not doing that."

"A freak show?"

"Well, we're all freaks, aren't we?"

Suddenly Akim was there in the conservatory, standing beside Genevieve. He was holding a black silk robe, long, voluminous, embroidered with purple and red poppies, and he draped it softly over her shoulders, patting it around her with rather more attention than the job required.

"For now, Akim will take care of you," Wrobleski said. "Akim's good at taking care of things."

8. BACKLESS

A long basement room, not quite a cell or dungeon, but small and dark, with one narrow, high, barred window, a row of a dozen or so single beds, a TV playing in the far corner, and on the wall a framed cartoon map of Manhattan, faux 3-D, with a goofy King Kong hanging off the Empire State Building. It was morning and Genevieve had slept well enough once Akim had finished taking care of her.

She woke now because there was somebody standing in the room, the woman she'd seen briefly last night in the conservatory, Laurel, and she was carrying a tray, delivering breakfast, part maid, part jailor, part would-be friend. Laurel's morning attire wasn't so very different from her evening wear, heels, a backless sheath dress. She put the tray down and turned to make sure that Genevieve got a good look at her tattooed back. Genevieve scrutinized the tray and Laurel with equal suspicion.

"What's this about?" she said.

"It's just breakfast," said Laurel. "It's bacon and eggs. Want me to be your food taster?"

Genevieve shook her head and began to eat, slowly, methodically.

"I meant, what's this whole thing about? Who is he? What is he? What is this place? Why did he have me brought here?"

"He's Wrobleski. He's a crook. This is his place. He had you brought here because of the tattoos."

That answered all Genevieve's questions, and it answered nothing.

"What? He really likes tattoos?"

"No, he really likes maps. But tattooed maps: those he doesn't seem to like so much. They worry him. I don't know why, but they do."

"Yeah, well, we've all got our worries," said Genevieve.

"Wrobleski doesn't like being worried."

Genevieve chewed sluggishly.

"Is that meant to sound scary?" she asked.

"Mr. Wrobleski can be very scary indeed."

"What happened to you?" Genevieve asked, although she thought she already knew.

"I'm a call girl, okay?" said Laurel. "High class, whatever that means. I'm expensive. I'm tough. I got called to an address. I drove myself there, went alone. It wasn't a bad part of town, but the address didn't exist; the street did, but not the number. While I was wondering if it was my mistake, I got dragged out of the car, blindfolded, tied up, taken to a basement. And then this happened."

"Sounds familiar," said Genevieve. "You never saw his face, right?"

"Right. But I survived, and I had money, and I thought about getting the tattoos removed or maybe getting new tattoos done to cover up the old ones, but the weird thing was, while I was thinking about it, I found I could make more money with these crappy tattoos on me than I ever made without them."

"Yeah? What's that about?" asked Genevieve.

"I think it's because most men are totally fucked up, and they like women who are totally fucked up too." Laurel shivered just a little.

"So you kept the tattoos to make money?"

"And because the men are right. I *am* totally fucked up. Maybe the tattoos stop me forgetting what I am."

"Who needs reminding?" said Genevieve.

"And then," Laurel continued, "I got another call, to come here and service Mr. Wrobleski. His guy Akim made the arrangements, brought me here. And at the time obviously Wrobleski didn't know about the tattoos, had no idea. But we started, and we did this and that, and eventually I got completely naked and he turned me over and started fucking me from behind. He must have seen the tattoos then, of course, must have seen them straightaway, but I guess he was distracted at first, didn't take a really good look at them, or maybe it took a while for him to realize what he was looking at, but then suddenly he saw something there, something in the tattoos, and I didn't know what, and I still don't, but it made him go crazy. Totally fucking crazy. I thought maybe he was going to kill me then and there. But he didn't, and I've been here ever since."

"How long?"

"A couple months maybe. It's hard to keep track of the time, you know. I'm like a trusty around here. It's good to have some company."

"Is he planning to kill me?" Genevieve asked.

"I don't know about that. I honestly don't. But at least he doesn't seem to be in any hurry."

"You think he really wants us dead?"

"I think it's one of his options. But we could give him other options."

9. SCARE

Zak Webster got on with his life. What else was there to do? The events of the other night had been pretty strange, but he found it impossible to calibrate the degree of strangeness. Looked at from one perspective, it all seemed random enough, just big-city weirdness, but from another, there was something less than random about it, something ominously specific that seemed to involve him and Utopiates.

A couple of days passed. Zak did his job, sold a set of mid-priced eighteenth-century maps of Peru, talked to Ray McKinley on the phone, said nothing about the tattooed woman. He wouldn't have known what to say, and why would Ray even have been interested? He got through the working hours, and the genuinely random universe seemed to be asserting itself. That was a good thing, right? And then there was a counter assertion.

It was another long, restless evening, and again it was nearly time to close the store, but then Zak glanced out the window and saw the battered metallic-blue Cadillac parked a short distance away. His heart sank. He felt disappointed, anxious, and somehow inexplicably angry. He looked up and down the street, thinking perhaps history was about to repeat itself, that perhaps some other tattooed woman was out there, just waiting to strip naked and show herself, but no, this time the street was thoroughly empty.

Zak watched as the driver got out of the Cadillac, strutted along the sidewalk, looked very briefly in the window of Utopiates, then ambled inside. Zak gave him a nod of tentative welcome, but initially the guy ignored both Zak and the contents of the store. He moved slowly and purposefully around the space, briefly entering the back room, as though staking it out, looking for exits or trapdoors or hidden gunmen. Zak suspected he might be in some trouble. Absurdly, he found himself saying, "Can I help you?"

The visitor didn't reply at first, then asked, "How's business?"

Billy Moore sounded genuinely interested, which only alarmed Zak even more.

"It could be better," Zak said truthfully.

"Always," Billy said. "Business could always be better."

He looked at Zak with what might possibly have been sympathy, though Zak suspected it might equally well be contempt. This didn't look like a man who'd have much respect for someone who worked in retail.

"Who buys this kind of shit?" Billy asked.

"People who like this kind of shit," said Zak, with just a hint of defiance in his voice.

Billy Moore nodded slowly, considering the answer, and when it had sunk in, he said, "You on your own here?"

Zak wanted to say no, no, there were a couple of samurai lurking in the basement, just dying to come up and start trouble, or finish it, but he said, "For now I am, yes."

"Good," said Billy Moore. "I've got a message for you."

"Who are you?" Zak asked.

"It doesn't matter. And why would I tell you anyway? The message is just this: the things you saw the other night, the woman, the tattoos, the Caddy, me . . ."

"Yes?"

"You didn't see them."

"Oh, okay," said Zak. "I think I get the message."

"Well, there's the problem. It's not just a verbal message. I'm here to scare you. Are you scared yet?"

"I'm anxious," Zak said.

"That's not the same thing."

"Okay, then, let's say that I'm scared," said Zak, but there was a certain insolence in the way he said it, suggesting that he might not scare so easily after all.

"That's not enough. I have to make sure."

"How are you going to do that?"

"I'm going to hurt you. It's nothing personal."

"Couldn't you just hurt my feelings?"

"Are you trying to be funny?"

"A little," Zak said. "Trying to, you know, break the tension."

"If you're trying to be funny, then you're not nearly scared enough, are you?"

Zak could see he had a point. "What does 'hurting' mean exactly?" he said.

"Maybe break something."

"That would definitely hurt," Zak said.

"Something in the face maybe," Billy suggested. "Nose, teeth, jaw, whatever . . ."

Zak conducted a brief mental inventory of his face. Every part of it seemed infinitely breakable, as fragile and brittle as any of the antique maps and globes that were on sale in the store.

He said, "I really didn't see anything. And even if I did, I didn't know what I was seeing. And I definitely wouldn't tell anybody. I've nothing to tell. I really am quite scared."

"You're getting there."

"No, I'm right there. You can leave it at that." Zak was trying to sound resolute, reasonable, and robust, but he wondered if he might have done better to sound pathetic. He added, "You don't have to hurt me. You've delivered your message. I'll do what you say. Now you can just fuck off."

Zak was a little surprised to hear those words come out of his mouth, though not nearly as surprised as Billy Moore. They both knew it was absolutely the wrong thing to say.

"Are you telling me to fuck off?" Billy said.

"Only metaphorically," Zak replied, and then he wished he hadn't said that either.

Billy Moore positioned himself between Zak and the front door of Utopiates. There'd be no chance for Zak to escape in that direction, and there was nothing to be gained by running into the back room: Billy had already established that was a dead end. Lacking other options, Zak squared himself up. He'd been in very few fights in his life and, given the choice, would never have been in any whatsoever. Still, he wasn't going to beg or plead; and he was certainly going to do his best to fight back.

He didn't get the chance. Billy Moore zipped up his leather jacket, a sign that he meant business. He took half a step forward and landed a precise, effortless punch in the core of Zak's body, as though his navel were a bull's eye. So, not the face after all, Zak thought, but that was no consolation. He was amazed by the pain, as though a battering ram had penetrated his body. Fighting back suddenly didn't seem to be a possibility. His legs lost their stability. The air was too thin, his lungs too feeble. He started to fall and another blow hammered him in the eye before he'd hit the floor.

Once there, Zak clutched himself and again tried to breathe, but he seemed to have lost the knack. Billy Moore stood over him, nicely positioned to give him a good kicking, a process he began by slamming his foot into Zak's left kidney. Zak squirmed, his arms and legs twitched, motor coordination was a thing of the past.

Another kick landed. From what had been said, Zak didn't

believe this man had actually come to kill him, but he suspected that guys like this often made mistakes; they got carried away, enjoyed their work a little too much. Then, dimly, from very far away, Zak heard the front door open and close. Somebody had come into the store, and then a woman's voice that sounded only vaguely familiar was issuing commands—"Stop that. Stop that right now. Leave him alone. Stop kicking him"—and to Zak's great surprise he was no longer being kicked.

The female voice persisted. Zak recognized it now as belonging to the woman with the tortoiseshell glasses. She was angry and outraged, or was at least pretending to be. Either way it was impressive. From his quasi-fetal position, Zak couldn't tell exactly what was going on above him, but he sensed that his assailant was moving away.

"Get out of here. Go on," the woman shouted. "And shame on you."

Billy Moore was calm, and he didn't seem remotely ashamed. He straightened himself, ran a hand through his hair, though, in fact, his assault on Zak had left him entirely unruffled. It seemed he was about to leave the store, just as he had been told to do, but the woman wasn't finished with him yet.

"And that poor creature from the other night," she demanded, "the one you put in your car, where is she now? What have you done with her?"

Zak was certain these questions would not be answered, and that even asking them was a very high-risk activity.

"It's none of your business, is it," said Billy Moore, flatly.

She marched up to him. She was carrying a backpack and she swung it in a wide, shallow, urgent arc, slamming it into the side of Billy Moore's head. He flinched, surprised but certainly not hurt: not even conspicuously angry. He looked at her sadly.

"You know," he said, "there are some guys who pride themselves on never hitting a woman. I'm not one of them."

He delivered a single punch, not nearly as hard as either of the ones he'd landed on Zak—something more delicate, something for the ladies, but not a bitch slap either, more of a jab, a straight shot with a closed fist that landed neatly on the woman's left eye. Her head snapped back, her spectacles went flying, and she went down too, ending up on the floor, not far away from Zak. Billy Moore showed just a modicum of concern as he watched her fall, but once he was satisfied that she hadn't cracked her skull open, that she was down but not completely out, he was content to unzip his jacket and leave. He'd driven away before either of his victims was able even to contemplate getting up from the floor.

10. DEVIATION

"Why did you come back?" Zak asked when he could finally breathe and speak. "I thought the place gave you the creeps."

"It did. It does. And I don't know why, and that kind of intrigues me in itself."

They had, in due course, managed to raise themselves from the floor, inspected their own and each other's injuries. Both had facial bruises that would soon flower into black eyes. They had even managed to introduce themselves: "I'm Zak Webster"; "I'm Marilyn Driscoll."

"You said you didn't know what you saw the other night."

"I still don't," said Zak.

"I can help with that." She took a scuffed, bestickered laptop out of her backpack. "I took some pictures. They're not great, but they're a start."

Zak was inclined to ask, "The start of what?" but he held his tongue. He also wondered why she'd been taking pictures. Was she a tourist? A street photographer? A student of urban renewal? He didn't ask any of that either. Recent events suggested he might be much better off not knowing what he'd seen, but it was already too late for that.

Marilyn Driscoll brought the laptop to life, and there on-screen appeared thumbnails of the pictures she'd taken on what Zak was increasingly, and ever less ironically, coming to think of as "that fateful night." She clicked through a handful of quickly taken, not especially clear images. In one of them Zak could see himself standing in the doorway of Utopiates, looking awkward and profoundly unphotogenic. He didn't like seeing pictures of himself at the best of times. They moved on to another image, one that showed the battered Cadillac: that wasn't exactly fascinating either.

Then Marilyn brought up an image of the driver and zoomed in on his face. That was more revealing in a way. You could probably have identified the guy from it, though Zak could have identified him perfectly well without a photograph. In any case, there was nothing very special about him. To Zak he looked like just another bruiser, a petty crook, not a rarity in this city or any other.

Marilyn opened up the next picture, the one that seemed by far the most important, showing the pale, tattooed skin of the naked woman's back. The photograph had been taken from an oblique angle, so that the camera's automatic focus had struggled to find a center, and the framing was haphazard, but at least Zak could see that his impression had been right: it really was a map.

"Pretty crude," said Marilyn Driscoll.

"The photographs?" said Zak.

"I meant the tattoos. Which is to say, a very crude map."

"Yes," Zak agreed, "although in general, the cruder the map, the clearer the mapmaker's intentions."

He hoped that didn't sound too pretentious. It was true, as far as it went, but he was aware that he was saying it with more gravitas than it merited. He was playing the scholar, trying to impress this woman, attempting to do an impersonation of a shrewd, wise man.

"I can enhance it a little," Marilyn said.

She played with the image of the woman's back, sharpened it, adjusted the brightness and contrast, the shadow and highlight function, until it became a little clearer, though scarcely less enigmatic. Zak could now see, at the center of the woman's back, running shakily down either side of her spine, two long, rough tattooed lines. One of them, in red, looked somewhat like the representation of a road. The other, a black line with cross-hatching, could have been a railroad track. Two other, more or less parallel, blue lines snaking lazily, horizontally across the woman's shoulder blades might possibly have been the banks of a river or canal. Elsewhere on the exposed flesh were scattered squares and rectangles that you might interpret as buildings, though you could just as easily have interpreted them as something else. Dotted and zigzag lines might have signified routes or directions, but then again they might not.

"So what are we looking at here exactly?" Marilyn asked. "You think it's a real map?"

"All maps are real," said Zak, hoping that he wasn't pushing his luck too far.

"But where's it a map of?" said Marilyn. "Is it an actual place or an imaginary one? Can we use it to get somewhere? Is it maybe just decorative? Maybe it doesn't have any use at all."

"Every map has its use," said Zak. "The problem may be working out what that use is. And it may be even harder to work out who's the intended user."

Marilyn Driscoll nodded thoughtfully. She seemed to be impressed: he liked that.

"And what's that thing there?" asked Marilyn.

She pointed at a small round tattoo located right on the flesh of the woman's coccyx. The image was especially unclear in that area, but Zak knew well enough what it was.

"That's a compass rose," he said. "The kind of thing you'd see in the corner of a map or chart, showing cardinal directions—

north, south, east, west—sometimes the intermediate ones too. Must hurt like hell to have it tattooed there."

"You think?" said Marilyn.

"They're called roses because some of them are very ornate. The first one was drawn by a sixteenth-century Portuguese cartographer named Pedro Reinel. And originally they were called wind roses because early mapmakers made no distinction between a direction and a wind that came from that direction."

"You're good," Marilyn said.

"Are you glad you came back?"

"Glad might be overstating it," she said, delicately touching her eye where Billy Moore had punched her.

"And of course," said Zak, "as far as that goes, the early roses made no distinction between magnetic north and true north. That's called deviation. I could go on."

"I imagine you could."

It might have been a putdown, but he didn't think it was. She seemed happy enough to hear him spout his cartographic expertise. She looked at him approvingly, but then with some concern.

"We're both going to have black eyes," she said. "People will think we've been boxing each other."

"Well, they'll think you won. Mine's going to look worse than yours."

"Maybe we need to get a bag of ice."

"Funny thing," said Zak. "Where they have ice they often have alcohol."

"Don't tell me you know some sleazy watering hole where cartographers go to lick their wounds?"

"I don't actually hang out with cartographers," Zak confessed. "But I do know a sleazy watering hole where I go to lick *my* wounds."

"Good enough," said Marilyn.

11. PLASMA

Wrobleski didn't like having to sit in one place in order to be informed, entertained, or sedated: he found the passivity excruciating. That's why he'd bought the biggest TV he could find—panoramic, high-def, as large as his own bed, all the bells and whistles and klaxons—and wall-mounted—once they'd reinforced the wall of his living room. When there was something he really needed to see, he could watch it while still pacing around the room.

The screen currently showed two women and a man sitting uncomfortably in gawkily stylish, primary-colored chairs. Behind them an electronic backdrop showed ever-changing "then and now" images of the city. One woman was the interviewer, young, eagerly serious, but unthreatening, unlikely to give the other two a hard time. The other woman was familiar to Wrobleski, and to everybody else in this city. It was the mayor, Margaret "Meg" Gunderson, a big, severe-looking woman, a bruiser with a background in the transport unions, worn only somewhat smooth by her years in city politics. She'd been pushed through media boot camp, taught when and how to smile, to speak slowly and display a certain quirky charm, but she still looked like someone you wouldn't want to tangle with in a street fight.

The man, if you wanted Wrobleski's opinion, was a ludicrous, pretentious clown, albeit one for whom Meg Gunderson apparently had some use at that moment. The interviewer introduced the clown as Marco Brandt, a member of the mayor's select committee on inner-city regeneration, and described him as a "futurologist with a special interest in speculative urbanism," but Wrobleski had stopped listening before she'd gotten around to explaining what the fuck that meant.

Brandt's exoticism was conspicuous but oddly nonspecific. His voice, when he acknowledged the introduction, seemed to be conducting its own world tour of accents. He was an older man trying to look young. The clothes were all black but featured asymmetrical angles and various fabrics that showed different degrees of luster: velvet, brocade, leather insets. His white hair was spiked and upright, and he wore spectacles that looked like ornate miniature scaffoldings on a long, thin face that would otherwise have appeared bland.

The three TV heads were talking about the future of the city. Mayor Gunderson was giving it her all, being as genial as she could manage, but also comprehensible, talking about the need for the city to get off its butt and press on with new developments. And she had a pet project. The old Telstar Hotel, which all on-screen agreed was a great example of sixties architecture—though Wrobleski had only ever thought of it as that closed-down dump that used to have a revolving restaurant—was now about to be included on the National Register of Historic Architecture. Gunderson had worked hard for this, become personally identified with the campaign that put the Telstar at the heart of the next phase of renewal. She said she cared deeply, was passionate about the plans. She said she was prepared to put her reputation on the line here. For all that Wrobleski despised and distrusted politicians, he was almost inclined to believe her.

He looked over to the other side of the room, where Akim was meticulously, if unenthusiastically, polishing the glass on a wall full of framed maps. Wrobleski couldn't trust just anyone with a job like that.

On the TV screen, Brandt was now unleashed. Before long Wrobleski was not so much listening as fighting to stop himself from riddling the screen with bullet holes. He heard Brandt utter formulations about shifting paradigms of urban policy, sustainability, streetscapes, environmental enhancements, social inclusiveness, synergy, metropolitan hegemony.

It was only after this had gone on longer than any sane human being could possibly tolerate that the interviewer decided it was time to bring things to a close. She talked directly, and a little too brightly, to the camera for a few moments, and as she spoke, Meg Gunderson (off microphone, but by no means off camera) looked across at Brandt and mouthed the words "You twat."

"You know," said Wrobleski to Akim, "the more I see of this woman Gunderson, the less and less I feel like killing her."

12. IN AND ON THE GRID

The "sleazy watering hole" was named the Grid. Originally it had been a minor outpost of the telecommunications industry, a squat bunker of a building that housed an arcane and obsolete form of telephone exchange. Now it had been "repurposed" into an inky, angular, high-ceilinged bar, with tight pools of blue and purple light, and miscellaneous chunks of antique electronic equipment half-visible in dark recesses. It was the kind of place that casual, uncommitted drinkers would peer into and immediately realize, rightly, wasn't for them. There were TV screens above the bar, but no sports had ever been shown on them. The management preferred to screen classic noir and European avant-garde masterpieces, played in slow motion with the sound off.

In the corner, on a tiny raised stage, an extravagantly muscled, hairless man was playing an electronic keyboard. He looked as if he might have been a biker, maybe a laid-off steelworker, maybe a gay bodybuilder. His repertoire heavily favored Satie, Philip Glass, and Stockhausen. He called himself Sam, though nobody thought that was his real name, and in any case, few people had ever said to him, "Play it again." He nodded to Zak and to Marilyn, though it was a general rather than a specific greeting.

"That's Sam," said Zak. "They say he used to be a cop. Whether a good cop or a bad cop, I'm not sure. One of those 'profiler' guys, I think."

Otherwise the crowd was a mix of hipster, nerd, and borderline-criminal element. The woman behind the zinc-topped bar looked like a ruined Bettie Page, something both reinforced and contradicted by a tattoo of Bettie Page on her forearm. Zak and Marilyn took up places at the bar and ordered drinks from the "special" cocktail menu. Something celebratory seemed in order. Nothing quite brings people together like being beaten up at the same time, in the same place, by the same guy. The drinks came, in elegant, conical cobalt-blue glasses, though the bases were severely chipped.

"This is where you come for kicks?" Marilyn said.

"One of the places."

"And what else do you do for kicks, Zak?"

"Oh, you know . . . I read, I watch movies, I walk. Actually what I like best is urban exploration."

"Yes?"

She didn't seem as impressed by that as she had been by his knowledge of maps. He tried to explain.

"Urban exploration: investigating the city, creative trespass, going where I'm not supposed to, getting into abandoned structures, factories, closed-down hospitals, derelict power stations. You know?"

"So you spend all your workdays dealing in representations of places, and you spend your free time exploring actual places."

"Does that sound weird?"

"Not to me. What do you think I was doing the other night when I found Utopiates? Walking, looking at the city, taking pictures."

"A woman after my own heart," Zak said, and immediately felt like a fool. At least he hadn't used the word "soulmate."

Without being asked, the bartender delivered two bags of ice, suitable for the care and treatment of black eyes. Zak remembered why he liked this place so much.

"Yeah," he continued, "on my days off, I get in the car, go to some disused flour mill or iron foundry or whatever, and you know, just poke around."

"You have a car? You don't look like a car owner."

"How do car owners look? It's just a company car, a big brown station wagon, good for hauling stock and not much else."

"But still," said Marilyn, "it creates possibilities."

Zak took a moment to consider what these might be.

"You got any tattoos, Zak?" Marilyn asked.

"No."

"Ever thought about it?"

"Not really," said Zak. "I wouldn't know what to get. It's a big commitment. Not that I'm afraid of commitment."

"How about a tattooed map?" Marilyn suggested.

"Even bigger problem. Of where?" he said. "Atlantis? Pangæa? The Batcave? And I definitely never thought of having one on my back."

They suckled on their drinks.

"We got beaten up," said Marilyn, "just because of something we saw."

"I don't think the guy even knew that you saw it until you told him. In any case, I reckon you got beaten up because you hit him with your backpack."

"It seemed like the right thing to do," she said. "So I guess we're not going to call the cops, are we?"

"No," Zak agreed. "Calling the cops would involve telling them what I saw, and according to the guy who beat me up, I didn't see anything."

"But doesn't that kind of make you want to tell everybody everything?"

"Not really," said Zak. "And I still don't know what I saw."

"Not quite true," said Marilyn. "We know what you saw, we just don't know what it means."

"Now you're starting to sound like me."

"And where do you think that poor woman is now?"

They both knew it was an impossible question to answer, but Zak suspected it wasn't quite a rhetorical one. He felt she was testing him, seeing how his imagination worked.

"Oh, I'm sure she's living a life of quiet contentment somewhere in the countryside," he said dryly.

"Or maybe she's lying dead in a ditch," said Marilyn. "Either way it would be good to know."

"Would it?"

"Yes. Don't you feel some responsibility?"

"Not really," Zak admitted.

"Some basic human concern?"

"Well yes, okay, maybe a little of that."

"Then don't you feel we ought to do something?"

"Like what?"

"Maybe track down this guy and his Cadillac, see where he lives and who he is. Find out what he did with that woman."

"Are you serious?"

"Well, do you have a better idea?"

Zak had several, and none of them involved tracking down a Cadillac and its violent driver, to who knows where, in order to find a tattooed homeless woman who might not want to be found. He didn't see how this could lead to anything other than another beating. At the same time he didn't want to destroy the feeling of connection he had with Marilyn, and he certainly didn't want her to think he was a wimp.

"Look, Zak," Marilyn said, "you could help me on this. You know about maps, you know parts of the city that I don't. I could really use your help."

The idea of being a help to Marilyn, even the idea of being "used" by her, did have a certain appeal.

"I like to help."

The muscle-bound keyboard player was tinkling some unexpectedly conventional cocktail piano, a little Sinatra, and he was even singing, in a surprisingly sweet, light baritone. The lyrics insisted that love is the tender trap, and Zak was happy enough with that sentiment, but the line that really spoke to him was the one about hurrying to a spot that's just a dot on the map. Most places are a dot on some map or other; some dots are bigger than others, and sometimes the size of the dot bears no relation to the importance of the place. In any case, there are very few you really need to hurry to. He wondered if the universe was sending him a message, and if so, what it said. He was pretty sure the sensible thing to do was go home and stay out of trouble. And after a couple more drinks he did go home, alone. No surprise there; and besides, Marilyn said she had to get up early the next morning. She had to see a woman about a tattoo.

13. SUIT

Billy Moore's parking lot, early morning, the air pigeon-gray with haze, the lot empty except for his two trailers. There were no cars there because a dump truck was currently depositing a load of white one-inch pea gravel at the lot's center and a small gang of day laborers were waiting with shovels and rakes. Billy Moore stood in the street watching, next to his Cadillac, with his daughter beside him: a man in a leather jacket, a girl in a camouflage hoodie and graffiti-patterned sneakers. Quite the family group, he thought. Billy Moore: landowner, entrepreneur, patriarch. Carla Moore: heiress.

"How's it going, Sanjay?" Billy shouted to a young man in a short-sleeved pink shirt with a crimson bow tie, black suit pants, shoes glossy as a freshly buffed eggplant, who was supervising the laborers and largely being ignored by them. Sanjay raised two overoptimistic thumbs.

"Who's Sanjay?" Carla asked.

"He's my employee," Billy said, pleased though not yet comfortable with the term. "The world's best-dressed parking attendant. He's from one of those loser countries that had to change its name, used to be a student back home, now he's here trying to better himself, paying his way through college. Eventually I'll get him a little hut with a chair and a baseball bat in case of trouble. He'll collect the money, keep an eye on the cars, and he can read his textbooks or whatever when things get quiet."

"Like all great plans it's really simple," said Carla.

"You know, sarcasm is really unattractive in a twelve-year-old."

"I don't do it to be attractive."

A part of Billy was still fretting gently about having hit the guy and the girl at the map store. It had been necessary, sure, but it hardly fell within the boundaries of keeping out of trouble, let alone going straight. And behind that, there was a more shapeless kind of fretting about what Wrobleski was going to do with Genevieve and maybe Laurel, and the other women he might be told to haul in. It was better to be concerned with something practical and uncomplicated: the graveling of a parking lot.

"You really think you're going to make a fortune in the parking business?" Carla asked.

"Yes and no."

"Then why?"

"Let me explain," said Billy, thinking it was no bad thing for a man to explain himself to his daughter. "Look, I know this isn't the most desirable bit of land in the world. But that's the whole point."

"Yes?"

She walked deliberately along one edge of the lot, as though she were pacing it out. Billy found himself trailing after her, explaining.

"Yeah, see if you own a nice piece of land, something with grass and trees on it, or a nice old building, and then you want to develop it, put a big new building on it, well then, people get all upset because they think you're screwing up the environment or something. But if you own a parking lot, well, everyone thinks the environment is pretty screwed up already. Everybody says, 'It's just a parking lot; anything's better than that.'"

"Maybe," said Carla, less than convinced.

"So that's what I'll be doing. I'll run this place as a parking lot for a while, but then at some point I'll sell it on to a developer who wants to build some butt-ugly apartment block, and it'll be easy to get planning permission because everybody says, 'Well, it's a butt-ugly apartment block, but at least it's not a parking lot.' And then I take the profit from that deal, buy another parcel—"

"Parcel?"

"Yep. That's what they call it, a parcel of land. Then I'll make another parking lot and start again."

"So we'll be moving?" said Carla, a flare of alarm in her voice.

"That's the beauty of a mobile home," he said, as reassuringly as he could. "In the meantime, I'm trying to make it a really good, secure parking lot. There's a crew coming this afternoon to put up a fence. And I've got a chance of a city contract. A subcontractor wants to park his trucks here while they're working on the Platinum Line. How about that?"

"Kudos," said Carla blankly.

A fast-food box blew across the street toward the lot. Carla stomped on it, then picked it up, doing a little light housekeeping.

The dump truck was ready to depart. Sanjay was shouting something incomprehensible to the driver, and Billy watched the guys with the shovels and rakes as they began to spread the gravel. They were working a lot harder and with a lot more enthusiasm than he'd have been able to muster.

"And does this all lead to riches and luxury and world domination, Dad?" Carla asked.

"It leads to me being able to live with my daughter," said Billy. "That's the main thing."

She looked at him with a seldom-seen sweetness.

"You know, Dad," she said slyly, "if you're going to be an entrepreneur, you might want to lose the leather jacket."

"Yeah?"

"You don't want to be less well-dressed than your parking attendant."

He could see her point.

"Yeah. I can see you in a really nice suit," said Carla.

"Pinstripe?"

"No," said Carla, "pinstripe is way too obvious. I see you in elephant gray, exposed stitching, two-button, notched laps, front flap pockets, side vents, vermilion lining."

"You really see me in that?"

"Yeah."

"You sure you don't just want a different kind of dad?"

"I want the same dad, I just want him to look good."

14. THE FLASH

"Old tattooists never die, they simply lose their flash."

The person delivering this piece of hoary tattoo wisdom to Marilyn Driscoll was an old woman by the name of Rose Scarlatti. They were sitting in Rose's small, dark apartment, the air clouded with the sweet, marginally corrupt smell of clove cigarettes. Marilyn had found Rose online. She'd been looking for somebody who knew some history and wasn't afraid to repeat it. Her initial word searches had combined "tattoo artist" or "tattooist" or even "tattooer" with other relevant terms, such as "knowledgeable," "scholarly," "erudite," "cerebral." There had been no shortage of hits, and so to limit the field, she'd added the word "female"—a shot in the dark, but she sensed it would be easier to talk to a woman about this stuff—and Rose Scarlatti was the only one within a hundred miles. Marilyn wanted a face-to-face meeting.

There was a small, unruly, neglected website, graced with a banner—*Rose Scarlatti: The Lady Tattooist and Scholar*—and a small online gallery that showed her work and the woman herself, and although the site suggested she'd hung up her tools, there was also the implication that if the right project, the right body, came along, she'd be perfectly prepared to get back to work.

Marilyn e-mailed her. Funny how if you're a young woman and you send an e-mail to some old person and say you're really interested in their work, and that you'd really love to talk with them in person, they're likely to say come right on over as soon as you like.

Rose Scarlatti lived alone in an apartment building called the Villa Nova: low-rise, coated in French-blue stucco that had seen better days, but the sign on the front was in a cursive faux-retro typeface, and the individual apartments had balconies where many of the residents were trying hard to establish some greenery.

Rose's apartment was on the third floor, in the very center, right above the gap between the words "Villa" and "Nova," and as Marilyn pedaled toward the entrance, she looked up and saw Rose sitting out on her balcony, surveying the street, smoking. She was a thin, dry, neat woman, careful with herself, but not delicate. She peered down, saw Marilyn, waved with her cigarette, and went inside to buzz her up.

Rose's den was part personal museum, part smoking lounge. Marilyn's eyes darted around the place, not knowing where to settle, scanning the items of tattoo memorabilia: framed newspaper articles and photographs of tattooed men and women, carnival posters, design sheets, shop signs—too much to take in all at once, though a fierce-looking crossbow mounted above the door to the kitchen was hard to miss. Needing something else to focus on, Marilyn let her eyes settle on an old photograph of a woman who would have appeared severe, respectable, even matronly, if it hadn't been for the patterns inked all over her.

"That's Nora Hildebrandt," said Rose Scarlatti. "The first tattooed lady to be exhibited in America. Daughter of Martin Hildebrandt, German immigrant and tattooist. His glory days were in the Civil War. He went from camp to camp tattooing soldiers on both sides. In his downtime he obviously tattooed his daughter as well. But maybe he thought that would seem a little strange, or maybe not strange enough, so when she went on stage they made up a story, that they'd both been kidnapped by the Sioux, and the Injuns had forced Daddy to tattoo his daughter, every day a new one, once a day for a whole year, 365 of them. Then they set 'em free."

"Nice story," said Marilyn.

"Sure. Everybody needs a story. Doesn't need to be true. Why don't you sit down, tell me what's on your mind?"

Marilyn sat down in an unstable, swamp-colored recliner. Her mind was racing. It was an unsettling experience to sit in a room with this trim, benign-looking, gray-haired lady who was dressed in corduroy pants and a crew-necked, long-sleeved cashmere sweater, and to know that beneath the corduroy and cashmere there was a riot of brilliant, obsessive tattooing: the usual in some ways (snakes, flaming skulls, dancing girls, birds of prey, pirates: no maps as far as Marilyn was aware), but with something special and flowing, free-form and spontaneous about it.

She knew all this from the pictures on the website that showed Rose as a much younger woman, more or less naked, more curvy, more arrogant, wilder. But there was also something unfinished-looking about Rose's tattoos, still a lot of bare skin. Marilyn had seen those pictures of people whose tattoos were like bodysuits of ink, neck to ankle and wrist to wrist, but Rose's weren't like that. Hers were limited to certain areas: the legs, the chest, the right arm, while her back, her buttocks, and her left arm were all completely bare. The asymmetry created the effect of a work in progress, not that she'd lost interest or been forced to abandon it halfway through, rather that she was still awaiting new ideas, leaving space for fresh possibilities and inspiration.

Marilyn Driscoll liked that the tattoos were covered up now. It showed a certain reserve, a sense that Rose's tattoos were a private matter. In public Rose might pass for a retired schoolteacher, but get her alone and naked in a room and she would become something very different.

"I'm doing a project on tattoos and tattooing," said Marilyn as innocently as she could.

"A project, eh?"

"That's right."

"Are you thinking about getting a tattoo?"

"Not really, no."

"Why not?"

"I think I'd live to regret it."

"What's wrong with that? That's the whole deal with tattoos. You make a choice. And if it turns out you made a bad choice, you live with the consequences, you take responsibility, you don't blame anybody else. That's life, right?"

"Sure," said Marilyn. "Unless you didn't actually choose to have the tattoos done."

"Ah right, now you're talking," said Rose, and something in her brightened. "Enforced tattooing. A long and shameful tradition."

"Yes?"

"Oh sure, the Greeks and Romans used to tattoo the words I'M AN ESCAPED SLAVE across the foreheads of their slaves so they'd never be able to become escaped slaves. Clever, huh? And the Nazis, of course. And outlaw bikers sometimes tattoo PROP-ERTY OF on less than willing girls.

"In India before the British Empire, they used to tattoo con-victs with images of their crimes: a bottle if they were drunks, cock and balls if they were adulterers. I guess it might have been a deterrent *before* the event, but once you'd got the tattoo on you, there wouldn't be much incentive to stop being a drunk or an adulterer, would there? You might as well live up to your image. And then, of course, some criminals tattoo themselves to show what crimes they've committed. They're proud to wear their crimes on their skin. And I don't even want to think about what those damn Russians get up to."

Marilyn could feel that Rose was looking her over intently, professionally, not undressing her with her eyes, but coating her with imaginary ink and imagery.

"You sure I can't talk you into letting me tattoo you?"

"Really, no," said Marilyn.

"That's okay," Rose said. "It's good not to pretend. Some people would have come in here and tried to butter me up by saying they wanted me to work on 'em. I don't care. I like talking about my work, and I like talking to young women; so y'know, I ain't complaining. Besides, I'm retired."

She laughed, as though this were a joke she'd repeated many, many times, to the point where she was the only one who still found it funny.

"Why did you retire?" Marilyn asked.

Rose put her cigarette to her mouth and Marilyn could see that her long, thin, pale fingers were knotted tightly at the joints.

"Physical things partly," Rose said. "Arthritis in the knuckles, carpal tunnel problems, and my hand just wasn't as steady as I wanted it to be. And you know, the sad fact is, a lot of young people don't want to be tattooed by some old lady. They want somebody their own age, from their own tribe. But the real deal, the real reason I quit: the area where I had my studio, it got *gentrified*."

She spat out the word as if it implied a combination of moral degeneracy and self-inflicted disease.

"The rent kept going up," she continued, "and the yuppie scum kept moving in. There was no room for any of the old trades. We all got driven out. Like rats."

Marilyn Driscoll pictured a procession of knife grinders, rag-

and-bone pickers, button molders, hounded from one part of the city to another, a contagion being driven to the borders, Rose reluctantly but defiantly bringing up the rear.

"Have you tattooed a lot of women, Rose?" Marilyn asked.

"Sure."

"Is it very different from tattooing a man?"

"Well, it's a lot more fun, if you like women. But I couldn't afford to be picky. I didn't discriminate."

"How about maps? Did you ever put a map of a city or a country on somebody?"

"Sure. This is a service industry. If a customer asked for a map, I'd give 'em a map. People want to be reminded of where they come from, or where they did a tour of duty, or where they met their wife, or whatever. Doesn't seem to me it's the kind of thing you'd forget, but I was happy to do the work."

"Did you ever tattoo a map of Utopia?"

Rose filled her lungs and looked skeptically at Marilyn.

"Nah. But I once did a map of the planet Mongo—y'know, Flash Gordon. You'd be too young to know what I'm talking about. But sure, the world's a big place. So why not a map of Utopia, whatever the hell that looks like. The fact is, somebody somewhere is having the most idiotic thing you can imagine tattooed right across their chest at this very moment."

"Or across their back," said Marilyn.

"Well, the back's always a strange choice, if you want my opinion. You never get to see it except in a mirror, and even then you see it left to right reversed. All those guys with gang names or American flags or Stations of the Cross on their back: they never see them as the world sees them, except maybe in photographs. What's the point?"

"I can see that," said Marilyn. "And all tattooists have their own style, right?"

"If they're any good they do," said Rose. "If they're not any good, they just buy some flash and copy the designs, which is no more than tracing, if you ask me. You might as well buy a coloring book."

"So if I showed you a picture of a certain tattoo, could you maybe tell me who did it?"

"Jeez, girl, you want a lot. I call myself a tattoo scholar, not a psychic. Sure, the ones who are really, really good do stand out, but given the number of people in the world who do tattooing, it's a tiny percentage. The ones who aren't any good, and that's most of 'em, the work all looks pretty much the same as far as I'm concerned."

"Want to try anyway? I'll show you a photograph of some tattooing, and you tell me if you recognize who did it."

"Do I get a gold star?" said Rose.

"You get my deepest gratitude."

Rose's face indicated that she didn't consider that much of a prize, but she didn't object as Marilyn got out her laptop and showed Rose the same image that she and Zak had pored over. Rose stared at it with concentration, then incomprehension, then growing distaste.

"What exactly is this?" she asked suspiciously.

"You tell me."

"First thing, it's fucking incompetent, is what it is. But you don't need me to tell you that. The guy who did this wasn't any kind of tattooist. He was an amateur. I'd say he was a butcher. In fact, I'd be inclined to say he was a fucking lunatic."

"Do you know any amateurs-slash-incompetents-slash-butchers-slash-lunatics?" Marilyn asked.

"Who are also tattooists? Nah."

Rose concentrated even harder on the image, and suddenly reacted as though she'd received a sharp sting somewhere in her lower back.

"Wait a damn minute," she said. "What's that?"

She jabbed her cigarette toward an area of the laptop's screen and Marilyn zoomed in on a detail of the image.

"That's not right," said Rose. "That's very fucking wrong. See there, that thing there?"

She peered hard at the screen, at the tattooed woman's backside.

"It's called a compass rose, isn't it?" said Marilyn, pleased to have some useful knowledge.

"Yes. That's what it is, all right. And it's mine. The compass rose is Rose Scarlatti's fucking trademark."

Rose pulled up the right sleeve of her sweater, to reveal on her forearm a small circular tattoo of a compass rose. It was intricate, delicately done, and bore very little resemblance to the one in the photograph as far as Marilyn could see, which was why, she supposed, she hadn't noticed it when she'd looked at Rose's images online.

Rose tapped her forearm and said, "That's the first tattoo I ever did on myself."

"I don't get it," said Marilyn. "So whoever did this is copying you?"

"Copying, stealing. They've made a lousy job, whichever it is."

"Why would anyone do that?"

"I don't know. But if I found him I'd slap his head till I found out."

Rose was about to say more, perhaps much more, and then she stopped herself. It was abrupt and defensive, as if she'd realized, suddenly, out of nowhere, something crucial and secret, and maybe forbidden, and she wasn't remotely convincing when she said, "Okay, leave it. You know, I'm probably being silly. I'm overreacting."

"I don't think so, Rose."

"Yes, I am."

"What's up, Rose, what do you see? What have you realized?"

"Nothing. Nothing at all."

"What is it? What's going on, Rose? What's happened?"

"Nothing's happened."

"You know who did this tattoo, don't you?"

"I don't know anything."

"Why don't I believe that?"

"I don't care what you believe. And if you're not going to believe me, you might as well get out of my apartment."

Rose distracted herself briefly by lighting a fresh cigarette. She inhaled deeply, then released a swirling band of smoke. She didn't quite blow it in Marilyn's face, but she might as well have.

"Rose, I'm sorry," said Marilyn. "I didn't mean to offend you."

"But you did."

"And I'm sorry, I apologize. There's lots more I want to ask you."

"Yeah, well, I got nothing more to say."

"Please."

"Another time maybe. Or maybe not."

"Rose, I really am sorry."

"So you keep saying."

"Is there nothing I can do?"

"Not unless you're prepared to let me put some ink on you."

Marilyn slowly stood up, gathered her belongings, made a move toward the door.

"I'm going to have to think very long and hard about that," she said as she departed.

15. RAY OF LIGHT

Zak Webster lolled at his desk. His head and eye and back all ached, his mind was full of things he might have said or done to avoid getting a beating yesterday, and also of the things he might have said or done to make Marilyn declare, "I have a meeting with a tattooist tomorrow, but what the hell, let's make a night of it." He had not come up with any of the right imaginary words or deeds before he saw Ray McKinley's sleek, butter-colored convertible pull up outside the store. Ray was making one of his irregular and unscheduled visits. That would be a distraction, though not of the kind Zak wanted.

He dreaded these visits. Ray was loud, vulgar, wealthy, all too keen to make sure Zak knew it. His conversation was full of expensive restaurants he'd been to, new cars he'd bought, and short, madly exotic weekends he'd been on that cost more than Zak earned in a year. And although Zak didn't doubt that Ray was telling the truth when he said that Utopiates was one of his least important enterprises, did he have to say it quite so often?

Ray's business card announced that he was a property developer, and maybe there was always something murky about that business. You didn't hear of real estate empires built by lovable nice guys who got where they were by being compassionate and unassuming. Maybe you had to play rough; still, Zak thought Ray reveled in it a little too much. There was often gloating talk of evictions and repossessions, and when a local journalist described Ray as a "slumlord," he reacted as though it was the greatest compliment he'd ever been paid.

Ray also liked to insinuate that somewhere farther offstage he had an even darker life. Details were always kept sketchy, but he liked to drop hints about money laundering, political bribery, connections to some very dangerous elements. Zak had no idea whether any of this was actually true.

Now, scarcely inside the door, Ray began a monologue about a sushi restaurant he'd been to the previous night, and he was some way into a detailed description of fatty toro, sea urchin, and monkfish liver ("so fucking pricey, so fucking worth it") before he noticed Zak's black eye.

"What happened to you?" Ray asked.

It was a question vague enough to allow Zak to answer in any way he saw fit.

"I walked into a door," he said, not expecting to be believed.

"A door with knuckles," said Ray. "That'll happen. Anything I need to know about?"

Zak still didn't know if it was really any of Ray's business, but since the whole drama had unfolded in and around the store, it didn't seem unreasonable to mention it.

"Maybe," said Zak. "Do you know a guy who drives an old blue Cadillac? Wears a beat-up leather jacket. Isn't afraid to hit women."

"That's not a lot to go on," said Ray.

"In that case, do you know a woman with a map tattooed across her back?"

Ray laughed, arched his eyebrows high and wide.

"Sounds like something we could sell. But no, afraid not."

"Then you know even less than I do, Ray. And it's probably best to keep it that way."

Ray looked at Zak with amused interest. "You know, I always hoped you might have a secret life. Well done. But seriously, Zak? Want me to get you a Taser, a sawed-off shotgun?"

"No," said Zak.

"If you want me to deal with this, I can. I don't like people hassling my employees. I know people, right?"

"I think that might make things worse."

Ray shrugged: it was a point of view, though not one he necessarily shared.

"You're going to rely on your intelligence and charm, are you?" he said.

"It's served me well enough so far," said Zak, though this wasn't exactly true.

"Okay, we'll leave it there. Now let me show you the latest treasure you're going to sell for me."

He handed Zak a cylindrical map case, sometimes called a kit case: a leather-wrapped tube finished with straps and brass buckles, four inches in diameter, perhaps two feet long.

"Tell me what you think of this," said Ray.

Zak unbuckled the case, extracted a scrolled map from the felt-lined interior, and opened it out across the width of his desk. The map was complex, hand-drawn in multiple colored inks and pencils, of a city he didn't recognize: no labels or street names, no unmistakably defining features. It didn't look especially well done, obviously not the work of a professional mapmaker. In fact, there was something very naïve, perhaps primitive about it; still, it was appealingly detailed and obsessive, and dotted all over: not at random, though without any obvious pattern, were squares, circles, stars, triangles, diamonds, in various colors and sizes.

"So what do you think?" asked Ray.

"I don't know what to think," said Zak.

"You ever hear of Jack Torry?"

"No."

"I'm not surprised. He wasn't one of your A-list psychos. He never even killed anybody, though he came close. Basically he was 'just' a rapist, but prolific, a volume dealer, at least a hundred. And he was clever. There was no pattern to give him away, no standard operating procedure. And apart from being a rapist, he was clean, he wasn't in any of the files.

"Maybe the cops would have caught him eventually, but in the end they didn't need to. He turned himself in. Confessed to everything. Maybe he had a conscience, couldn't live with himself. That's the charitable explanation. But maybe he wanted everybody to know what a big shot he was.

"Of course he didn't know the names of most of his victims, but he knew where and he knew when, so he drew the cops a map—that's what you're looking at, Zak."

"What do all the symbols mean?" Zak asked.

"That's the big mystery. He didn't provide a key. Age, race, hair color, how many times? Your guess is as good as anybody else's. Maybe you can sit there and stare at it and you'll be the man to crack the code."

"I don't think so," said Zak.

"Whatever. Still, quite an item, isn't it?"

"Kind of disgusting," said Zak.

"Or titillating, depending on your point of view."

"How did you get this?" Zak asked.

"You wouldn't want to know."

"No. And I don't really want to be in the business of selling it, either."

"But you will, Zak, because that's your job. Not much of a job, I know, but it's all you've got."

Zak wondered if he might "lose" the map somehow, destroy it and claim it was taken by some brilliantly clever and compulsive map thief: there were plenty of those around, preying on libraries and archives as well as stores. But no, he was too conscientious for that as well, and Ray McKinley knew it.

"You think you can find a customer for it?" Ray asked.

"Maybe," said Zak wearily. "There's always Wrobleski."

"No, I don't think it's his kind of thing."

Zak thought it was precisely Wrobleski's kind of thing, but he didn't argue.

"I'm not very happy with our Mr. Wrobleski right now," Ray said, by way of unexpected explanation. "I want you to try one or two others first. Call 'em up. Give 'em some patter. See if you can get a couple of 'em interested, play 'em off against each other, drive up the price."

"Yes, Ray, I know how this works."

"Of course you do, Zak. And by the way, don't be surprised if you hear a bit of a ruckus down here in the next night or two. I'm having one of my soirees."

Zak knew all too well what he was talking about. A couple of weeks after Ray took possession of Utopiates, Zak was woken in the middle of the night by a racket going on in the store below. There were voices and laughter and the sound of breaking glass. Zak immediately thought burglary, but what kind of burglars made that much noise?

He got out of bed, got dressed. The apartment didn't connect directly with the store—access to Zak's living quarters was through a separate rear entrance—so he had to go outside, walk around to the front of the building, and peer in through the store window. He wasn't sure if he was relieved or not to find Ray partying in there: he'd only met him once or twice at that point. Ray was with a handful of other guys and a couple of women, and it seemed they were playing strip poker. Zak didn't think grown-ups ever really did that. Ray saw Zak's face staring in at him, got up from his chair, and lurched toward the window, beckoning for him to come in. Ray was shirtless and Zak saw he had a couple of nipple rings: hardly a shocker, but something he'd have preferred not to know about his new boss. Zak suspected that Ray was glad enough when he declined to join them. Zak was in no position to complain about these nocturnal gatherings, but given the number of properties Ray McKinley owned, it was hard to believe that this dingy little map shop was the best venue he could find for them.

"Well, Zak," Ray said now, "gotta get going. Can't spend too much time on this irrelevant little outpost of the McKinley empire."

He took a last, admiring look at Zak's black eye and said, "There are supposed to be techniques where you can beat people up and it doesn't leave any marks. Nice trick if you can do it. But of course a lot of people don't want to. You should find someone to kiss it better."

"I think maybe I've already got someone," Zak said, sounding a good deal more confident than he felt.

16. WHAT HAPPENED AT THE LOFT

Billy Moore was on the morning run, driving his daughter to school, when the second phone call came from Akim. "Call me back in fifteen minutes," he said into the phone, and put it away.

"Who was that?" Carla asked.

"One of my parking associates," said Billy. "I didn't want you to have to listen to all that boring business stuff."

"Are you keeping a secret?"

"Yeah right," said Billy. "The parking business is full of classified information. Hey, when are we going to go buy me that suit?"

"You're changing the subject."

"You noticed. So when?"

"This weekend—if you don't chicken out."

"Are you calling me chicken?"

"Of course not—so long as you buy that suit."

"You know, for a twelve-year-old, you're pretty much manipulating at an adult level."

"Oh, Dad, you say the sweetest things."

He delivered her to school. He was pleased that he and his Cadillac looked so completely out of place amid the clean, safe, caring parents and their clean, safe, caring cars: not that Billy wasn't caring. In fact, he reckoned he cared a hell of a lot more than most of these smug civilians. And as he drove away, with just the slightest hint of tire squeal, his phone rang again.

Akim said, "I don't like being told to call back."

"You know, I didn't think you would," said Billy.

"Your second job," said Akim. "I've made you an appointment."

"What kind of appointment?"

"To see a property. One o'clock. Banham Towers. There'll be a realtor there to show you a waterfront loft. She'll be expecting you. Her name's Isabel Sibrian. She's the one, even if she doesn't look like it. She's been told your name's Smith."

"Very inventive," said Billy.

Akim ignored that. "She may be a more difficult customer than the last one. But you'll deal with it. You'll bring her here."

"That's what I'll do, is it?"

"I believe so."

"And what if I say, 'I'm going to have to turn down Mr. Wrobleski's kind offer'?"

"It's already too late for that. Clear?"

Billy Moore knew better than to challenge Wrobleski, but he had no such inhibitions with Akim.

"Some of it's clear, some of it isn't clear at all."

An impatient grunt indicated that Akim didn't have much interest in clarifying things for Billy's benefit, but Billy wasn't deterred.

"You see," Billy said, "I get it that Wrobleski is way too grand to run around picking up these tattooed women."

"Very perceptive," said Akim.

"But what I don't get is why he needs *me* to do it. Why doesn't he have *you* pick them up for him, since you seem to know where they are?"

An insulted silence rippled through the phone and Billy thought Akim might hang up on him, but he didn't. Perhaps he was the one who needed to get things clear.

"Dragging women into cars," said Akim, "isn't really my style."

It sounded like the only answer Billy was going to get.

"Let's hope your style doesn't go out of fashion, Akim," he said.

Billy got the address of Banham Towers, one he vaguely recognized as part of an ongoing dockland development, a cluster of former bonded warehouses that were being converted into luxury apartments that people with real money and a taste for real luxury wouldn't have used to kennel their dogs.

He drove out there a little before one. It was evidently some way from complete or habitable, yet there was no construction work going on, no activity whatsoever. There was just one car in the parking lot: the realtor's, he assumed. He made his way inside the building and followed some freshly printed signs up to the show apartment on the second floor.

The woman waiting for him was tall, fleshy, with an artful tangle of dense, ink-black hair. She looked businesslike, though glamorous in a way, and overdressed for the occasion, as though she might be going to a gala afterward. There was a scent of lilacs about her, and her heels clacked on the loft's hardwood floor. Hollow light flooded the room, picked out some long, low, cut-rate furniture, and the angular, anonymous art on the walls. Yes, there was a cheapness to it, and a brittle fakery, but there was certainly a lot more room to stretch yourself here than in a trailer.

"Miss Sibrian," said Billy.

"Mr. Smith," she said.

"I thought a loft would be on the top floor," said Billy.

She smiled unconvincingly. Maybe she'd heard that one before. She was some way from being friendly, and Billy reckoned she must have made up her mind about him the moment she saw him, realized he wasn't a serious buyer, which of course was perfectly accurate. Even so, she went through the motions, showed him a thick, intensely colored, embossed brochure demonstrating the virtues of the place, which she then spelled out, talking about the apartment's many advantages, the "flow" from kitchen to living room to balcony, the quality of the soundproofing, the neighborhood, a little frayed at the edges right now but changing; a mall was planned, wine bars were opening, there was a fitness center, and, of course, the new Platinum Line subway would run close by. But her heart wasn't in it.

"I can see you're not impressed," she said, without any particular disappointment. "That's okay. If the place isn't right, it isn't right. We can work together. What are you really looking for?"

Billy could see it might help to play along.

"I guess I'm looking for something more . . . genuinely industrial."

"Yes? There's a new development in the old steel mill a couple of miles up the road. Can't get much more industrial than that. I can take you there now if you like."

"Okay, but we go in my car. I don't like riding bitch."

She laughed, not sure if he was joking.

"It's a little phobia of mine," he said. "Call me crazy. I don't like being driven by other people. Indulge me. I'll bring you right back."

It seemed she was prepared to indulge him. Maybe it had something to do with his smile, and after all, a potential sale was a potential sale.

As she was locking up the show loft, Billy said, "Do you always work alone?"

"Pretty much," she said. "Realtors don't usually hunt in packs."

"Don't you ever worry about what might happen?"

She gave him a frank, questioning look.

"What do you think might happen?" she asked.

Billy gifted her his smile again.

"*Anything* might happen," he said.

"Are you flirting with me, Mr. Smith?"

"Sure. It's what I do."

They took the elevator down to ground level, went out to the parking lot. Isabel Sibrian eyed the Cadillac and was not impressed. She hesitated, took half a step toward her own car.

"What?" said Billy. "My car's not good enough for you?"

"It's not that."

"So, we'll do it now, right?" he said. "You can trust me. I'm a good guy. I have my own business. I have a daughter."

"Well, I . . ."

She didn't get in with any enthusiasm, but she got in. Billy slid into the driver's seat, locked the doors, but left the windows open: the smell of lilacs was getting to him. He lurched the car into life, and Isabel Sibrian gave him some overdetailed directions to get to the steel mill development. He tried to look as though he were listening.

"You were right," Billy said as they drove away. "I do think that apartment's a piece of expensive crap."

"Do you?"

"Yeah, and I think you know it too."

"We all have to make a living."

"That's so true."

They drove for a while in silence. She looked out of the side window. They were passing a cemetery, a fire-damaged mall, some freshly built big-box stores. He was no longer following her directions. She hadn't a clue where they were. She suddenly got very nervous.

"Why don't you stop," she said, as calmly as she could. "Let me out here and now if you're not interested."

"I am interested. But I'm not here because of any apartment. I'm here because of the tattoos."

The woman's fear arrived like a rolling wave.

"What tattoos would those be?" she said with forced, exaggerated calm.

"The ones on your back."

He wondered if she'd deny it. He even wondered if he, or Akim, might have got the wrong woman. But no.

"How do you know about them?" she said.

"Why? Is it a secret?"

"From most people, yes. What do you know?" she demanded. The fear hadn't completely blotted out her essential curiosity.

"Less than you do, that's for sure."

"Do you know who did it to me?"

"No," said Billy. "I kind of want to know. But then again, I kind of don't. In any case, I'm here to take you to somebody who knows a lot more than I do."

"You're really freaking me out here, you know."

"I'm not trying to, but it's all the same whether you're freaked out or not."

"Stop the car. Stop the car. Please."

"Please is nice, but it won't do it."

He saw her hand snake into her purse and she took hold of her cell phone.

"You know that's not going to work either," said Billy.

He stopped the car for a second, grabbed her hand, peeled her fingers from the phone, and tossed it out the side window before driving on.

"Why don't we try again?" she said. "Why don't you tell me what you want? Is it money? Is it sex? Everything's negotiable."

"Don't insult me," Billy said. "I'm not some fucking . . . opportunist. I don't want money or sex from you, right? I just want you to come quietly. And look, if I were really a bad guy, I'd have walked in there, knocked you unconscious, and then carried you out to the car."

She gave him a look of finely regulated distaste and condescension, and then her hand was in her purse again, grabbing something small, black, and cylindrical: a pepper spray.

"Now that's just annoying," Billy said, and he slammed on the brakes again.

She lurched forward, her black hair falling around her face like a hood. He hit her once, good and hard so she understood the situation, then took the pepper spray and blasted a jet of the stuff into her face. She fell back in the seat, coughing, retching, and he popped her again, just to be sure. He almost felt justified.

"There's more where that came from if you don't behave yourself," he said, hating the sound of his own voice.

She whimpered indignantly and behaved herself. Billy delivered her to Wrobleski's compound, received the envelope of money; this time he didn't even bother to see how much was in it. It would again be too much, maybe even more than before. He knew he hadn't earned it. He looked at his watch. He was in good time to pick up Carla from school. He hoped she wouldn't notice the scent of artificial lilacs or the sting of pepper.

He thought he was doing well. Carla smelled nothing, but then she pulled something out from under the front passenger seat, an embossed real estate brochure. Billy hadn't noticed it; Isabel Sibrian must have put it there, and he knew that was bad, he was supposed to be aware of these things. Carla turned the few heavy pages, looked at them in deep fascination.

"Wow, we really are moving up in the world," she said.

"We're not moving *there*, that's for sure," said Billy.

"No? Why not?"

Billy could think of a lot of reasons, all of them plausible, but he wasn't sure which one would satisfy Carla.

"I didn't like the realtor," he said at last.

"Why not?"

"Just a feeling."

"What? She didn't treat you right? She didn't show enough respect?"

Billy wished he'd never started this. "Sure, something like that."

"You see, Dad," Carla said triumphantly, "if only you'd been wearing a suit . . ."

17. OFF THE WALL

Early morning, Marilyn got on her bike and rode out of the city center, thinking about Cadillacs in general and one Cadillac in particular. Supposing, she asked herself, you drove a classic metallic-blue Cadillac, where would you take it to have it serviced and maintained? You'd want somebody who knew what he was doing. But given the distressed state of the car, it obviously hadn't been looked after by a fancy dealership or restoration boutique. Chances were it had been taken to some cheap, halfway-honest, gritty establishment out in the boonies. It would be a place that knew the car inside out and also, obviously, they'd know the name, phone number, and maybe even address of the owner. If she could find that garage, and charm a mechanic into revealing some or all of the above information, well then . . . well, she wasn't sure exactly what, maybe another punch in the eye somewhere along the line, although she would try very hard to resist hitting him with her backpack if she saw him again.

She had made herself a map of sorts, actually more of a loosely schematized list, names and addresses of garages that fit the bill to a greater or lesser extent, arranged by location and what she imagined to be relevance. She was surprised how many there were, less surprised that they were located in some exhaustingly out-of-the-way parts of the city, places she'd never been before and would never go again. It was a brave old world out there, one of industrial parks, service roads, freeway on- and off-ramps, chemical plants and landfills, waste lots littered with sagging huts made out of sheet metal. Were these the kinds of places Zak had said he liked to explore? She wished she'd asked him a few more questions. She also found herself wishing, to her considerable surprise, and not only because he had a car, that she'd brought him along. But that was not to be: he had a day job and a sense of responsibility. She imagined the latter could eventually be diluted, but for now this was something she had to do by herself.

She started optimistically enough, and met a lot of hardworking men, caked in oil, grease, and road gunk. They seemed like good guys, but once she started asking questions, they all became similarly surly and tight-lipped. Showing them a picture she'd printed out, of the Cadillac and a man in a battered leather jacket, didn't melt their hearts any.

One or two wanted to know why she wanted to know. She tried a few fake answers: the guy in the picture was an old friend she needed to reconnect with (although this story capsized when it became evident she didn't actually know his name), or she wanted to buy the Cadillac from him, or she'd accidentally scraped the car while it was parked and she wanted to do the right thing and pay for the damage. Her stories were greeted with sullen disbelief. The guys all said they knew nothing, and although they wouldn't have any reason to tell her the truth, she suspected they weren't actually lying. Her black eye surely was no help. She'd tried to cover it with concealer, but it was hard to keep makeup intact while riding a bike through various more or less threatening interzones.

The day slithered on, used itself up, and although Marilyn tried to sustain an air of energy and commitment as she pedaled, eventually she no longer knew for whose benefit she was keeping up appearances. The project had been a bust: there were still more garages to try, but they were long shots, they were miles away, and they might well be closing for the day by now. In any case, her legs and her butt ached: she'd had enough.

And then, as she was pedaling back into the city, she saw another garage, not one from her list, a cube of purple-painted cinder block, with two metal shutters in the front, the first wide open, the other rolled firmly shut. There was no name on the building, but on the side wall was a clumsy and garish mural, a broad black road narrowing through sand dunes into a high vanishing point. On that road was a line of classic, cartoon-style Cadillacs.

She slammed on her brakes, skidded the bike to a halt, and went to look more closely. She was aware of two men inside the garage, one older, one younger. The older man was elbow deep in the guts of a pickup truck; the younger was sweeping the floor with exaggerated care. She could hear a radio playing loudly inside, tuned to a religious station, a voice blustering something about grace and redemption.

She stood and stared, saw that the mural was signed *Carlos*, and before long the man with the broom, not much more than a boy, she saw now, came out to talk to her. He had a wide, goofy smile; she hadn't seen many smiles in the course of the day.

"I did that," he said, pointing at the mural with a little too much enthusiasm.

"You're Carlos."

He seemed both astonished and infinitely proud.

"Yes, I am. My dad's called Carlos too, but I'm the one who did the painting. How did you know?"

"Your fame is spreading," Marilyn said, hoping that didn't sound like she was mocking him.

He considered this. "Yeah," he said, "yeah, my fame is spreading, yeah it is."

The older man now stepped out of the garage.

"Hey, Carlos, how's that sweeping coming along?"

"Really well," said young Carlos, and he returned obediently to the job in hand.

Carlos senior was an unthreatening Latino, short, fleshy, with a thick head of glossy hair, a thin band of mustache across his upper lip, and a tattoo of the Virgin Mary on his oil-streaked forearm. He looked at Marilyn, looked at her bike, and said, "Yeah?"

"Just admiring your son's mural."

"It keeps the kid out of trouble. Mostly."

"Do you specialize in Cadillacs?"

"The kid likes Caddies. I specialize in whatever anybody brings in."

She continued to gaze admiringly at the mural, and she hoped she sounded suitably casual as she said, "I used to have a boyfriend with an old Cadillac."

"What kind?"

"Oh," she said archly, "I never know about years and models and that stuff. But actually I do have a picture."

She rummaged in her backpack and pulled out the photograph of the metallic-blue Cadillac and its owner. She showed it to the older Carlos, who looked at it, but looked away just a little too quickly, or so she thought.

"Nineteen eighty-one Seville," he said. "Not one of their best years. The Eldorado is the one you want."

"I'm sure you're right."

"You always carry your old boyfriend's picture with you?"

"He's pretty recent. I really need to see him actually. I thought if you specialized in Cadillacs he might bring his car here. A long shot, I know."

"I'll say."

The guy still didn't seem very interested, but she decided to take a chance. He was good to his son, and it seemed he had some religious leanings. She patted her stomach.

"It'll be showing soon."

That stoked the man's curiosity just a little, and maybe his sympathy. She turned her face so he could get a good look at her black eye.

"He just left you?"

"He's disappeared. I don't even know where he is."

Carlos junior found a reason to sweep very close to where the two of them were standing. He tilted his head to get a look at the picture Marilyn was holding.

"Hey," he said, "it's Billy Moore."

The father's face puckered, and showed the briefest flare of anger before settling into a more customary resignation.

"You'd better step inside for a moment," he said to Marilyn.

They walked into the garage. It was hot in there and smelled as much of French fries as of gasoline. An industrial-sized swamp cooler stirred the air to no noticeable effect. The radio station was now playing choral music. Marilyn checked out a row of hubcaps on the wall, some with bullet holes, and next to them was a pinup calendar showing a girl draped over a hot rod, and beside that was a picture of the Pope.

"What's the story?" Carlos senior asked.

"Billy's disappeared," she said, picking up on the name. "He won't answer his phone. He always did move around a lot. I have no idea where he is now. I hoped maybe you did."

"You're not lying about being pregnant, are you?"

"No," she said, sounding offended. "It would be terrible to lie about a thing like that."

"Yes, it would."

She hoped he wasn't going to make her swear on the Bible.

"See," he said, "I don't know much about the guy. He brings

his car here, that's all. I know his car, not him. I'm sorry to hear about your troubles, but I think maybe you're better off without this Billy Moore."

"Can't you give me his latest address? Maybe where he works?"

"I got nothing. All the work I did was off the books. No invoice, no sales tax. I got no address for him, nothing."

At which point Carlos junior edged into the garage, not wanting to be left out. Besides, he had some important information to deliver.

"I'm not sure where he lives," the kid said. "But I know where he parks his car."

"You serious, Carlos?" the father said.

"Sure."

"Really sure?"

"Cross my heart."

"So where does he park?"

"In a brand-new lot on the corner of Hope Street and Tenth."

Carlos senior shot Marilyn a look that said his son wasn't always wrong about things, and he raised his splayed hands in her direction. It could have been a benediction, but it might also have indicated that he wanted to wash his hands of the whole business.

18. SWING

"You've brought me to a high place," said Wrobleski. "Again."

"Is that a bad thing?" Ray McKinley asked.

They were on a rooftop, twenty-one stories high, on the edge of Chinatown, at an underpopulated nighttime golf range. On three sides the parapet of the roof supported green netting that towered and billowed like perforated sails. Spotlights trained down from a great height, turning the darkness hazy and bordering it with white velvet flare.

"I fucking hate golf," said Wrobleski. "I hate the people who play it, people who watch it, everything about it."

He glanced at the nearest pair of golfers, a young Asian couple, three tees over, driving balls haphazardly into the netting. They were too far away to hear what he said. He thought that was a shame.

"Maybe it'll grow on you," said McKinley.

"If it grows on me, I'll hack it off."

McKinley feigned amusement. Wrobleski did not.

"You hit. I'll watch," said Wrobleski.

The tees were automatic: balls popped up from the ground at the golfer's feet, and one appeared now in front of McKinley. He concentrated, addressed the ball, did an exaggerated wiggle with his ass, drew back the club, swung, hit the ball effortlessly, straight, clean, if perhaps with more height than length. Even so, he looked quietly satisfied.

"I hear you've been buying real estate," he said.

"It's not a secret. Looks like easy money to me. I see you buying and selling property. I think, How hard can it be?"

McKinley didn't take the bait. He said, "Maybe you should sell that compound of yours. Turn it into quirky luxury apartments."

"No."

"Too many memories, eh?" Ray said, smirking. "Look, are you all right? What is it? Money troubles? Women troubles? Whatever it is, you can talk to me about it."

"No, I can't. And I don't want to."

"Okay then, just enjoy the view," Ray McKinley said. "I like it here. You can see half the city from here. Don't you like it?"

"I'd like it better without the nets and the lights and the dicks playing golf."

"You have to see past all that stuff," said McKinley. "That's what I do. I look beyond. I see possibilities."

"Yeah, Ray, you're king of all you survey."

"No need to be a jerk about it."

"Oh, that's right," said Wrobleski, continuing to be a jerk. "You can see the tower of the Telstar Hotel from here, can't you? You still own a piece of that?"

"You know I do. Otherwise we wouldn't be having this conversation."

"I hear the mayor's plans are going pretty well."

"Plans are made to be changed."

They looked out across the city, to the dimmed stillness of the empty Telstar. There were one or two lights dotted randomly amid the grid of its windows: squatters. Ray lofted another ball, harder, straighter, even higher.

"Don't tell me," said Wrobleski, "you just want to talk."

"Is that so terrible?"

"It's a conversation we've already had," said Wrobleski. "You're going to ask me to do a job I've already told you I'm not going to do."

"I think you should be allowed to change your mind."

"There are jobs and there are jobs. This one is just suicide."

"What? You're scared? The old Wrobleski wouldn't have scared so easily."

"What's wrong with being scared?" said Wrobleski. "Only an idiot's never scared. And you can't just rub out the mayor because she's in the way of one of your development deals."

"Oh, I think you can," said McKinley. "The mayor goes. Her little restoration plan collapses. The Telstar gets demolished. I make a killing."

"And I'm the one who *does* the killing."

"Sure. It's what you do, isn't it?"

Wrobleski didn't respond, but he didn't deny it.

"Look," said McKinley, "I'm not asking you to *enjoy* it. But I can't see any other way. I've tried reasoning with her. I've tried bribing her. You got rid of the other old dude for me. That ought to have got her attention, made her rethink her position. But it didn't. So what am I supposed to do?"

A news helicopter, black and white, insectlike, hacked through the air not so far above their heads. There was a man in the passenger seat, leaning out, pointing a video camera down at them. McKinley raised thumb and index finger and mimed shooting down the chopper.

"The mayor has people," said Wrobleski. "She's never alone. She has armed security. She has cameras on her twenty-four hours a day."

"What is it?" Ray asked. "Are you trying to go straight, Wrobleski?"

"No."

"Or maybe you're squeamish about women."

Wrobleski didn't answer.

"Really? Is that it? Well, aren't you the gentleman assassin?"

At last Wrobleski picked up one of the golf clubs McKinley had rented for him. He held it like an ax. McKinley addressed the new ball that had appeared before him. He swung, the ball flew away, fast, straight, and low this time.

"Why don't you pay one of your other goons to get rid of the mayor for you?"

"You're the only goon I can trust," said Ray. "I want to keep it neat. I want to keep it in-house."

"You could always do it yourself."

"What do you think I am?"

"I know what you are," said Wrobleski.

"You sure?"

Wrobleski at last stepped up to a place at the tee. A ball was there waiting. He wound himself up, took an almighty swing, as though he was trying to burst the netting, send the ball far across the city, to the outskirts, to the empty brown land beyond. The ball sliced fiercely, viciously off to the right, smacked the young Asian man standing three tees away, hit him clean and hard in the right shin. He fell down as though he'd been shot. Wrobleski strolled across, stood over him, and offered a thoroughly insincere apology.

"You have to keep your head down and your elbows in," said McKinley, unhelpfully.

19. MARILYN'S OWN DEVICES

Marilyn Driscoll wafted into Utopiates, a certain elasticity, maybe even bounce, in her step. Zak wondered if this was a good sign; at the very least it suggested that the place no longer gave her the creeps.

"Your black eye's not looking so bad," Zak said by way of greeting.

"You think?" said Marilyn. "Under the makeup it's looking more purple edged with yellow than black. I guess that's a step in the right direction."

"And how was your tattooist?"

"My tattooist was a cranky old lady who has a lot more information than she's prepared to give me. Especially about compass roses."

"I can tell you more about the compass rose if you like."

"Sorry, Zak, not that kind of information."

Again Zak felt a pang of not quite explicable hurt.

"You ever worry, Zak, that the printed map might be a dying form?"

"I *know* the printed map is a dying form, but I don't worry about it."

"So what do you think of this?"

Marilyn flipped open her laptop, and on the screen was a computer-generated map of the city, with a tiny, stationary red spark flashing at its center.

"What's that?" Zak asked.

"It's Billy Moore's car," Marilyn said.

"Billy Moore?"

"Our friend with the Cadillac."

"You know his name?"

"Yeah, and I know where he parks his car, on some new lot that's opened at the corner of Hope Street and Tenth."

"Is that worth knowing?" said Zak.

"Yes. And now I know he lives there too, in a trailer, with his daughter. I've seen them. And I know some of where he goes. Not very far, not yet anyway, but I haven't been tracking him very long."

"What kind of tracking?"

"With a portable tracker. That's the thing flashing on the map on-screen. You stick it underneath a car, like if you have a fleet of delivery trucks or traveling salesmen, so you can see they're not goofing off or speeding or going somewhere they shouldn't. You could use it to keep track of an errant wife if you had one."

"It all sounds very high tech."

"It cost seventy-five dollars on Amazon. No bigger than a pack of cigarettes. Thirty days' battery life. *Ideal for rugged outdoor use* is what it says on the package."

Even if Zak had no illusions about the printed map being a dying form, he hadn't realized how out of touch he was with new developments.

"So far," said Marilyn, "our man's been from the parking lot to a school and back every day, his daughter's school presumably. And the other day he went to a tailor's."

"You've been following him?"

"Only on-screen. And the fact is, Zak, there are real limits to how much you can learn that way."

"You want a printed map?"

"No, I want us to follow him in the real world."

"Us?"

"Yes. I don't want to come across as a girl, Zak, but I'd like you to come with me. There's safety in numbers."

"Two's a very small number."

"I don't want to have to go up against him alone."

"I don't want to 'go up against him' at all."

"Come on, Zak, there'll be some urban exploration."

"Oh, that'll make everything all right."

"I want you as a partner," said Marilyn. "A partner with a big brown anonymous station wagon."

"And we follow him where?"

"To wherever he goes. Maybe to where he's keeping that woman. You might have to close the store a little early."

"For you, I'd be prepared to do that," Zak said. He hoped she realized what a big step that was.

20. BILLY MOORE'S NEXT JOB

A third phone call.

"A woman who goes by the name of Chanterelle," Akim said lazily. "She's a dancer, stripper, whatever. She's working a late shift at the True Gentlemen's Club. You heard of that?"

"I'll find it," said Billy.

"When she finishes there, she has to go to another club across town, the Oracle. You'll step in, tell her you're a driver sent by the Oracle."

"She'll believe me?"

"You'll convince her and then do the usual."

"What about the real driver? Won't he turn up?"

"Believe me, he won't turn up."

"You know, Akim, I've thought of something else to ask you."

"Have you really?"

"Yeah," said Billy. "See, I can understand that Wrobleski's too grand to pick up the women, and I'll buy that you think it's not your style, but how do you even know who these women are and where they're hanging out?"

"Because I make it my business to know."

"That's a strange business to be in, isn't it?"

Billy wasn't expecting much, but there was an arrogance and a vanity in Akim that made him keep talking.

"I've been keeping track of them."

"Since when?"

"Long enough."

"Since before or after they got tattooed?"

"Before they were tattooed they were of no interest whatsoever."

"And now they're *interesting*?"

"I just said so."

"Knowledge is power, right?"

"That's what Mr. Wrobleski says. But some people say ignorance is bliss."

"I'm not looking for bliss," said Billy. "Just one more question. *Why* have you been keeping track of them?"

"Because I knew it would come in handy one day. And it has, hasn't it?"

"Handy? Who for?"

"For Mr. Wrobleski, of course. Who else?"

Billy Moore couldn't remember when he'd last encountered a true gentleman, but he was pretty sure he wouldn't be meeting any in this club he was going to. It was out by the abandoned heliport, in a low-slung concrete building, wedged between a lumberyard and a pumping station. Above the club's entrance were flashing lights, a smear of neon, and a billboard-sized image of a fashion model who would look nothing like any of the dancers inside.

He was wearing his brand-new suit, as described and selected by Carla: elephant gray with a lining that flashed vermilion at irregular intervals. He knew he looked good, probably too good for this place. He paid his money, went into the club, past a couple of bouncers who looked about as threatening as Tweedledum and Tweedledee, and took up a position at the bar. The place was a pit of shadow and multicolored points of light, barely a quarter full, the customers an even blend of blue- and white-collar, mostly sedate single men, although one or two, incomprehensibly to Billy, had brought their dates with them.

Billy watched the acts of half a dozen dancers who were not named Chanterelle. None of them were bad-looking and a couple of them could really dance. One was voluptuous but somehow apologetic, while another—skinny, lank-haired, big-jawed— worked the room with effortless confidence. A redhead who looked old enough to be the mother of every guy in the club had them begging for real or feigned mercy.

Billy saw that every one of the dancers had a tattoo of some kind or other: a Tinker Bell, an ace of spades, a sleeve of koi and cherry blossoms, and one had seamed stockings tattooed all the way up the backs of her legs; but these were not the tattoos he— or rather Wrobleski—was looking for. And then the guy running the show, a chubby rockabilly guy with a pompadour and mutton chops in not quite matching shades of black, came out to announce the next act: Chanterelle.

He talked her up so much that anything short of Gypsy Rose Lee would have been a disappointment, and Chanterelle was no Gypsy Rose Lee. She strutted out wearing a futuristic gunslinger outfit: gold thigh boots, ray guns in a holster, and a loose vest with fringes and space badges that fell wide open at the front to reveal heavy, dark, natural breasts. She moved around the stage with chilly self-assurance, her body big and ripe, her oiled skin gleaming in the lights. The real problem was the face. It could have been an attractive face if it hadn't been so taut, if the features hadn't been set in an expression of hostile contempt, daring the men to make eye contact with her. Few did, not even Billy; he wanted to remain inconspicuous for now. He got just a few tantalizing glimpses of her back as the vest twirled and flapped around her, but that was as much as he needed. She didn't display the tattoos, but if she'd really wanted to hide them, she could have chosen a very different outfit.

Billy Moore glanced quickly around the bar to see if anybody was looking at him. He still took seriously Wrobleski's concern that he shouldn't be seen, but just how invisible could you be when you were picking up a woman at a strip club? And you couldn't beat up everybody who might possibly have noticed you, could you now?

He watched Chanterelle dance her way through three songs. At one point she pressed the sole of her boot into the face of a man in the front row: he seemed to like it. She fondled and licked her ray guns, and in the last song—"Ghost Riders in the Sky"— fired them to shoot cream or yogurt or something all over herself. The final applause was polite rather than enthusiastic.

She gave a bow that had a lot in common with a shudder, picked up her money, and descended from the stage. The dressing room was across the far side of the club, so she had to pass through the audience. On a busy night that would have made for a lively journey, but this evening she strode across the empty floor without hassle, and Billy was able to fall in step beside her. She looked as if she was going to tell him to fuck off, but before she could do that, Billy smiled and said, "Hi, Chanterelle, I'm from the Oracle. I'm here to drive you over."

She looked him up and down. He doubted that he looked exactly like a man who drove strippers from one gig to the next, but he thought that probably helped. Maybe she was even impressed by the suit.

"You're not the usual guy," she said.

"You just can't keep good staff."

She looked at him dubiously and shrugged. One driver was as good as any other. He followed her to the dressing room and waited briefly outside. She didn't bother to change into street clothes, simply cleaned herself off, picked up her bag, and put on a long fake-fur coat to cover her outfit. They went out to the parking lot, where she eyed the Cadillac indifferently. She moved to get in the back of the car, but Billy was having none of that.

"Why don't you ride up front with me," he said. "That'd be the friendly way."

"I'm not your friend."

"Well, there's no reason to be my enemy."

She got in beside him, though there was still nothing remotely amicable about her. They'd been driving for quite a while in icy silence before Billy said, "You've got some tattoos on your back."

"You're so observant."

"I wondered why you weren't showing them off."

"Because they're fucking ugly."

"Then I wonder why you were showing them at all."

"Yeah, I'm a mass of contradictions."

Billy wasn't prepared to let it go quite that easily.

"Looked like it might be a tattoo of a map," he said.

"Did it?"

"Well, is it or not?"

"You ask a lot of questions for a driver." And then, "Wait a minute, this isn't the fucking way to the Oracle."

"Sure it is," Billy said. "I'm taking you by the scenic route."

"If you're lost, just say so. Don't be a guy about it."

"You think I need a map?"

She'd heard enough. "Stop the fucking car."

"I don't think so," said Billy.

She slapped him across the right cheek, as viciously as she could, though the confines of the car stopped her getting her best swing. Billy stomped on the brakes, the car slewed to a halt, and he grabbed the stripper by the throat with his right hand. He rose in his seat to slam her head back against the side window.

"You should know I have no problem hitting women," he said, "and if you do that again, I'll smash your head through the glass."

She seemed to believe him. For a while she sat in a silence even icier than before, but that didn't suit her for long.

"So where are you taking me, you cunt?" she asked at last.

"I'm taking you to see a man named Wrobleski."

"I don't know anybody called Wrobleski."

"I never said you did."

"What does he want, a private show?"

"Maybe."

"And who are you, his pimp?"

"I'm just a guy who's doing what he's being paid to do."

"So you're his whore."

"You really do have a dirty little mind, don't you? Isn't getting paid reason enough for what *you* do?"

"Don't get me started," she said. "And don't think you know anything about what I do or why."

"Fair enough," said Billy.

There were plenty of things he'd done in his own past that he could neither justify nor explain, and why would you even bother? Shit happens, and then more shit happens. He drove fast and carelessly. He wanted this to be over. He didn't even notice the brown station wagon that was following them.

21. UNCOMMON PURSUITS

"Is this a car chase?" Zak asked. "I can't believe I'm in a car chase."

"No," said Marilyn. "I think this is a pursuit rather than a chase."

In truth neither of them knew exactly what it was. As Zak drove, he leaned on the steering wheel for support, and his head jutted forward as if he were peering through a mailbox rather than a broad glass windshield. Beside him, Marilyn sat low in her seat, trying to remain grave and determined, yet unable to keep a smirk of pleasure from her face. This was turning out better than she could possibly have imagined. She had hoped, at best, that Billy Moore might lead them to wherever he'd taken the tattooed homeless woman. But it was already bigger than that. First he had taken them to a strip club (damned shame they couldn't go inside, but Billy Moore would have recognized them), and then he'd picked up another woman, and now they were heading to a place where, Marilyn was confident, something would become clearer, where something, perhaps many things, would be revealed.

They were heading north; they passed the old, disused sports arena and a decaying varnish works that Zak had promised himself he'd break into and explore one of these days, but for much of the time they were in terra incognita. For now there was something strangely comfortable about following somebody else's tracks, being devoid of direct responsibility. As he drove, Zak realized that this business of following somebody in a car didn't require nearly as much skill as you might think.

Finally they were somewhere in sight of rail yards and land-fills. The traffic was thin; the Cadillac and the station wagon were among the few cars on the road. And then up ahead Zak saw a cluster of linked buildings: raised up, set back, brooding, with some fancy architectural additions on the roof. The Cadillac began to slow down: this looked like journey's end. There was a skinny old man at the gate, which opened up as the Cadillac approached, and Billy Moore drove inside. Zak continued to drive on at a stately pace, quick enough, he hoped, to seem unremarkable, but slow enough so they could get a look inside: a couple of ill-matched men waiting in the courtyard.

Zak drove on farther, skirted the compound, eyeing the height of its walls, the bars on the windows, the degree of impenetrability, the NO TRESPASSING and ARMED RESPONSE signs. He tried not to feel daunted. When they were far enough away, he did a U-turn so that the station wagon was now facing the compound again, and pulled off the road, down onto a gravel shoulder. He stopped in the deep shadow of a railway arch, between a couple of wrecked dump trucks, a place from which they could neither see the compound nor be seen from it. He killed the car's lights and engine, and he and Marilyn sat and waited, neither of them with much sense of what they were waiting for.

"You don't think that's Billy Moore's place?" Zak said, for the sake of having something to say.

"I'm guessing not," said Marilyn. "A guy who lives in a trailer in a parking lot generally doesn't have a second home."

"Still, nice Fortress of Solitude, whoever owns it. That's a Superman reference."

"Thank you, Zak."

"So what do you think is going on in there?" he asked—a dumb question for sure.

"Who knows? Sex, drugs, cartography?"

Time passed, but reluctantly. Zak thought of turning on the radio, but no, that would have been crass.

"You know," he said, "I'm pretty certain I could climb up those walls and get into that compound."

"You think?" said Marilyn dubiously.

"It's what I do—well, a part of what I do. I'm not one of those serious 'infiltrators' or parkour guys, but when you do a bit of urban exploration there's almost always some wall or fence that needs scaling."

"That would be quite a climb," Marilyn said.

"You think I couldn't do it?"

"I'm sure you could," she said, but it didn't sound as if she was sure at all.

"You want me to do it?"

"Let's wait awhile," said Marilyn.

They waited awhile: nothing continued to happen. Zak was getting very twitchy. He was also starting to feel reckless. He reached out and took Marilyn's hand. Her eyes arched above her tortoiseshell frames in quiet disbelief.

"What are you doing?" Marilyn demanded.

"Being affectionate," he said.

"You don't think sitting in the car holding hands is a little bit . . . juvenile?"

She shook her hand free.

"Well, we could do more than hold hands," said Zak.

"What, you think we should start necking? You think we should do some heavy petting?"

"No, no," said Zak. "I was just being . . . nervous."

"You know, timing is really all-important in these things."

He was silent for a long time, weighing the extent of his rejection and humiliation.

"Okay, then," he said at last, "I'm going in."

At another time and place Marilyn might have thought this was a fresh declaration of sexual intent, but in the circumstances she knew he meant that he was intending to climb the face of the compound and get inside.

"You sure that's wise?" said Marilyn.

"What's the worst they could do to me?" said Zak.

"Shoot you in the head?" Marilyn suggested.

"No, I don't think so. The way I see it, nobody who's really capable of delivering an armed response is going to put up a sign saying ARMED RESPONSE, are they?"

Marilyn could see no point in debating the many illogicalities of that premise.

"Maybe they'll just throw you in a cellar and have rats do terrible things to you for a few months," she said.

"And maybe they won't. Do you want to know what's going on in there or don't you?"

"I do," said Marilyn. "You know I do."

Zak emptied his pockets, handed Marilyn his wallet and keys, everything that would identify him if he got caught. He clambered out of the car and trotted briskly away in the direction of the compound, into the darkness, until Marilyn could no longer see him. She sat in the car, waiting, wishing that she smoked. Meanwhile, with a litheness Marilyn would scarcely have believed even if she'd been able to see it, Zak began to scale the nearest outer wall, like a surprisingly elegant spider monkey.

22. ZAK LOOKING IN

Zak ascended, negotiating a series of thin ledges and windows, a couple of loose drainpipes. He took it all in his stride, climbing skillfully, gracefully, without hesitation. He rather wished Marilyn could see him. At the top of the wall he paused just long enough to scan for cameras, motion sensors, trip wires, mantraps, and especially dogs, but there were none as far as he could tell. He hoisted himself over the parapet onto the building's flat roof.

He found himself close to the glass-walled living quarters, empty but brightly lit, and he glanced inside at the natty furnishings and some strange and interesting framed maps. Another man might have found this more surprising than Zak did: if you like maps, it doesn't surprise you that other people like them too. In any case, he didn't linger. He crossed a stretch of the roof, his thin-soled sneakers silent on the concrete, and he looked down into the courtyard below, where the Cadillac and a black, steroidal SUV were parked.

There were lights on in some of the lower windows surrounding the courtyard, and a couple of guys in overalls stood around down there, but they didn't look even remotely alert. Zak made a dash across a farther section of roof, to a cluster of vents and air-conditioning units that provided a decent hiding place, not far from the domed conservatory. That was apparently where the action was. Through the glass he could see people, move-ment, sharp, shadowy candlelight.

He moved closer, close enough to see while still remaining unseen, an outsider looking in: a role that suited him extremely well. He could see this wasn't a typical conservatory: not many plants, some kind of model of an island at the center. Under the glass, two men and four women were acting out an unfathom-able dumb show. The first man was Billy Moore; the other was a solid, gray-haired man, a dense center of dangerous authority whose face Zak couldn't see. The two men were fully clothed, suited, and they sat edgily on rattan chairs; the four women stood in a line and were completely naked.

To Zak they looked like contestants in a sad nudist beauty pageant, lined up for display and inspection. But even the most modest beauty contest demands some smiling and preening, a show of confidence and self-presentation, and there was precious little of that here. One of them he recognized as the homeless woman Billy Moore had scooped up at Utopiates. Nothing so very terrible seemed to have happened to her: in some ways she looked better, or anyway cleaner, now than she had then. An-other, he was pretty sure, was the stripper who'd just been brought there from the club; the other two were unknowns, a young, tough-looking little number and a fleshy woman with lots of dark hair.

Zak shuddered, only partly from the cold. A sharp-edged wind flapped in from across the city. He hunkered down, tried to make himself smaller. He watched the gray-haired man rise from his chair, and now Zak got a look at his face. It was not exactly famil-iar, but he definitely knew who it was. He'd just been talking about him with Ray McKinley.

This was Wrobleski, Mr. Wrobleski, a good customer of Uto-piates, though he wasn't someone who spent much time browsing the stock inside the store. On those few occasions when he'd been in, it was to buy directly from Ray McKinley, and he'd treated Zak like a serf. Meanwhile, Ray usually behaved as though he and Wrobleski were blood brothers, though that in itself didn't mean a whole lot: Ray treated a lot of people that way when there was something in it for him. The fact that he'd said he wasn't "very happy" with Wrobleski now seemed deeply, though incomprehensibly, significant.

Inside the conservatory the four women moved together, though still not with any coordination or poise. This time Zak had the impression of a very amateur chorus line in its early days of rehearsal. They revolved through 180 degrees so that they now had their backs to the two men and to him.

Zak sensed he was on the verge of something, as if some of the dots could be joined up, could be made to reveal a grand design. He felt both excited and disablingly anxious. This was what he'd come to see, but now a part of him wished he didn't have to look at it. He saw that each woman's back was marked with a bad, ugly, tattooed map. They were not identical to one another by any means, but you'd certainly assume they were all done by the same lousy tattooist: the clumsy lines and forms had a consistency about them. And it occurred to Zak that the tattooist wasn't simply inept but rather that he'd scrawled all over these women's backs as a deliberate act of desecration. The lower the tattoos came on the body, the more ugly and confusing they got, until they dissolved into a collection of abstract lines and patterns, circles, arches, spirals. And while the maps on the women's backs all looked different, below the waist they all seemed very much the same, including the presence of a compass rose, at the base of each woman's spine, just above the cleft of the ass, right on the coccyx.

Zak watched as Wrobleski stood up, took a few steps forward, and reached out to touch the women. His hands trembled just a little, both eager and faltering. With infinite gentleness his fingers made contact with the back of the woman from the strip club, began to trace the shapes of the tattoo, the rough gouges and grids that bore no relation to the shape of the flesh beneath. The woman whipped around, straightened her neck, and unleashed a gout of saliva that hit Wrobleski sloppily on the side of his broad, flat face.

Wrobleski steadied himself, raised his hand as though to slap the woman, but something stopped him, maybe something that Billy Moore said, or maybe some deep, personal uncertainty. He lowered his hand, and the woman turned her back on him, resuming her position in the line.

Zak moved forward, pressing right up to the wall of the conservatory. The light wasn't good, there were reflections and streaks on the glass, and his view was obstructed by a large golden barrel cactus, but the map-obsessive in him wanted to know more. He tried to get a better look at the tattoos. Those markings begged for interpretation. Zak was well aware, professionally aware, that all maps demand a degree of decoding, and these maps could surely make sense only to a strictly limited number of people. He clearly wasn't one of them.

He watched in taut anticipation, fascinated yet dreading what might come next, how this ritual would play out, but suddenly Wrobleski had had enough. He stepped back from the line of women. He stood very solemnly, held his chin up, and stretched his arms straight out to his sides at shoulder height. It would have been an ambiguous gesture at the best of times, a sign of affection, as if he were trying to embrace and enfold the women, an attempt to grow wings, an indication that he was ready for his crucifixion.

Then Wrobleski dropped his arms to his sides and turned

around, moved away from the women, toward Billy Moore, who remained gazing inertly at the spectacle, bafflement and dismay on his face. Wrobleski said something to him, but if it required a response, Billy Moore didn't give it. And then Wrobleski looked away so that he could stare at his own reflection in the glass of the conservatory wall, and now Zak got a perfect look at his face. There were long thick streams of tears running down his cheeks, bubbles of snot in his nostrils, and his mouth was contorting as he tried, but failed, to prevent himself from sobbing. Wrobleski couldn't bear to see his own reflection. He closed his eyes tight, and his head and shoulders quaked. To Zak he looked like a big, fat, murderous baby.

The show was over. Zak was relieved, more for the women than for himself. He watched as a young black man came into the conservatory, attentively helped the naked women cover themselves up, then led them away, solicitously, maybe even obsequiously, into some other part of the compound. They didn't resist; they went as if floating, sleepwalking. Billy Moore and Wrobleski remained behind, though they didn't seem to be talking to each other. They didn't seem to be doing anything.

Zak remained where he was, wondering what to do next, whether he should wait for something else to happen, and how long that might take. There were surely any number of inferences, though not conclusions, that might be drawn from what he'd just seen, but lurking in the dark on the roof of the compound seemed no place to do that. He decided he'd wait a while longer, make sure the coast was clear, and then he'd descend, go back to Marilyn. He'd be the proud hunter-gatherer returning with his stash of precious information.

Then he heard a man's voice, a deep, constrained whisper:

"And who the fuck are you?" At the same moment he felt a metal snout pressed into the side of his neck: a gun, he supposed, though he had never actually had a gun pressed into the side of his neck before. So the ARMED RESPONSE sign hadn't been bogus after all.

"I'm . . . Steve," he said. The hesitation was natural enough, and at that moment Steve was the only name he could possibly think of.

"And *what* the fuck are you, Steve?"

"I'm a trespasser," he said quietly.

"Yes, you are. But why?"

Out of the corner of his eye Zak saw that the man with the gun was the same one who'd helped cover up the women, an all-purpose assistant, it seemed.

"I'm an urban explorer," Zak said tentatively.

"You're a fucking what?"

"Well, in this case I guess I'm more of a builderer. A freak-climber. That kind of thing."

"I still don't know who the fuck you are, or what the fuck you're talking about," said Akim.

"There are a lot of us," Zak said, then quickly added, "but I'm on my own now. We climb buildings. We like a challenge. I saw this place, and wow, I had to climb it. Really. That's all. I'm done now. I was all set to leave. I won't make trouble."

"I know you won't."

Akim patted down Zak, went through his pockets, finding absolutely nothing. Still pressing the gun into Zak's neck, Akim steered him into the conservatory, into the presence of Wrobleski and Billy Moore. Zak couldn't help looking more closely at the relief map. He recognized it immediately as Iwo Jima, and he could tell it was a fine thing: he could think of quite a few collectors on the Utopiates mailing list who'd pay an arm and a leg for a specimen like that. Then he thought he ought to concentrate on matters at hand. Wrobleski turned to him. He no longer looked like a man who did much crying. He didn't look at all like a baby.

"Do I know you?" Wrobleski said to Zak.

"No, you don't," Zak said, and Wrobleski seemed prepared to believe that part of the story, at least for now. Zak was well aware that if this went on too long, then serf or not, he would surely remember him from the store. He set his features in what he hoped was an uncharacteristic expression.

"Do *you* know this guy?" Wrobleski said to Billy Moore.

Billy Moore looked at Zak for just a second, his face a mask of utter indifference, then said, "No. He's a nobody. How would I know him?"

Zak tried to breathe normally. He didn't understand why Billy Moore would say that, but he wondered if he was allowed to feel the very slightest relief.

"He says he's a freak," said Akim.

"A what?" said Wrobleski.

Zak tried again to explain the joys of urban exploration and freakclimbing, all the time keeping his head down, his face away from Wrobleski.

"Can you believe this guy?" said Akim.

"I have actually heard of this shit," said Wrobleski; then to Zak, "And what, you were going to spray your name on the side of my building?"

"No way," said Zak. "I respect the places where I trespass. And anyway, you can see I don't have any spray cans with me."

There was no denying that.

"You're not just some common or garden-variety burglar, are you?" said Wrobleski.

"No," said Zak.

"Can you imagine what I'd do to a burglar?"

"No, I can't," said Zak.

"That's probably just as well," said Wrobleski, and he scrutinized Zak's face, looking for evidence. Zak was terrified at what he might find.

"Is that a black eye you've got there?"

"Yes, yes, it is," Zak said, and allowed his eyes to turn just a couple of degrees in Billy Moore's direction. Billy remained reassuringly blank.

Wrobleski continued to stare at Zak. It was true enough that he didn't look much like a burglar, and just as he was carrying no spray cans or climbing equipment, he wasn't carrying any burglary gear either.

"What do you think, Billy?" said Wrobleski. "You think he's worth soiling my hands on?"

"That's your decision, Mr. Wrobleski," said Billy.

"Fucking right it is," said Wrobleski; then to Zak, "You weren't spying on me, were you, kid?"

"Who'd employ me as a spy?"

It wasn't a bad answer, and Wrobleski seemed inclined to accept it. Even so, he said, "You understand I can't just have people waltzing into my place. That would be very bad for business."

"I'm not trying to hurt your business," said Zak, having no idea what Wrobleski's business was.

"I believe you," said Wrobleski, "but you also understand that I have to do *something* to you, right?"

"No, I don't really understand that," said Zak.

"Do you know why I'm not going to kill you?" Wrobleski asked.

Zak shook his head gravely.

"Because nobody's paying me to," said Wrobleski.

Zak thought that might be a joke, but nobody was laughing, least of all him.

"Would it help if I said I'm sorry?" Zak offered.

"No," said Wrobleski. "It wouldn't help in the least. Billy, would you do the honors?"

Billy Moore crossed the conservatory, edged around the relief map, and, with a remarkable tenderness, put one hand on the back of Zak's head, pulling him forward. For one bizarre moment Zak thought Billy Moore might be about to hug him, but then Billy tightened his grip and, with a deft, intense force, slammed Zak's face down into the concentric, geometric heart of the golden barrel cactus. He twisted the head a little, rubbing it in, scuffing it around, then he changed hands, grabbed Zak's hair and the back of his shirt, and tossed him all the way across the conservatory.

Zak lay motionless on the floor, not the first time he'd been in such a position thanks to Billy Moore, though this time there was no supplementary kicking. There was no need for it. His face felt as though it had been in a losing encounter with a commercial-grade stapler, as if it had been excruciatingly refashioned, collaged into some new, though by no means improved, design, and when he raised a hand to touch his face, he felt the spines that remained in his flesh, perforating his lips, his cheeks, his nose, his eyelids. He could hear Wrobleski making some approving noises.

By the time Zak had regained his senses, both Wrobleski and Billy Moore were gone from the conservatory and Akim was dragging him to his feet, pushing him out of the door and across the flat roof. Zak could barely open his eyes and had only an approximate idea of where he was going, into a descending elevator, it seemed, then out and through a room with many more framed maps on the wall. Akim pressed his lips way too close to Zak's ear and said, with a horrible intimacy, "He's getting soft. The old Wrobleski would have shoved that cactus up your ass and then thrown you off the roof," and then they were in the courtyard, by the outer gate of the compound. The old man slid the gate open just a couple of feet. Akim looked out suspiciously.

"You really on your own?" he said to Zak.

"Would I lie to you?"

"Yeah, you probably would," said Akim.

What did it matter either way? Akim wasn't about to go searching the streets. He kicked Zak in the butt, ejected him, booted him out into the real world beyond.

Zak still had enough wit to stagger off in the direction away from the station wagon, and he kept going long after he'd heard the gate shut behind him. When he reckoned Akim and the guy on the gate were no longer able to keep an eye on him, he doubled back, plunged into the shadows, and kept going, eyesight smeared, his face erupting, until he could just make out the two wrecked dump trucks and the brown station wagon parked between them. He hoped Marilyn was the kind of woman who knew some first aid.

23. THE PEDAGOGUE

Late night, a lumbering darkness, the smell of solvents and hot dogs hanging low in the downtown air, and even at this hour Sanjay, Billy Moore's sole employee, continued to tend the parking lot, to *guard* it. He paced the perimeter, inside the fence, taking slow, ponderous strides across the white pea gravel. There were no cars parked there now, not even his boss's Cadillac, only the trucks from the subcontractor of the Platinum Line, not that they didn't need guarding too.

There was also the matter of Carla Moore. Sanjay could see that even though her father's trailer was dark and he was obviously absent, Carla remained in the smaller trailer, the lights on, visible through the uncurtained side window, conspicuous and exposed. She was sitting at her desk, reading, making notes, and he found that touching: she was quite the little scholar. He also noticed that she had her father's old leather jacket draped around her shoulders.

He was experiencing some mixed feelings toward Billy Moore at that moment. He had signed on as a parking lot attendant, not as a babysitter, much less as a guardian, and in one way, being left alone here with the little girl in the middle of the night felt like far too much responsibility. At the same time, he felt flattered that Billy Moore trusted him with his own progeny. He was not entirely uncomfortable with this paradox: he thought paradoxes were to be embraced.

His circuit of the lot took him right by the trailer window, and although he tried to be discreet and quiet, the sound of his footsteps made Carla look up and put her face to the glass. Sanjay smiled, tried to look benign, gave a wave that he hoped might appear avuncular or fraternal, and she waved back and motioned for him to come to the door.

He did as bidden, but he was reluctant to cross the threshold into the child's private space. As an immigrant, an alien, even a well-educated one, he knew you couldn't be too careful in these matters. He remained teetering respectfully on the trailer's doorstep.

"When did you last see your father?" he said archly.

Carla realized he was probably quoting somebody or something, but she just said, "A few hours ago."

"And do you know where he is?"

"Away on business, I suppose."

"But isn't this parking lot his business?"

"What can I say, Sanjay? He's a man of many parts."

"That he is," said Sanjay. "And what are you doing, Carla?"

"Homework. I'm learning about skin."

"Ah, skin, a very large organ," he said, then wondered if perhaps he hadn't phrased that very well.

"I'm learning about sweat," said Carla, "and I'm kind of puzzled."

"How so?" He liked to help people with their questions. He was proud of his pedagogic instincts.

"You see," said Carla, "it says here that we sweat in order to cool down."

"Quite so," said Sanjay.

"But my problem," said Carla, "is that I often hear people complaining about being hot and sweaty. But I never hear anybody say they're cold and sweaty, so it seems the sweat doesn't work."

"Sometimes," said Sanjay, "people go into a cold sweat."

"Sure, but that's different. It's not like they start out hot and sweaty and they cool down and go into a cold sweat and that makes them feel comfortable. They go into a cold sweat because they're scared or nervous or whatever."

"You make a good point, Carla, and, of course, I can understand why you might be fascinated by the subject of skin, given your disease."

"It's not a disease," said Carla. "It's a condition."

"Ah, no doubt as you say, Carla. The human body is not my area."

"What is your area, Sanjay?"

"Back home I studied business and geology," said Sanjay with quiet pride. "I was hoping to go into the mining industries."

"Maybe you still will."

"At the moment it seems unlikely."

Carla didn't argue with him.

"You know," he said, and this was evidently something that had been on his mind for some time now, something he had to get off his chest, even if only to the boss's daughter, "it seems to me there are certain liabilities in having these subcontractors' trucks here on the lot."

Carla didn't say, "Why are you telling me this?" though her face certainly conveyed that. Sanjay was not deterred.

"The drivers seem a little lax," he said. "If they scrape the fence or each other's truck, they seem to find it quite the joke. And besides that, many of the trucks have signs on them saying HAZARDOUS MATERIALS, in one case even CAUTION: EXPLOSIVES. But these workers and drivers do not seem aware of the hazards, and they certainly don't seem cautious."

"Have you talked to them?"

"I have. I suggested that there might be certain elements in this city who would be all too keen to get their hands on some illicit chemicals and/or explosives."

"And?"

"And, Carla, I'm afraid they did not treat my suggestions with the respect they deserved."

"Have you told my dad?"

"Oh no, Carla. That is not the way. My job is to bring him solutions, not problems. I learned that on my very first day at business college."

"And have you got a solution, Sanjay?"

Sanjay thought long and hard.

"No," he said, "but your father did very kindly supply me with a baseball bat."

24. TREASURE

Marilyn had moved into the driver's seat in case a quick getaway was needed, but as Zak staggered back to the car, he looked damaged rather than hurried, and he opened the door and got in beside her with surprising delicacy, as if he were a package of fragile goods, already broken but perhaps still partly salvageable. Marilyn looked at his face with fresh, pained alarm.

"What happened?"

"Cactus," Zak said, through thick, barely mobile lips, though he knew that explained nothing.

"We need to do something about that," said Marilyn.

"I was thinking . . . same thing," he said. It hurt.

Marilyn began to drive, with purpose, though not fast. Zak slumped beside her, the skin of his face zinging under a web of small, sharp, stabbing pains. Below that was a deeper, spreading ache, and deeper still a more general feeling of nausea now that the adrenaline was curdling inside him. As they drove, he explained as best he could, as economically as possible, what he'd seen and done, and what had then been done to him. The only thing he couldn't tell her was what any of it meant. Marilyn was a good deal less sympathetic than he'd hoped for. He wanted her to be caring, compassionate, concerned for his welfare; instead, she was all business.

"So we now know the guy's name: Wrobleski," she said. "And you say he's a customer of Utopiates."

"Yes, a collector."

"Is that why he wants these women? Could it be that simple?"

Zak grunted.

"Okay, maybe that's not simple at all," said Marilyn. "And he didn't recognize you, why? Because you're a nobody as far as he's concerned?"

"Right," said Zak.

"But if he ever comes in the store again, he'll definitely recognize you. God knows what happens then. And Billy Moore *did* recognize you, he must have, but for some reason he pretended not to. But it seems he's just a nobody too, just a guy whose job it is to bring these women to Wrobleski."

"Sometimes being a nobody has . . . advantages," said Zak.

"At least the women seemed to be okay," said Marilyn. "Well, as okay as you can be when you've got tattoos across your back, when you're being kept in a compound by some blubbering weirdo, and you're being paraded naked in a conservatory."

"Yep, these things . . . comparative," said Zak.

He looked out of the windshield through one half-closed eye, couldn't make out where they were.

"Where are we going?"

"Back to my place," said Marilyn.

"In other circumstances that would make me so happy," said Zak.

"I think I might still be able to make you happy, Zak. Once I've done my stuff with tweezers and rubbing alcohol."

"Where . . . you live?"

"I live in a squat," said Marilyn.

"Yeah?"

"In a hotel. The Telstar. You know it?"

"Everybody knows the Telstar."

•

Like Wrobleski, like many others, Zak was inclined to think of the Telstar as "that place that used to have the revolving restaurant." More correctly it had had the Canaveral Lounge, a space-themed bar up on the twenty-third floor that had delivered a complete panorama of the city, 360 degrees, every sixty minutes. It had stopped revolving a long time ago.

The Telstar Hotel was, or at least had been, an optimistic statement in steel, tinted plate glass, and exotically colored concrete, an embodiment of 1960s ideals and design tics, with grounds that took up most of a city block. Its base was a four-story chunk with walls that flowed and ribboned, and rising from one corner was a tower, a little too short to be considered genuinely phallic. From directly above, in outline, in aerial photographs, or on a map, the effect was of an amoeba and its off-center nucleus, or perhaps, according to some, a fried egg. Inside, the vestibule had looked like a psychedelic planetarium; the honeymoon suite resembled NASA headquarters; in the basement there was an Op Art disco with floor-to-ceiling aquariums.

Critics, of which there were plenty, said it was too cool a building to remain cool for very long, and they were dead right. When business slackened, when room occupancy fell, when the conference trade evaporated, the place came to seem very old hat, and stilling the revolving restaurant was the first, all too symbolic, money-saving measure. But it wasn't nearly enough. The Telstar had been closed and shuttered for the best part of a decade now, but it wasn't quite empty or uninhabited.

Even before Mayor Meg Gunderson came into office, there had been ambitious, if amorphous, plans to revivify the place, to turn it into apartments, or a college, or a museum, or some combination of the three. There had always been other plans, of course, to demolish the damn thing. After it had sat empty for a few years, as the early discussions reached stalemate, a group of politicized, leaderless squatters occupied the building. They called themselves the Homesteaders: part Woody Guthrie, part Road Warrior, radical, anarchic, surprisingly media savvy. They moved in with their many children and dogs, and started holding press conferences. Speeches were made about social control, homelessness, deprivation, corporate evil: it played pretty well.

Meg Gunderson was mayor by then, and she stepped in and organized a provisional compromise. Utilities would be reconnected to the hotel (though not enough to spin the Canaveral Lounge), and the squatters could remain so long as there was no trouble, until a final decision had been reached about the Telstar's future development. They were still waiting.

Naturally, Zak had thought about the Telstar as a suitable object for his urban explorations, but he'd been deterred by a number of things. First, it was said the place was a death trap: walls, floors, staircases were all likely to collapse under the weight of the naïve infiltrator, but Zak rather doubted that. The mayor was hardly likely to let the squatters stay there if the building was going to kill them. He had been more inclined to believe that the squatters themselves were the real threat. It was said they were a fighting, feral bunch. True, that didn't square with what he knew of Marilyn, but perhaps that was only an indication that he knew nothing at all. Then the last time he'd scouted the perimeter fence, there was an armed guard with a sorrowful, angry dog, though it was unclear to Zak whether the pair were there to keep the public out or the squatters in. He hadn't investigated. As his excursion into Wrobleski's compound had just proved, urban exploration was sometimes a lot more fun to contemplate than actually do.

Now Marilyn parked the station wagon half a block from a side gate of the overgrown hotel grounds, where a different security guard and his hound stood sentry. Marilyn walked up to the guard, said, "How's it going, Bob?" pressed a couple of bills into his hand, and patted the dog. Bob looked at Zak, at his distorted face, speckled with blood and cactus spines, and decided it was none of his business.

"Can't complain," Bob said, as he opened the gate and waved Marilyn and Zak inside.

Marilyn took Zak's hand (he liked that) and guided him through the obstacle course of the grounds, scattered with concrete buttresses, barbed wire, giant buddleia, a blackened school bus. They got into the hotel via a rear service entrance, passed through buckled metal doors into a long corridor, patchily illuminated by a line of bare bulbs hung from the ceiling like decaying fairy lights. The corridor led past cavernous, festering kitchens, skirted furnaces that resembled the innards of some scrapped steamship, past a giant laundry that was now a shantytown of stacked gray linens. The corridor walls were scorched with graffiti: grinning robots, dwarves with oversized genitals, political slogans—*It's the Insurrection, Stupid.* At the far end there was a small, solid pool of light and an emergency generator adjacent to the rusted doors of a freight elevator. They encountered nobody, though Zak thought he could hear a band rehearsing somewhere up above.

"Want to risk the elevator?" Marilyn asked. "It's a hell of a climb otherwise."

In his punctured state, Zak didn't want to risk anything whatsoever, but he wanted to climb even less. He found himself in the elevator, a makeshift and decrepit thing. Marilyn punched a set of numbers into a keypad in the wall, and they began a rattling ascent, up through a great many floors until the cage stopped with a shudder. The doors opened, a good two feet below the level of the floor outside, and Zak, stepping up and out, stared blearily into a strange slice of shadowy, glass-walled space. They were at the very top of the hotel, inside the Canaveral Lounge, the unrevolving revolving restaurant.

"Oh God," Zak groaned. "Now I'm in an alternate universe, right?"

The Canaveral Lounge said sixties all right, though it spoke in a stuttering, muted fashion. There were plastic pods and blobs, white egg-shaped chairs, though all the plastic had crazed and developed a pale yellow patina. On the floor, the carpet showed a pattern of stars and planets, seen through a veil of plaster dust. The walls were decorated with memorabilia that looked authentic enough: tattered flags and banners, portraits of alarmingly youthful-looking astronauts, sections of charred rocket fins and satellite housings. There was a map that Zak, even in his present state, recognized as a lunar landing chart for the Sea of Tranquillity, still visible through cracked glass that had developed a thin film of mold.

"You really live here?"

"Sure," said Marilyn. "A view property."

"Why?"

"Who needs a reason?"

"Isn't it like living in a Kubrick movie?"

"*The Shining* or *2001?*" Marilyn suggested. "Or were you thinking *Spartacus?*"

"Not sure," said Zak.

"Sit down at one of the tables," said Marilyn. "I'll get the first-aid kit."

She disappeared into the dark hub of the restaurant, into what had once been the bar, and returned with rubbing alcohol, tweezers, a freezing spray, and began the long, delicate, painstaking process of extracting the cactus spikes from Zak's face. She started at the top, by the hairline, and worked her way down.

"Jesus!" Zak yelled, as she made her first incursion.

"If you could find some way of distracting yourself while I do this, that would be great," said Marilyn.

"What?"

"Just talk."

"It hurts when I talk."

"Okay, then," Marilyn said, "I'll start with the mouth."

Zak gritted his teeth as Marilyn cleared the area around his lips. Not talking hurt too, but once she'd cleared the area, operating like some kind of cosmetic bomb disposal expert, detonating tiny controlled explosions as she went, he was increasingly able to string some words and thoughts together, while she went back to working on his forehead.

"You know," he said, "those maps on the women could be parts of something bigger. Sectional maps aren't unusual. If, say, a group of you is going on a secret mission behind enemy lines, you may not want every member to know where you're heading, so each of you has a piece of the map. Oh shit, Marilyn, that really fucking hurts. So you need each other, but you're also keeping secrets from each other. And if one of you gets caught, the whole mission isn't blown."

"So what's the mission in this case?" said Marilyn. "And who's the enemy and where's the line?"

It sounded like something he'd have said. Marilyn continued her task, concentrating on the eyelids.

"No idea. Wrobleski is surely putting the pieces together," Zak said.

"I guess," said Marilyn. "But how many segments are there? How many maps? How many women?"

She sloshed alcohol onto a raw area of Zak's inflamed cheek, so that he experienced a new kind of dense, flooding pain as he considered an answer.

"You'd think it can't be very many," he said. "Nobody makes a map with, say, a hundred sections, because it's too hard to get a hundred people lined up in the same place at the same time. Shit—did you train as a sadist in a previous life?"

"No, I learned it all in this one," she said. "And the question remains, when we put the sections together, what do we get? What's it a map of? It looks like a city, but is it *this* city?"

Zak said, "Could be, but the maps are so bad, it's hard to recognize anything. And they're probably coded anyway."

Marilyn worked steadily, methodically, moving down the topography of Zak's face, following the random pattern of spikes, creating fresh contour lines of pain. Zak felt as if his face were melting, turning to hot clay. He wanted to scratch it, tear at it, drive his fingers right down to the bone. He felt like bawling.

He said, "And why was Wrobleski crying?"

"Maybe because he doesn't understand the maps any better than we do," Marilyn suggested.

"Or because he understands them too well," said Zak.

Marilyn's tweezers dug into the rear of Zak's jaw this time, into the hinterland between cheek and ear. He took a big, greedy swallow of air.

He said, "But what if Wrobleski is assembling a human treasure map?"

"Say?"

"There are arrows and lines on the women, they could be marking a route or a destination, and the symbols could be like *x* marks the spot."

"Hurrying to a spot that's just a dot on the map," Marilyn quoted.

"Maybe the compass rose marks the spot."

"Right at the base of the spine, just above the ass. Well, there are worse spots. But what's the treasure? And who buried it? And why?"

"There you've got me," said Zak.

She did indeed have him. She abruptly stood back, looked at Zak's face, admired her own handiwork.

"I can't get any more out," she said. "You'll have to let nature take its course with the rest."

"Oh no, not nature . . ."

She reached across and took Zak's battered face in her palms, and searched for a neutral spot, eventually selecting a small area below his black eye, not the most erogenous of zones, but good enough, and she touched her lips there softly. It hurt him only a little.

"You stay there," she said. "I'll be right back."

He had no intention of going anywhere. Now at least he could open his eyes and look out the restaurant window at the city below, at the web of lights, the intermittent traffic patterns, the busy glow of streetlights spread on the horizon. He was high enough to feel above it all, though not exactly superior to anything down there. From this vantage point he could see the logic of patterns, lines, grids, but he knew they were just diagrams, schemata, they didn't tell even a fraction of the real story. Down at ground level there was all that confusion, all that necessary, deceptive human clutter; and below the street surface it got even worse: tunnels, sewers, drains, concealed voids, unmapped spaces that he knew absolutely nothing about. As for Marilyn, it seemed he didn't know a damn thing about her either. What kind of person would want to live her life alone up here, squatting in the unrevolving restaurant of an abandoned hotel?

When Marilyn came back, she no longer looked remotely like herself, or like anybody Zak knew or ever expected to know. The glasses, the bookishness, the hipsterism, the baggy clothes, they'd all gone. She was now wrapped in an enveloping floor-length iridescent black . . . well, he couldn't quite put a name to it . . . a robe, a gown, a cape? And was it real leather or fake? Or some kind of man-made material, perhaps developed as a by-product of the space program? And could those strips of leopard skin around the hem and the cuffs be as authentic as they looked?

"Zak," Marilyn said briskly, "there are one or two things you should know about me before we get started."

"I want to know everything," said Zak. It seemed like the right thing to say, but mostly he wanted to stare.

"I'm not talking about innermost hopes and dreams. I'm just talking about sex, okay? I'd like to lay down some ground rules before we start. It saves time."

"Okay," said Zak, although saving time wasn't uppermost in his mind.

"Well," said Marilyn, "I'll swallow if I like the taste; I'll spit if I don't. You shouldn't take it personally."

"Then I won't," said Zak.

"I don't mind being held down, but I don't want to be *tied* down, and I definitely don't want the ball gag and the hand-cuffs."

"Good."

"Sex toys are fine, but I don't like actual *equipment*. So a pony harness, no, but vibrators and butt plugs are fine, and available on request."

"Okay," said Zak.

"And you know, I really do like dressing up: boots, lingerie, fetish gear if it isn't too ridiculous. On the other hand, I absolutely, positively don't want *you* to dress up."

"I'm glad," said Zak.

"If you want to take some dirty pictures, that's fine, but I don't want to see them all over the Internet, at least not showing my face, and definitely not under my real name."

"I can understand that," said Zak.

"Spanking's okay, but I think it's more blessed to give than to receive. Water sports, well, all right, if you really want, though frankly it doesn't strike me as much of a sport, though I do understand the nature of territorial pissing."

"The map is not the territory," said Zak, then wished he hadn't.

"And I guess we should use condoms," Marilyn continued. "You don't look like a guy who barebacks with other guys, but how would I know? Oh, and if you want me to wear a strap-on, I will, but I can't promise to keep a straight face."

"That won't be an issue," said Zak.

He understood the advantages of talking to women: learning what they wanted, telling them what he needed. Nobody liked everything, and nobody liked everything equally. Even so, he thought it might be better if you worked those things out as part of the process, rather than as preconditions. Marilyn seemed to be giving him a map of her sexual landscape, but there were times when it was much more fun to be without one, to find your own way, to get lost for a while. Even as he thought this, Zak wondered if he might be too immersed in the business of Utopiates.

"Other than that," said Marilyn, "you can do whatever you like."

She stood up and let the robe or gown or cape, or whatever it ought to be called, fall away. Zak took a deep, desperate breath. She was wearing a strange, gorgeous, ornate halter corset—he thought "steampunk" was probably the word to describe it—made mostly of leather, though there were bands of suede and silk, some laces, metal clasps and buckles, studs. It was a substantial and devastating piece of costume, curling up around her neck and shoulders, cupping her breasts and framing her crotch, while at the same time leaving them completely, emphatically exposed.

"Fuck," said Zak.

"That's the general idea," said Marilyn.

25. WHAT HAPPENED IN GREENLAND

Zak Webster had never believed those narratives where the hero wakes up in a strange bed with a strange woman and doesn't know quite where he is or how he got there. Zak always knew where he was when he woke up: not much of an achievement, since it was invariably in his own bed, in the apartment above Utopiates, usually wishing he was somewhere else. And that morning, however strange it seemed to be waking up in the non-revolving restaurant at the top of the derelict Telstar Hotel, and admittedly not strictly in a bed but, rather, on an inflatable mattress, on the floor, in a tangle of sheets, he knew perfectly well where he was.

But as he stirred and floated up to full consciousness, he realized Marilyn was no longer next to him, and looking out across the room, he saw that she was already up and dressed in her familiar, quasi-hipster street duds, sitting at one of the many tables scattered around the Canaveral Lounge, finishing her coffee, drinking from a mug bearing the Telstar logo of an atom and a communication satellite. Last night's erotic fancy-dress extravaganza seemed a very long time ago.

"Shouldn't you be getting ready for work, Zak?" Marilyn said.

He looked at his watch, and yes, he could see he was going to be a little late. After a night like the one he'd had, a different man might have thought he was entitled not to go to work at all, but Zak was not quite that man, and it seemed that Marilyn knew it. Unless, of course, she just wanted to get rid of him.

"Are you trying to get rid of me?" said Zak.

She didn't say no, but offered the perfectly reasonable observation that "You're never going to be able to get out of here without me."

Zak thought of the guard, the dog, the dubious elevator, the reputedly feral squatters, and saw the truth of this. He got up.

"How's the face?" Marilyn asked.

"It doesn't feel like mine," he said.

"Still looks like yours," she said. "More or less."

She crossed the room, patted his cheek briskly, as though she were dismissing some rather unlovable nephew. Ten minutes and a quick mouth-wash later Zak was outside the hotel, at the gate, being seen off by Bob the security guard and his dog.

Zak decided he would play it cool. He wouldn't call Marilyn in the course of the day, would avoid seeming pushy or besotted or desperate. Instead, despite some serious misgivings, he'd call one or two collectors, tell them he had something special for sale, something rather unusual, perhaps a little macabre, not for everyone, just for connoisseurs: the infamous Jack Torry rape map. "You never heard of that? Oh well, perhaps it's not for you. Oh really? Well, let me describe it for you . . ." This would not be a display of the highest moral character, but it was what his job entailed. He was looking at a list of clients, wondering who to call first, when Billy Moore strode into Utopiates.

Zak jumped in his chair: Billy Moore had again succeeded in scaring him. Zak suddenly saw the attraction of having a Taser or a sawed-off shotgun, though he also had a feeling that waving a weapon at Billy Moore would only be likely to make things worse. Billy, like Marilyn just a short time before, scrutinized Zak's face closely.

"You're in a state," he said.

"You should know," said Zak. "Look, if you've come here to beat me up, why not go ahead and get it over with?"

"I'm not going to beat you up," said Billy. "Not yet anyway. But I do want to know what the hell you were doing there last night."

Zak thought he might as well tell the truth.

"I was trying to impress a woman," he said.

Billy considered this. It wasn't the most improbable thing he'd ever heard.

"Did it work?"

"I guess it kind of did, yes."

Each in his own way was quietly surprised by this admission.

"You know, your face could have been a lot worse if I'd wanted it to be," said Billy.

"Am I supposed to say thank you?"

"No, just so long as you don't expect me to say sorry."

"The thought had never crossed my mind."

"You're smarter than you look."

Zak watched Billy Moore do a silent circuit of the store, then stop at a framed reproduction of Buondelmonte's map of Constantinople, the only survivor from before the Turkish siege: turrets, city walls, a hippodrome, a drawbridge that seemed to end in the middle of water.

"Look, I don't get it," Billy said at last. "I just don't get this whole map thing."

"Does that matter?" said Zak.

"Yeah, it does. You're the smart guy. Help me on this."

"Why? Why do you want to 'get it'?" Zak said.

"Because I'm trying to understand what I'm involved with. Just like I think you are."

Zak was reluctant to consider that he and Billy Moore had anything in common. But if Billy was telling the truth, then yes, maybe they did share a basic urge to comprehend the situation they were in, and perhaps an urge to be free of it. Also, Zak couldn't quite resist the opportunity to demonstrate his expertise. In exchange maybe Billy would share some information that Zak could take back to Marilyn.

"Basically, of course," Zak began, as simply as he could, "maps tell us where we are and how to get where we're going. And not just in a literal way, but in a political, metaphorical, and philosophical way too. No map can ever show everything, so every map involves selection, putting in what's considered important and leaving out what isn't. Every map shows the concerns and prejudices of the mapmaker."

Billy Moore nodded slowly.

"And maps are always nostalgic one way or another," said Zak, "always referring to the past, to something that no longer quite exists, because no matter how current a map is, whatever technology you're using, whether it's printed on paper or created by a satellite or a computer, it's out of date as soon as it's been made. Maps can only ever tell one fragmentary, temporary version of the truth. But that's okay. And a map doesn't even have to be 'true' to be useful."

He couldn't tell if Billy Moore was looking at him with grudging admiration or confusion or contempt.

"Let me show you something," said Zak.

He took the cylindrical leather map case from a drawer in his desk and removed the Jack Torry map, unrolling just a couple of feet of it.

"Take this map here," said Zak. "You couldn't use it to get anywhere, but you *could* use it to learn about certain events."

"Like what?" said Billy.

"It shows where certain rapes occurred. So it's only partly a map concerned with place: it's more of a map concerned with recording actions."

"Who'd want a map like that?"

"Some people just do."

"Sick fucks?"

"Not always," said Zak. "But let me try a less loaded example."

Putting away the Torry map, Zak crossed the store and pointed out a framed eighteenth-century map of Greenland, or *Carte de Groenland*, according to the uneven italic script along its lower edge. It was a copper engraving with an elaborate cartouche, bright coloring, not large, not really all that valuable.

"Let me tell you about Greenland," Zak said. "Let me tell you about Alfred Wegener."

Billy looked at him suspiciously.

"Don't worry. It's not rocket science. It's barely even cartography."

Billy was not immediately reassured.

"Alfred Wegener was a meteorologist who spent a lot of time looking at maps. And one day he looked at all the ins and outs of the Americas and he saw how they could be fitted into all the outs and ins of Europe and Africa. And he came up with this wild idea of continental drift.

"Everybody thought Wegener was crazy. Maybe he even had some doubts himself. But then he went on an expedition to Greenland, and while he was there, he kept looking at old maps, and he made some new maps of his own. Then he compared the two, checked the longitude and latitude of the coast, and he calculated that over the previous hundred years—between the making of the old maps and his new one—the coast had moved a whole mile, which is a colossal amount of movement for a landmass. This was great news for Wegener. As far as he was concerned, this was absolute proof that his continental drift theory was right."

"Yeah?" said Billy Moore.

"And the continental drift theory *is* right, more or less. But Wegener was completely wrong about the coast of Greenland. It hadn't moved at all. It was right where it had always been. Wegener was a better mapmaker than his predecessor, that's all. The old map had simply been inaccurate; it had put the coast of Greenland in the wrong place by one mile."

"Okay. I get it, I think," said Billy. "Or maybe I don't. What are you telling me?"

"I'm telling you that the inaccuracy didn't matter. The old map was 'false,' but it showed Wegener something that turned out to be true."

"And that's a big deal?"

"It can be," said Zak. "Take those maps tattooed on the women. We don't know what they mean. Maybe they're maps of real places, maybe they're not. Who knows? But they've got to be a map of *something*. Maps always mean something to somebody, and they always mean more to some people than to others."

Billy stared at the map of Greenland, thinking about what Zak had said, and thinking about much else.

"So you don't know a damn thing about these maps on the backs of those women?" he said.

"No," Zak admitted.

"You don't know who did them or why. You don't know what they mean to Wrobleski or why he needs these women taken to him. Or what he's going to do with them."

"I'm afraid not," said Zak. "I was hoping you did."

"So correct me if I'm wrong: for all your knowledge about maps and meanings and continental drift, you don't know any more than I do."

"Well . . ." said Zak.

Billy Moore's cell phone rang. He saw it was Akim, and he knew that his lesson in cartography was over.

"Zak," Billy said, "maybe you aren't any smarter than you look."

Zak was left with his phone and his list of customers. He wondered when, if ever, it would be appropriate to try getting in touch with Marilyn. Probably he should wait for her to call him. Maybe he could distract himself by doing a little research into the history of the Telstar Hotel.

26. MARILYN OFF THE GRID

That night, Marilyn returned alone to the Grid. Although Zak had said he sometimes went there to lick his wounds, and he surely had plenty to lick now, he wasn't there, and she was relieved. Sex complicated everything. She probably shouldn't have taken him back to the Telstar. She wondered how long it would be before he called her: too soon, she was sure.

The place was a lot less welcoming and a lot more crowded than when she was there the first time: there was nowhere to sit. She bought herself a drink and took up a spot standing, wedged in by the piano, where she could listen to Sam, who was now playing something melancholy and formless and, she assumed, improvised. She found that encouraging. She dropped a couple of bills into his tip jar, and when he took a break, she offered to buy him a drink. Funny how if you're a young woman and you offer to buy a drink for some guy and say you're really interested in his work, he can be surprisingly willing to talk to you. He slid along the broad piano stool so Marilyn could sit next to him.

"My friend tells me you used to be a cop," Marilyn said.

"Who's your friend?"

"Zak Webster. Map guy. Comes in here once in a while."

"I don't remember names," Sam said. "Or faces."

"Wasn't that a problem when you were a cop?"

"It was the least of them."

"You were one of those profiler guys, right?"

"Aren't you the little Nancy Drew?"

"Seriously, can I ask you a question, Sam?"

"Don't tell me you're a writer? Journalist? Documentary filmmaker?"

"No, no," she said quickly. She was ready with a lie or two she'd worked out. "I'm an actress."

He looked her over. Yes, he could believe she was an actress, though he couldn't believe she'd ever be a very successful one.

"I'm working on a part," Marilyn explained quickly.

"Lady Macbeth?"

On another occasion she'd have been prepared to be insulted, and to deliver an insult in return. Instead, she said, "No, it's a brand-new play. It'll be the premiere. We're workshopping it, doing some improvisation. So I need some background."

"You're playing a cop?"

"No, I'm playing the murderer."

He smiled at her just a little condescendingly and said, "You don't look the type."

"Well, that's the whole point."

"So, what do you want? Help with your motivation?"

He exhaled a small snort of ridicule.

"What's wrong with that? Don't cops try to work out motivation?"

He snorted again, but he didn't argue.

"The thing is," said Marilyn, "I can totally understand why people kill people. That seems the easy part. But I want to know what they do next."

"What does your playwright say?" .

"That's the problem. He keeps changing his mind, doing rewrites, so I'm trying to give him some input."

"He'll love that," said Sam, and ran his fingers along the

keyboard, played some suspended chords, then a few cop show stabs and arpeggios.

"Some people just shrug it off," he said, "and they get on with their lives like it never happened. No guilt, no remorse. Nothing. I guess we call them sociopaths. Or psychopaths. I can never remember which is which. They can both be pretty hard for the cops to catch."

"And really hard to portray on stage, I guess," said Marilyn.

Sam shrugged exaggeratedly, to show this was not his territory. He said, "And some murderers go directly to the nearest cop and confess everything. That kind of takes the sport out of it."

"Doesn't make for much of a play, either," said Marilyn. "But what if they don't go to the cops yet still feel the need to confess?"

"Like to a priest? A family member? Only a fool trusts a priest. Or his own family."

Marilyn smiled at him sweetly, as if she knew he was only pretending to be so cynical.

"What if they wrote down their confession, like in a diary?" she said. "Is that possible?"

"I've seen that. Gets it off their chest, and if they're really twisted, then they have the thrill of reliving the murder all over again."

"Right," said Marilyn with what she hoped sounded like no more than professional enthusiasm.

"It's a dumb thing to do, though," he said. "People have a way of finding other people's diaries, and they always read them."

"What if it was in code?"

"That would make life trickier. And a lot less plausible."

"Or what if maybe they burned the diary after they'd written it?" Marilyn suggested. "Like a sacrifice, burning the sins away."

"No, it'd just be burning a diary. The sins would still be right there."

Sam's fingers moved up and down the keys again, in exaggerated ecclesiastical scampering. A weary drunk leaning against the bar turned around and blessed himself.

"What if you drew a diagram of the murder?" Marilyn said. "Like a map. So there wouldn't be any actual words saying 'I did it.' In fact, depending on how you drew the map, somebody could look at it and still not realize it was showing a murder. You wouldn't have to draw knives, body parts, pools of blood. Is that the kind of thing murderers ever do?"

"I'm sure somebody somewhere has done it at some time."

"So how about this? Our character commits the murder . . ."

"This is *your* character?"

"Yes."

"Why does she commit the murder?"

"For money."

"Female hit man? You know, you're making it harder and harder for me to suspend my disbelief, but okay, carry on."

"And afterward," said Marilyn, "she's all crazy and worked up, maybe goes into a kind of fugue state. Drives around the streets. And in order to get the murder out of her system, she grabs some random woman from the street. Do you buy *that*?"

"I wouldn't even want to rent it."

"Stick with me, Sam. She drags the victim into a van, takes her into a basement, straps her down, strips her naked, gets some tattoo equipment, tattoos a map on the woman's back showing all the details of the murder."

"Man, I really want to see this show of yours. Why does she do that?"

"So that it's gone. The confession's been made. The murderer feels free. And the tattooed woman goes back to the streets. The fugue state disappears. Then sometime later, I'm not sure how long, these women with the tattoos start showing up. Yes?"

"This playwright of yours—who's his biggest influence? David Mamet? The Three Stooges?"

Marilyn raised her hands in a "search me" gesture.

"I don't know," she said. "We've still got a lot of exploration to do."

"I would think so."

Sam stared down at the keys but kept his hands folded in his lap.

"Do you believe in this bullshit you're giving me?" he asked.

"I don't know."

"Do you *want* to believe in it?"

Marilyn had no answer to that.

Sam continued, "I guess I'm supposed to say something wise and profound about now, yeah? Follow the money. *Cherchez la femme*. Round up the usual suspects."

"You're not taking me seriously."

"I'm taking you as seriously as I can. And the truth is, I think you're miscast. I think you'd make a much better victim than you would a murderer."

He played a few deep, rumbling, sonorous notes on the bass keys.

"Still, if you need somebody to do the incidental music for the show—give me a call," he said. "I'm not easy, but I'm cheap."

27. THE COACHING MANUAL

"So what's a life coach?" Billy Moore asked his daughter.

"Search me," said Carla.

"Look it up for me, will you?"

Carla was sitting at the fold-down desk inside the Lofgren Scamp, laptop open in front of her, and she tapped the words into a search engine.

"Okay, here we go," she said; then quoted, " 'Life coaching is a practice aimed at facilitating psychological or emotional growth, that helps individuals identify and achieve personal goals, using a variety of techniques, including psychology, sociology, counseling, mentoring, and motivational methods. It is not to be confused with psychotherapy in that it does not focus on examining or diagnosing the past.' "

"Yeah well, I'd hate to be confused," said Billy. "Tap in the name Dr. Carol Fermor, would you?"

A few moments later, the website for *Carol Fermor: Change and Inspiration* popped up: a background with a big sky full of melting clouds, and at its center an image of a sleek, serious, confident woman, dark lips, pale eyes, and stylishly sharp gray hair.

"Oh yeah, you'll like this," said Carla. " 'Go confidently in the direction of your dreams! Live the life you've imagined. As you simplify your life, the laws of the universe will be simpler.' "

"Did she really say that?"

"No, some guy called Thoreau said that. She just put it on her website. What the doctor says is 'Do you have two selves? Is the self you present to the world in better or worse shape than the self you keep private? Would you like to heal the separateness you experience even as you extend yourself to others?' Then there's some stuff about holistic empowerment. You planning to get empowered?"

"It couldn't do any harm, could it?" said Billy.

"Well, it'd make the social worker happy."

"That's what I live for."

He seemed suddenly distracted and sad. Carla decided he needed cheering up.

"I've been thinking about tattooing," she said.

"For the love of God, why?" said Billy, and instantly realized that he was overreacting. The last thing he wanted to do was alarm his daughter. "I mean, aren't you a bit young to be thinking about tattoos?"

"I'm not thinking of *getting* one," Carla said.

Billy was thoroughly relieved that they weren't having *that* conversation.

"The thing is," Carla said, "I don't understand how anybody ever starts doing it in the first place. I mean, who's going to get a tattoo from somebody who's never done any tattooing before?"

Billy gave a small, uninterested grunt that he hoped was enough to stifle the conversation.

"Maybe most people start on themselves," said Carla, immune to his tactics. "And I hear that some people practice on a pig, but it's going to have to be one very docile pig, isn't it?"

"Maybe a dead pig," Billy suggested.

"But that's where I could come in, isn't it?" said Carla. "Somebody could practice on me. They wouldn't use a real needle, just a blunt stick, like a knitting needle, something that wouldn't break the skin. And they could draw a pattern on me, all over my body if they wanted, and then when they'd finished, they'd see if it was any good. And if they didn't like it, then they'd just wait awhile till it disappeared and then start all over again, keep on doing it until he (or she) got really good. Then move on to real ink. It could be a great after-school job."

"Tell me you don't mean any of this," said Billy gloomily.

Her attempts to cheer him had been a conspicuous failure.

"You really think you need some life coaching?" she asked.

"Nah," said Billy. "I just need a life."

Akim had set up the appointment for late in the afternoon. That allowed Billy to pick up Carla from school and take her home before doing the job, though Akim had surely not taken that into account when making the arrangement. The doctor's office was on the ground floor of a grand, red-brick, three-story house in one of the leafiest, safest, most expensive parts of town. Access to the office was via a side entrance, and Billy guessed that the doctor lived in the house upstairs, presumably not alone, given the size of the house. For now, however, there was just one car in the drive, and that promised to make things easier. He parked the Cadillac in front of it, boxing it in.

Billy tapped on the office door and tried the handle. It was unlocked, and he stepped into a tiny reception area where Carol Fermor, looking rather less confident and sleek than on her website, was hammering at a keyboard and scowling at a computer screen.

"I'm looking for Dr. Fermor," Billy Moore said, though he knew he'd found her. "Dr. Carol Fermor."

"That's me."

"Oh, okay. I thought you might be the receptionist."

"I don't have a receptionist," she said, and it sounded like a complaint. "And this computer is killing me."

"I'm your five-thirty," he said.

"Right, of course. Hello, Mr. Smith. William Smith, is it?"

So Akim had made the appointment using half of Billy's real name. He tried to calculate the degree of insult and the degree of risk.

"Sounds like a fake name, doesn't it?" he said.

The doctor simply replied, "Go on through and take a seat in my office. I'll be right with you."

Billy moved through the reception area and, via a frosted-glass door, into a large, bright room that looked out onto a trim but lush square of garden. To the limited extent that Billy had any preconceptions of what a life coach's office would be like, he had imagined something between a hospital room and a hotel gym. This place was homely: worn rugs, unmatching furniture, a huge flabby couch. There were table lamps in the shape of ballerinas that looked like they revolved and a shelf displaying a row of Minnie Mouse figurines. And although there were framed certificates on the wall, there were also pieces of children's art and a photograph of a younger Carol Fermor standing thigh-deep in a trench, with Egyptian ruins in the cloudy yellow distance behind her. Billy was still looking at that picture when she came into the room, but he pretended he was looking at the certificates, examining her professional credentials.

"Are you a real doctor?" he asked.

"I'm not a medical doctor, no. My doctorate was actually in archaeology and anthropology. Then I had a long career in human resources. I've been a life coach for a decade or so. And you?"

"No, I'm not a real doctor either."

She offered a wintry smile.

"Why don't you sit down?" she said.

Billy selected a plain, straight chair that had its back to the window. Carol Fermor sat down on a chair just like the one he'd chosen, angled at a careful 45 degrees to his. She balanced a yellow legal pad on her knee, took out a slender gold mechanical pencil. Very old-school, Billy thought, though he had no idea what new-school would have looked like.

"Well, Mr. Smith, how are you? You sounded a little anxious on the phone."

"Yes," he said. What point was there in saying it hadn't been him who'd made the call?

"So, Mr. Smith, William, what do you think I can do for you?"

"Tough questions first, eh?"

There was no smile from her this time, and nothing at all from Billy.

"All right," she said, "let me tell you how this usually works. At a first session like this neither of us should expect too much. We'll talk. I'll ask you a few questions. You'll ask me a few questions. I'll explain what I do. You'll explain what you hope I can do. And if we decide to move forward, there are various personality tests and questionnaires we might find useful as a starting point."

"Sounds good to me," said Billy.

"We should both come without fixed ideas, but there is one very simple thing I'd say: you must be ready for change. Are you?"

"Fuck yes," said Billy. "Oh sorry. Yes, yes, I'm ready for change."

"Good."

She allowed him to sit in an awkward silence for a while, until he felt obliged to say, "I feel like a bit of a fraud coming here really."

"It's not unusual to feel that way. That's often part of the problem. There's no need for those feelings."

They sat in silence for an even longer spell, and this time she cracked first.

"Well," she said, "Freud—though you won't find many Freudians around these days—tells us that love and work are the only therapies."

"Smart guy," said Billy.

"He had his moments, yes. So, William, how's work?"

"Hard," he said. "Too hard."

"How so?"

He was only briefly tempted to describe the stresses of the parking business. Instead, he said, "My boss is the real problem."

"Bosses so often are. What line of business are you in, exactly?"

"Well, that's part of the problem. I'm not sure."

"You're not sure what business you're in?"

"I work for a guy," said Billy. "I do what he tells me to do. He isn't a guy you can ask a lot of questions, not about what business he's in or anything else."

"That must make your work very difficult."

"You think?"

"And how do you feel about that?"

"Worse and worse."

"That's why you're ready for change."

"You got it."

Billy knew he should have made his move already, and yet he couldn't help feeling that this woman might be pretty good at what she did. In some absurd way he'd taken an immediate liking to her. He wanted to talk to her, almost as much as he wanted this to be over. He was also finding it hard to believe that her back was covered in tattoos. He knew it was a dumb thought, but she just didn't look the type.

"And what's preventing you from simply quitting your job?" she said.

"I think I won't be allowed to."

She looked away, kept her head and eyes down, inviting him to say more.

"My boss is a crook, okay?"

"Okay," she said, though she didn't sound as though she thought it was okay at all.

"A real crook. I mean, he isn't some guy who cheats on his taxes or buys and sells things that fall off the back of a truck. The guy's . . . the real deal."

"And you've been assisting him with this?"

"Well, part of it, yeah, but only a really small part. Do you want to know exactly what I've been doing?"

"Do you want to tell?"

Billy opened and closed his mouth, but nothing came out.

"You know," said the doctor, "in the circumstances, it might be better if I don't know. It might create certain professional difficulties for me."

"Maybe you could meet my boss," Billy said, "use some of your counseling on him. I could take you there now."

"I'm afraid that's not how this process works."

The sun had gone down appreciably, so that it now shone from directly behind Billy, turning him into a substantial, gloomy silhouette. Carol Fermor got up and lowered the blind a foot and a half. She didn't return to her seat.

"Mr. Smith, I'm going to be honest with you, I think I'm out of my depth here. I can see that your situation is very difficult, and your desire for change seems sincere, but I'm not qualified to deal with the situation you find yourself in. I'm sorry."

"You're sorry?" he said.

Very gently she replied, "Yes, I am, and I'll give you the name of someone else who I think will be able to help you. He's a very good man."

"Somebody else won't do."

"That's simply not true, William." She turned away from the window and took a couple of steps toward the door. "I'll pop into the reception area and get his details."

"No," said Billy. "I came here for you. You're the one I want."

"We're going to have to wind things up now, I think."

Billy stood up rapidly, swept past her, placed himself between her and the office door. The look she gave him was a beauty, stern but sympathetic, authoritative, earnest, cautious but unafraid, the look you'd give a dog that had wandered into your backyard: beloved pet or rabid stray?

"Don't you want to hear about my problems with women?" Billy said.

"No, I don't. You need to leave now."

"No, that's not what I need. Now shut up and listen."

"This is getting out of hand, Mr. Smith. Step aside."

"You're not like the others. They were homeless or strippers or prostitutes, and sure, one was a realtor, but you're in a different class. Did you just get over it, shrug it off? Or did the tattoos *motivate* you or some shit like that?"

That really got her attention.

"I think you're mistaken, William. I think you have the wrong woman."

"I'd like to believe that," he said. "Not that it would make any difference. Like I said, this whole thing is a complete fucking mystery to me, and I've got a feeling some of it's a mystery to my boss too, but you'll see for yourself."

"You've rather eloquently convinced me that I *shouldn't* see this boss of yours."

She clutched her gold pencil, as though she might use it as a weapon, or might crush it between her tense fingers.

"Well, that's not an option, Doc. Neither of us has a choice about it."

"We all have choices, William."

"You know, I really fucking hate it when people call me William."

It all happened very quickly after that. He hit her just once, nothing fancy, and then she hit him back, which meant that he had to hit her that much harder, which knocked the fight out of her and gave him time to drag her from the office, to his Cadillac.

"I'm sorry I had to do that," he said, which he knew sounded stupid.

He also realized she'd pull herself together and be ready to fight some more long before they got anywhere near Wrobleski's compound, and he didn't want to have to hit her again to subdue her. He really didn't want to hit anyone anymore. So he settled the issue by bundling her into the trunk of the Cadillac and locking it. He felt sure that other, more elegant solutions must be available, but he couldn't think of any, and in any case, elegance was pretty low on his list of priorities just then.

28. TRUNK

As Billy Moore drove, he could hear the sounds of muffled banging and screaming from behind him, from inside the trunk of the Cadillac. Fists and feet, and very possibly elbows and knees, and possibly even a head, slammed pointedly and pointlessly against the car's internal panels. He was glad his car was already a wreck: a man who drove a better vehicle could have gotten really upset about a thing like that. He turned on the radio and found some dull classic rock to drown out the noise. Yes, music had its uses.

Once the car was inside the courtyard, where Wrobleski and Akim were waiting, the improbable double act, the old firm, Billy popped the latch on the trunk, and Dr. Carol Fermor slowly pulled herself out. Now that there was nothing to kick against, she stood quietly, trying hard to exhibit dignity, looking at all three men, making steady eye contact with each. Perhaps it was a professional gaze, thorough, diagnostic, or perhaps she was simply committing their looks to deep memory, anticipating a time when she might take revenge. Billy Moore stared at the ground.

"Who are you people?" Carol Fermor said. "What do you want? How do you think this can possibly end?"

"That's a lot of questions," said Wrobleski.

"I'm a respected professional. I have a husband and a family. I'll be missed. People will be looking for me. I can't just disappear."

Wrobleski stroked his scalp distractedly.

"People like you disappear all the time," he said. "People better than you."

He made the smallest gesture to indicate that he was bored, that Akim should take this woman out of his sight. She went reluctantly but without too much of a struggle, though Billy reckoned that might have a lot to do with the syringe in Akim's hand. Wrobleski took an envelope of money from his pocket and held it out to Billy, but Billy turned away, keeping his hands down, in his pockets, spoiling the lines of his new suit.

"I don't need it," Billy said.

"What? You're working pro bono these days?"

"No, Mr. Wrobleski. Have this one on me. I think I'm done."

"Have you found alternate employment?"

"Well, yeah, I'm trying to run my parking lot, but in any case, I'm the wrong man for the job."

"Don't you think I'm the best judge of that?"

Billy said nothing. Only a damn fool would tell Wrobleski there was something wrong with his judgment.

"It's okay," said Wrobleski. "I understand your position. You're confused. You want to know what's going on. Am I going to hurt these women? How long am I going to keep them? You want to know what the fuck these maps are all about."

It was true, Billy did want to know these things, but it had occurred to him that knowing exactly what Wrobleski was up to might be worse than being in the dark.

"Well, I could tell you, Billy," said Wrobleski. "But then I'd have to kill you."

Wrobleski didn't laugh or smile, because he never did, and Billy tried to console himself with the notion that all the best jokes are told with a straight face, not that this particular joke explained anything.

"Billy," said Wrobleski, "I'm not the worst guy to work for. There are many far worse than me. But I can't have you picking and choosing, coming and going as you please. I can't have anybody doing that. You're working for me, not for yourself."

As before, Billy was inclined to ask, "Why me?" but he knew it was far too late for that. He had been selected, perhaps for a good reason, perhaps on a whim, but once Wrobleski had made his selection, there was no room for further bargaining.

"But I'm not going to be a cunt about it," Wrobleski said. "So how about this? You do one more and that's it. Then you'll have picked up your last tattooed woman. You'll be your own man again. That's fair, isn't it."

It wasn't a question, and it would have made no difference whether Billy thought it was fair or not.

"Okay," said Billy. "One more and then it's over." But he didn't believe his own words any more than he believed Wrobleski's.

29. THE SKIN UNDER THE CITY

Sunrise on a landscaped slither of real estate, formerly nameless, now Columbia Park, a canal-side house of cards, a public and private partnership: shiny, flimsy new buildings, office blocks and apartments in unequal numbers, built by developers who'd been given an easy ride on planning regulations in exchange for cleaning up the chaos of territory alongside the canal. Ray McKinley had been one of the first. Now there was a bike path, a pedestrian walkway, some fanciful lampposts and benches, a laughably small "green space" containing an even more derisory "nature trail." At lunchtime this place would be densely populated with office workers, but now, with the sky barely light, it was deserted, static, and Wrobleski sat in the passenger seat of his SUV, Akim at the wheel, waiting.

Wrobleski had never made the mistake of thinking he was free. He knew he was scarcely even independent. He always operated for other people, did their dirty work: that was the cleanest way of working, nothing personal about it, no motive, no anger, no connection. But it also meant that he had to wait for a call, just the way his man Billy Moore did. And if Ray McKinley wasn't exactly the best or most considerate employer, at least they went back a satisfyingly long way: McKinley was the devil Wrobleski knew, or hoped he did.

When the call came, McKinley said, "Okay, so you won't

deal with the main woman for me, but you'll have no problem dealing with her 'advisor,' will you?"

"Who?"

"Brandt. The one Meg Gunderson called a twat on live TV. Remember?"

"I remember."

"Seems that our mayor is a very good judge of character. Mr. Brandt and I had a meeting. I said it would be worth his while to decide that the mayor's plans were unworkable, that we should start again, demolish the Telstar, get back to a clean slate."

"And how did that go down?"

"Seems our man has integrity. He threatened to call the cops. Then he threatened to set his dog on me."

"Big dog?"

"Dalmatian."

Wrobleski stared into the SUV's wing mirror and at last saw a man and his dog approaching along the canal's former towpath. Brandt looked older than on TV, but taller and leaner too. He was wearing a different pair of elaborate eyeglasses, like goggles, and he was dressed as though for some exotic and nameless sport, in something black and red, and all-enveloping, somewhere between a leotard and a space suit. The dog was a particularly restless and energetic example of his breed.

There were security cameras along the towpath, but Akim had been along last night and thoroughly vandalized them. Wrobleski watched man and Dalmatian as they went past the SUV, then he got out and started following. Brandt's progress was constant, faster than a power walk, slower than jogging. Wrobleski had to extend his stride in order to keep up. They'd gone no more than fifty yards when Brandt, without stopping, turned his head and glared at Wrobleski.

"Can I help you?"

That accent again: another country, or continent, or planet.

"No," said Wrobleski.

"Is there a problem?"

Wrobleski let his jacket hang open to reveal the leather strapping of a holster. He took out the gun. Brandt's face took on an expression that Wrobleski had seen often enough before, a confusing and contradictory alloy of disbelief and growing realization.

"Yeah. I can't decide whether to kill you first or the dog first."

While Brandt was trying to fathom that remark, perhaps hoping it was just a joke in very, very poor taste, Wrobleski had his problem solved for him. The dog bounded toward him, reared up, and though it looked more like neurotic enthusiasm than actual aggression, in general dogs disliked Wrobleski as much as he disliked them. The fucking animal sank his teeth into Wrobleski's left hand, between the thumb and forefinger. That settled it: dog, then man. He pulled the gun from its sheath, fired just two shots, and then that part was done with; from here on, it was business as usual.

The park remained static and empty, and the surface of the canal was slick as glass. Wrobleski wondered if a dead dog would float or sink: only one way to find out. He nudged the Dalmatian off the towpath into the water. It sank slowly. By then Akim had driven up alongside in the SUV and stopped. He got out and opened the back door, glaring consistently at Wrobleski.

"Yeah, yeah, I know," said Wrobleski. "This isn't making the best use of your talents. Duly noted."

Akim was aware that his complaint was being mocked even as it was being acknowledged. With as much dignity as he could manage, he took hold of Brandt's feet, leaving the shoulders for Wrobleski, and together they hefted the body into the vehicle. The bite on Wrobleski's left hand was starting to hurt like a son of a bitch.

•

Charlie opened the gate of the compound, and Wrobleski reversed the SUV into a tight, cluttered, neglected corner of the courtyard. He got out, and he and Akim opened the rear of the SUV. On the ground, cut into the tarmac, was a flat metal hatch, a trapdoor made of steel diamond plate: he'd had it fitted specially. Akim lifted the door to give access to a set of descending concrete steps, narrow with steep risers. There were various hard hats and flashlights hanging on the wall, and they both jammed on miner's helmets. That always felt pretty stupid to Wrobleski, but the helmets had lamps on the front to light the way as they went down, leaving their hands free to deal with the body, which, with Akim's grudging assistance, Wrobleski now lifted onto his own shoulders. They had got this down to a crude but efficient art.

Wrobleski always had a sense of the figure he was cutting, something monstrous yet also unavoidably comic: the Phantom of the Opera, Quasimodo, one of the mole people, a Morlock, accompanied by a sulky, rebellious assistant. As they negotiated their way down the steps, Wrobleski felt the rising coldness, detected the smell of dilute ammonia and maybe spoiled meat, and heard a thick roaring sound that grew louder with each step, as if he were entering the mouth of a gigantic seashell. Suddenly there was a muffled boom, something grand but far away inside the earth. There were noises like that down here all the time these days, muted blasts as they worked on the Platinum Line. Wrobleski refused to let it bother him.

Wrobleski and Akim pushed on, went deeper, through ash-gray concrete chambers, bunkers, rusted spaces that might have served as industrial bear pits, into a coarse intermeshing of tunnels that led ever farther into varieties of receding darkness.

Wrobleski knew his way down here well enough, knew how to get in and out, how to get where he needed to go, but he didn't know what most of these masses and vacancies around him were, what they did, had no idea how they related to the world above. And he was content to keep it that way.

It was cold, and yet he was sweating, from exertion and adrenaline. The tunnel they were in changed its direction, ran away in a taut, vaulted curve. The lights on the helmets picked out a broad, deep, semicircular arch, simple, functional, its apex and keystone scarcely higher than a man's head, an entrance of sorts.

They stepped through the arch and out the other side, into a long, straight, white-tiled space, with a low ceiling, regularly placed pillars, a few broken benches here and there, some peeling advertising posters, a tattered map on the wall. They were standing on the platform of a long-abandoned subway station, the ground scattered with coils of wire and lengths of pipe, rat droppings and discarded paperwork that somebody must have once considered really, really important. The first time Wrobleski came down here, years ago now, the place had seemed infinite and unfathomable: now it was simply the place where he finished the job.

A part of him was struck by how absurd it was for the city to be building a new subway line while this old station lay disused and apparently intact and serviceable. And yet the reason why it had been abandoned was obvious enough. As the rails left the station and disappeared into the tunnel mouth, they were twisted as if mauled by some giant, casually destructive hand. There had been a deep settling in the floor of the tunnel, a shift in the earth, a subsidence: a sinkhole had appeared beneath the railroad ties, black, wide, jagged-edged, and although it was obviously not literally bottomless, it was cavernous and capacious enough for his ongoing needs. You could lose a whole army of dead bodies down there: Wrobleski had only accounted for a small platoon. They never came back, never reappeared elsewhere, and the pit was deep enough that even the stench of death seldom made it up to the level of the station. Akim shivered, waited.

They stood at the platform edge, and Wrobleski heaved Brandt's body off his shoulders like an outsized sack of coal or potatoes, something that had already once been in the earth. Akim again took the feet, Wrobleski the shoulders, and they swung the corpse until it had enough momentum to carry it forward, away from the platform, down between the distorted rails, then away into the silent void.

Wrobleski took a breath, but not too deep: there were plenty of things you wouldn't want to inhale down here, quite apart from flesh rot. He stood listening, heard only the usual sounds of the earth. He nodded to Akim, not exactly in thanks, but in recognition that for better or worse he needed him and his talents. The second part of the job was done too. Now he was ready to go back aboveground, to spend some time with his maps, the ones on paper rather than on flesh.

30. MARILYN GIVES AN INCH, ROSE SCARLATTI TAKES A FOOT

"Thanks for coming with me," said Marilyn.

"Thanks for calling," he said, and realized this sounded a bit weak. "I'd have called you, but I didn't want to seem . . . whatever."

"You did the right thing. After a night like the one we had, I needed a little space."

"And now you need me again."

"I need you to be supportive, anyhow."

"I don't *feel* very supportive. I really don't know what you're doing here."

"Yes, you do, Zak. I'm going to get Rose Scarlatti to tell us more of what she knows about the compass rose tattoos, and why she reacted the way she did."

Yes, he did know that, of course.

They were standing outside the lobby doors of the Villa Nova apartment building, waiting to be let in. Rose Scarlatti was being a little slow to answer the bell, though in Marilyn's eagerness they were a little earlier than the agreed time.

"And you really think that getting a tattoo from her is going to help?" said Zak.

"That's what she said last time. And if you can't trust an old lady tattooist, who *can* you trust?"

The lock on the building's front door buzzed and opened at last. The apartment door was already open when they got to

Rose's floor, forbidding as much as inviting. Rose did not greet them. She was all business: her tattoo equipment—old-fashioned, workaday, looking like a gangly robot arm—was set up next to a hard, narrow daybed that had been moved to the very center of the living room. Her latex gloves were already on, the inks and needles laid out on a marble-topped table; a freshly lit clove cigarette was lodged tightly in the corner of her mouth.

"This is Zak," said Marilyn. "He's here to be supportive."

"Fabulous." Rose looked at Zak the way she might have looked at a suspicious stain on the bathroom floor, then said to Marilyn, "No second thoughts?"

"No," said Marilyn.

"And you only want a compass rose?"

"Right."

"Nothing more ambitious, more tribal? A mandala? A burning lotus? Scenes from the life of Elvis?"

"No," said Marilyn. "As agreed. Just a compass rose."

Marilyn seemed more nervous, more tense, than Zak would have expected. While she carefully, anxiously arranged herself on the daybed, he tried not to wear his resentment too conspicuously, tried not to alienate Rose still further, tried not to get in the way. He looked around the apartment, and despite himself, he could see the fascination of the clutter, of all the souvenirs and exhibits. If things didn't work out in the map business, he wondered if there was a living to be made buying and selling antique tattoo memorabilia. No doubt there was, though probably not for him. He reckoned you'd need some extensive ink on your body before customers took you seriously.

"How about your man there?" Rose said to Marilyn. "Does he need one too?"

Zak thought it best to speak for himself.

"No thanks," he said. "I had a grandfather in the navy. He

had a ship tattooed on the back of his hand. He said it was the worst decision he ever made in his life."

"Must have led a very tame life," said Rose; then to Marilyn, "And you're dead sure you want it on the top of your foot?"

"Certain," said Marilyn.

"And which way do you want north to be?" Rose asked. "Pointing up the leg or down?"

"Down," Marilyn said. "That way I can point my toes toward the North Pole."

Marilyn had already removed her boot, now she rolled off her sock and raised her long, lean, pale right foot. Zak didn't think its appearance would be improved one bit by the addition of a tattoo, but he was well aware that his personal tastes were not being pandered to here.

"At least a tattoo on the foot shows some commitment," said Rose. "It's going to hurt like hell, you know that? Top of the foot's just skin and bone, no muscle, no flesh."

"I know," said Marilyn. "You told me."

"And I don't want you wriggling, jumping around, making involuntary movements."

"I won't wriggle," said Marilyn. "Involuntary movements I can't do much about."

"You'll be just fine," said Rose, and she allowed herself the first smile of the day.

The tattoo machine buzzed into life. Rose cradled Marilyn's foot in one taut, nubbled hand, yet for all her talk of arthritis and unsteadiness, once she concentrated on the job, she was as sure and steady as a surgeon, or at least a pedicurist. She held the foot firmly and delicately, as though it were some small, nervous creature that needed to be soothed and calmed. She didn't use flash or a stencil, didn't even draw the design in advance: she was going freehand.

Rose's face showed determination and pleasure as the needles cut their first line into the flesh, drew their first ooze of blood. Zak found himself feeling just a little queasy as he watched, but fought against it: he was man enough not to throw up in the tattooist's living room. Marilyn felt as if her foot were being stung by an unusually active and persistent jellyfish, or perhaps by carefully aligned cactus spikes: she had no direct, personal experience of either, but she could imagine. She felt as though tiny licks of flame were sparking from her foot up her leg and into her core, but she managed to be a good subject, to keep her body still and controlled. She could even hold a conversation.

"Rose," she said, "did you ever tattoo a treasure map on anybody?"

"How's that?"

"You know *x* marks the spot, buried treasure, pieces of eight, gold doubloons."

"Like Long John Silver?"

"That kind of thing," said Marilyn.

"Can't say I ever did. But I would have if anybody had ever asked me to, though it seems kind of illogical to get somebody else to tattoo a treasure map for you. It means there's at least one extra person who knows where the treasure's buried. Why wouldn't they go and grab the treasure for themselves?"

"Unless the map is coded," said Marilyn.

It took a small effort on Zak's part not to insist that *all* maps are coded, but he knew he'd feel better for not saying it.

"A coded map?" said Rose. "What the hell is that? Still working on that 'project' of yours, are you? How's it going?"

"It'll be going a lot better when you tell me what you promised to tell me."

"Oh, you drive a hard bargain."

Rose Scarlatti was silent for a good long time, and it did cross

Marilyn's mind that the old lady might be about to welsh on the deal. It was too late for new negotiations: her foot already had some significant markings.

"Oh well," said Rose, "maybe it's nothing. It means something to me, but it might not mean anything to you. A long time ago, there was a kid, a weird little kid . . ."

31. THE DISAPPEARING KID

He blamed his mother. Why not? Anyone would. Everybody does. She was the one who made a man of him. And sure, his father played a part, did things to the mother that made her do things to the son, but Dad wasn't around much, and then he wasn't around at all. She decided the son wouldn't be like the father. She didn't have specific ambitions for him, none of the familiar, self-serving hopes for success, money, a good wife. She just didn't want him to be a weak, useless man like his dad. That was her special project, to turn her boy into a little tough guy: after that he'd be on his own. Was it tough love? Well, it was certainly tough.

It went pretty well. The boy didn't resist. He learned not to be soft. He learned that if he got into trouble, he had to get himself out of it. He liked the karate classes, the playground scuffles. He wasn't the biggest, wasn't the most volatile, but when it came to it, he was the meanest. The little boy in him started to fade away.

His mother wasn't such a bad bitch, he would decide long after the event. She did what she thought she had to do. And gradually her project became more refined. Later, when he tried to work out exactly how old he was when it first happened, he couldn't. It seemed to have been going on forever, seemed always to have been a part of his life, so it must have started when he was what? Eight years old? Six? Was that possible?

They were in the car. Mother and son traveling fast, no seat belts, no conversation. He figured she'd been drinking. They'd been on an errand on the other side of the city, buying something, selling something, delivering something, and they were coming back through a neighborhood he'd been in before, though not often—crowded streets, rough at the edges, poor but striving, and still a good way from home—when suddenly she pulled the car over and said, "All right, time to get out."

He wondered what he'd done wrong. His mother was an angry woman at the best of times. Anything might cause her to get mad: something somebody said to her, something she saw on TV, though more often than not it was his doing. But this time he was pretty sure he hadn't done anything wrong, and she didn't sound angry at all, which was even more scary.

"We're going to make a man of you," she said. "Get out of the car. I'll see you when you've found your way home."

She almost made it sound natural, like the kind of thing all mothers and sons might do, something that could be fun, a game, though since he was the only one playing it, he couldn't be sure about that.

"All right," he said, because no other reply was possible, and he got out of the car. He was still hoping, well, fantasizing more than hoping, because he knew how unlikely it was that she'd smile and say forget it, it was a joke, a test, that she was trying to make sure he wasn't a crybaby, which he wasn't. But he stood in the street and watched as his mother yanked the car door shut and drove away. She didn't wave goodbye.

He remained on the sidewalk, alone, dry-eyed, a long way from home, and he knew that in some sense he'd always be that way. He'd find his way back home all right. Of course he would. He knew his address, had a little money in his pocket and a tongue in his head, he could ask people the way, he could walk, he could get on a bus. He'd be just fine. And anticlimactic though it felt, he *was* fine. He got home soon enough, without incident that time, and without much fear, and he supposed his mother was pleased to see him, though she didn't show it. A week later she did it again, and again the week after that, again and again, dropping him off in ever more distant, dubious, and unfamiliar parts of the city.

He thought of buying a map and hiding it—his was the kind of home where it wasn't hard to hide things—but he didn't, because somehow that would have been cheating. And naturally he got lost once in a while, but never completely lost, and eventually he never got lost at all. Wherever he was in the city, he belonged there. And even if he couldn't have told you the name of the street or the neighborhood he was in, it was only a matter of taking certain bearings, tuning into the geography, feeling the contours of the city, noting the direction of the light, the angles of the skyline, and then he knew exactly where he was: right at home.

And as he walked he *looked*. He observed the various changing natures of the city, the characteristics of neighborhoods and communities, how people lived and *why* they lived that way, together or separately, in houses and hovels, in apartment blocks and tenements, richly or desperately, with dignity or defeat. He saw the clustering of life, of separate fates, the back and forth, the aggressions, the forms of symbiosis and parasitism, the flow, the exchange, the *business*. And although he was just a kid, and although he couldn't quite understand it all, and certainly couldn't have articulated what it meant, he knew that he wanted to be a part of it, and at the top of it, and that sooner or later he would be.

Increasingly he saw no reason to hurry back to his mother. He began to get into trouble, to make trouble for himself. It toughened him even more, and he reckoned that was the plan too. This wasn't an exercise in keeping a clean nose. It was about taking the long way home, digging himself into holes, then digging himself out, deciding what needed to be done, surviving, flourishing.

Trouble came in different forms. There was the obvious stuff that he couldn't help doing: minor theft, shoplifting, a bit of pickpocketing. He learned a lot from it, especially about the separation of cause and effect, the unpredictable nature of consequences. He'd go into a store and lift half a dozen CDs, or go into a comic-book store and steal as much as he could hide under his coat, and despite the cameras and the alarms and even the security guards, he'd get away with it completely. Other times he'd take a single apple from a market stall and find himself chased halfway around the neighborhood by some deranged stallholder. This was useful knowledge.

Adults were less of a problem than other kids. A boy on his own, even a tough-looking little kid, not from the neighborhood, that was an affront that couldn't go unchallenged. He had to be taught that he was in the wrong place. He was yelled at, taunted, tripped up, shouldered off the sidewalk, told to hand over his money. He always made them regret it. It wasn't that he always won the fights, yet somehow he had the knack of always making them feel like they'd lost. And when he had to, he ran. He saw no shame in running, and he wasn't a bad runner, though he knew he had his limits.

He found those limits one afternoon when he was thirteen years old. It happened on a bleak winter day, huddling under a furred gray sky, with the threat of snow in the air, and there on a corner were five kids who looked like fair game. They were foreign, very foreign, skins purple black, wearing the wrong clothes. They seemed out of place, and they'd have seemed out of place anywhere in this city. They were improbably tall, elongated, their limbs seemed to have too many segments. They were standing against a graffiti-tagged bus shelter, slouching, heads hanging, and still they towered above him: even so, he just couldn't walk past without doing or saying something.

Afterward he wondered if maybe they were young marathon runners in exile, but at the time that didn't seem very likely: they were smoking hand-rolled cigarettes. And as he walked by them, he said, couldn't help saying, "Hey, boys, don't smoke. It'll stunt your growth." And really, how bad a thing was that to say? But they reacted as if he'd said something filthy about their mothers.

All five boys straightened up, seemed to unfold simultaneously. They didn't say anything, either to him or to one another, but something in them changed, so that they now looked regal and infinitely dangerous, and he could tell they had plans to do something terrible to him. One of them showed him a brief glimpse of a knife blade. He made an immediate break for it. He started to run more determinedly than he'd ever run before. Why was he so scared? Was it because they were black? Maybe. Certainly it was because they were so alien. He didn't know what rules they'd play by if—when—they caught him.

They ran beautifully: even in his panic, looking back over his shoulder, he could see that. He felt himself to be a tangle of arms, legs, and lungs working at odds, but these guys were fluid, effortless, their spindly legs scarcely touching the ground. He didn't think they were even trying very hard; they were just toying with him. They could have pounced whenever they wanted to, but they didn't want to, not yet: for now they were just wearing him out, exhausting him for the fun of it. He kept going as long as he could. It wasn't a bad effort, but he knew he was running out of juice. Sooner or later, one way or another, the chase would come to a certain end.

He needed to get off the street, find some protected space, a shop, a café, maybe even a bank, somewhere they wouldn't follow and where they wouldn't dare attack him even if they did. His eyes were watering with the cold and the exertion, and the street around him looked blurred and grubby, but if there was going to be salvation, it would have to be here. There was a row of small shops: a liquor store, a head shop, a place that sold old-fashioned stationery. He didn't like the look of any of them, and careened past, and then he'd run out of all options but one. There was only one door, one store left. He had to go for it, whatever it was.

He dashed up to the glass front door, didn't even look inside, opened it just enough to slide through, then slammed it shut behind him and leaned up against it, gulping for air. His mind was empty and he didn't know what he'd walked into. He blinked about him. It was very bright and still in there, and his first thought was he might have come into a dentist's office. There was a noise coming from the back of the room that sounded like a dentist's drill, and there was definitely somebody laid out back there, a woman who seemed to be suffering.

However, the person doing the drilling didn't look at all like a dentist. It was a woman with long black hair and tight jeans and bare arms, one of which had a sleeve of tattoos. She stopped what she was doing, looked up casually, and said, "What's the matter, kid? Hellhound on your trail?" and that didn't sound like the kind of thing a dentist would say. Then he noticed there were pictures all around the walls, bright colors and clear lines: skulls, hula girls, dice, hot rods, devils. He was in a tattooist's studio.

"No," he said seriously, between breaths, "not hellhounds," and he looked out through the window and saw that the five tall, thin black kids had regrouped on the other side of the street and were now waiting, pacing up and down, displaying a chilly patience.

"Are those guys giving you trouble?" the tattooist said.

He wasn't a squealer, but in this case he didn't need to be. It was obvious what was going on. The tattooist said to the woman on the table, "Hold on there, babe," rummaged in a metal cabinet, and produced—he could hardly believe it—a crossbow. It appeared ultramodern, with a frame of brushed metal, a telescopic sight, and a rifle stock. It was a terrifying thing even to look at: he liked that.

The tattooist went to the door, opened it, cocked the crossbow, inserted a stubby arrow, and fired it across the street. She didn't seem to be aiming at anything in particular, and yet the arrow sliced a harsh, flat trajectory through the air, missing two of the boys by fractions of an inch, and lodging neatly, perfectly, in a telephone pole, making a sound like a bass string being thwacked. Alarmed and furious, the boys shouted something in an unrecognizable tongue and then sloped off, their composure and dignity re-forming around them as they went.

The tattooist shouted after them, "Fuck off, you little racists."

Back in the tattoo studio, the kid was very, very impressed, and just a little confused. He'd needed help, and a woman had come to his aid. That was very weird. And why did it feel so good?

"Come on, kid. Come over here and watch an artist at work."

Rose returned to her customer, to her tattooing. The woman on the table was lying prone with her arms bare and raised high above her head. There was a length of yellow silk draped across her breasts, though she didn't seem much concerned with modesty. Her eyes were open, but they weren't looking at anything. She was moaning quietly to herself, but the kid couldn't tell if it was pain or something else.

"Is she all right?" he asked.

"Yeah. She's fine," said Rose. "She's full of endorphins."

"What's that?"

"Chemicals. When you're in a lot of pain, the body releases these things called endorphins. They make the pain feel good after a while. Got that?"

"I think so," he said, though he wasn't sure he had.

"This young lady is in the middle of an endorphin rush," said Rose. "That's because I'm tattooing her armpits. That hurts like fuck, doesn't it, babe?"

"Oh yes," said the woman on the table. "Oh yes."

The kid peered into her left armpit, then the right. In the left, the tattoo was already complete, while the right was still a work in progress. When finished, the tattoos would be identical whirlpools of blue and purple foam, something both gothic and American Indian about them. They weren't the woman's only tattoos: she had swallows, poppies, butterflies, jungle creepers twining their way up her arms, a winged heart peeping out above the yellow silk, but the kid found himself transfixed by the armpit tattoos, the sheer weirdness of them. Why would she choose so much pain for a tattoo that so few would ever see?

"So come on," said Rose, "what's your story?"

While she continued with her work, the kid told her why he was there, about the "game" his mother made him play. Rose listened, and asked one or two questions, because at first she thought he might just be making it up, but the more it went on, the more sure she was that he was telling the truth.

"And your mother is doing this why?" she said.

"To make a man of me."

"You poor little devil," said Rose.

The tattooing went on for a long time, and although the kid could see it was a delicate, painstaking process, after a while the work itself wasn't so fascinating to watch. The woman's face, however, that was something else, something special. Within a frame of thick, tangled blond hair, her features were mobile and alive, alternating between certain pain and uncertain pleasure: lip-biting, tears in the eyes, a trembling mouth that was close to laughter but not close enough.

He stayed till the very end of the process, until Rose had finished and the woman was thoroughly inked and wiped down. She sat up and held a mirror to her armpits. He couldn't tell if the tattooing was any good or not, but maybe that didn't even matter. He was far more intrigued by how pleased the woman was, how happy Rose was with her own handiwork, how much it meant to them both.

"Can I have one?" he asked.

"What? A tattoo?" said Rose.

"Yeah."

"No, you can't."

"Why not?"

"Because I don't want to go to jail. Tattooing kids is still illegal in this city."

"Oh go on," said the newly tattooed customer.

"Are you trying to get me into trouble?"

"Always," the woman said, "but you could just do something really small, something nobody would ever see."

"Like in my armpit," the kid suggested.

"I don't think so."

"Go on, Rose," said the woman.

It seemed that Rose had a hard time saying no to her.

"Okay, but not the armpit. Kid, gimme your hand."

Eagerly, he extended his right hand, balled into a fist. He was already picturing a Viking or a fireball or a winged serpent emblazoned across his knuckles, but Rose grabbed the hand, rolled it over, and opened it up, and as quickly and as perfunctorily as possible, she tattooed a cluster of small, blue-black ink marks on his palm: a circle, and a pair of crossed lines, one of them an arrow marked with an N for north.

"What's that?" he asked.

"That's a compass rose," she said. "And if anybody asks, you did it to yourself."

"Okay," he said. But nobody did ask. He went home, went back to his mother, didn't say anything about the chase, or about Rose or the tattoo, and neither his mother nor anybody else ever said to him, "What's that on your palm?" No doubt there were other kids whose lives included the inspecting of hands, for cleanliness, honesty, maybe even punishment, but he had none of that. He kept his hand to himself. He looked at it only when he was alone, when he was sure nobody else was looking. Still, that was often enough to realize, all too soon, after just a couple of weeks, that the tattooed marks were fading.

At first he felt disappointed, then cheated. Rose must have known this would happen, that the marks would disappear. Later, he learned that's what always happens to tattoos on the palm of the hand: they won't stick, they just fade away. Rose had tricked him, treated him like a child. That really pissed him off. But then he started to feel differently about it. Maybe Rose had been pretty smart. She'd done the job, done what he and her friend had asked of her, and yet she'd also allowed for a reversal, for a kid's change of heart, and, of course, she was protecting herself too.

He needed to talk to her about this, and off he went, threading his way into the city to find her again, attempting to retrace the route that had taken him to her studio that day. Naturally, he'd had other things on his mind at the time, but even so, he was amazed how unfamiliar the whole area now looked, how hard it was to find a landmark that told him he was anywhere near the right place. He was pretty sure he'd found the bus stop where he first encountered his pursuers, and he had a sense of the direction he'd gone from there, so he headed that way now, but immediately he started to think he must be mistaken. The shapes of the buildings looked wrong, the streets weren't this narrow, he didn't remember that church or that convenience store. Perhaps he hadn't come this way at all. The kid who never got lost suddenly felt adrift and a very, very long way from home. He spent a whole afternoon covering the district, back and forth, pacing the grid, looking for clues, even buying a map from a corner gas station. And he also kept a lookout for five tall black kids who were good at running and might be eager for revenge. But he found nothing. He was both sadder and angrier than he could understand.

The endorphin rush from the tattoo on Marilyn's foot was small scale by most standards, and her eagerness to question Rose, to know what the story meant, cleared away both pain and pleasure. She pushed herself up on the daybed, just about managed to stay, or at least appear to be, calm.

"What was his name, Rose?" she asked. "What was the kid's name?"

"I don't know."

"What do you mean you don't know?"

"Oh come on," said Rose. "It was a long, long time ago. A lot of brain cells have died since then."

"It must be in there somewhere. Maybe we can jog your memory. Was the name Wrobleski?"

"I don't think so, but I never knew his surname anyway."

"So you did know his *first* name."

"Yes, I did. Once. But I don't anymore. It's gone, I'm old. I barely remember what happened yesterday. I'm all used up."

Unexpectedly, two thin streams of tears ran down from the old woman's eyes, making their way into the creases on her cheeks and around her mouth, tributaries heading for an inert inland sea.

32. TECTONICS

"How's your foot?" Zak asked as he guided Marilyn down the stairs of the Villa Nova.

"It hurts," said Marilyn. "It's going to hurt for two or three weeks if Rose Scarlatti is to be believed."

"You think she is?"

"About the foot, sure."

"And about the rest?"

"I don't even know what the rest is," said Marilyn. "Some time in the distant past, some random, nameless, traumatized kid went to Rose Scarlatti's studio. She gave him a tattoo she knew would disappear. And that gave him a taste for renegade tattooing? So now he's wandering the streets picking up women and tattooing coded maps on their backs, along with Rose Scarlatti's trademark, because . . . because he just likes it? Because it's a sexual fetish? Because he's fucking nuts? Sure. Who wouldn't believe a thing like that?"

"You think the kid was Wrobleski?"

"Even if it was, it doesn't explain everything else. Maybe I should just go and ask him," said Marilyn.

"Yeah, right."

"You think I'm not serious?"

"I don't know what you are right now, Marilyn. I don't know why you care so much. I don't know why you care at all."

They were at the ground floor. She looked at him with both sympathy and regret.

"I'll explain," she said. "But not here."

"Where?"

"Your place," said Marilyn. "After we've fucked."

Zak had taken twenty or so illuminated globes from Ray's unwanted stock and arranged them strategically around his bedroom, in various places, at different heights, to disguise the exact shape, size, and dreariness of the space. The globes glowed rather than shone, with a pale consistent blue from the expanses of water, quiet browns, greens, and yellows from the landmasses: the poles were plain white. The effect was like being in space, surrounded by a solar system of identical, unmoving planets.

"Quite the bachelor pad," said Marilyn.

"I do what I can."

"Oh, I think we can do better than that."

She took hold of him, tenderly, but with purpose and determination. Her hands moved rapidly down his clothed body, accelerating, a lightning raid, opening buttons, a belt, a zipper, then pulling fabric aside, not stripping him naked, but exposing only the areas she needed. She lay on her back on the dense, grubby blue carpet, and he did for her what she'd done for him: a series of strictly functional openings and unfoldings, all that was needed, just the moving parts. It felt good not to have to think about Marilyn's house rules.

Afterward Zak rolled onto his back beside her, sweating, breathing hard, pleased with himself. Who needed a road map? He put his arm around her and they stared up at the dark, distant ceiling above the globes. The world felt satisfyingly far away. He knew it wouldn't stay there.

"Tell me about your grandfather," he said.

He felt Marilyn's body clench and slip away. "What?"

"I've been doing some research. Karl Driscoll was your grandfather, wasn't he? And he was the architect who designed the Telstar. Is that why you live there?"

"You're quite the little gumshoe, aren't you?"

"I never left my desk. And I still don't know the half of it. I know he got kicked off the project before it was finished. I know he never built anything ever again. I know he's not around anymore."

"That's way too much already."

She started to get up, to fasten her clothes, ready to make her escape. Zak put his hand on her, hoping it didn't seem like a grab. And he hoped it didn't sound either too insistent or too whiny when he protested, "You said you'd explain. So explain."

Marilyn moved away across the floor, sat with her back to the wall, wrapped her clothes and her arms tightly around her body.

"My grandfather was a good man," she said. "He raised me after my parents died. Car crash. Drunk driving. Unheroic stuff. He did his best. His big thing was walking through the city with me, pointing out buildings, architectural styles and features. I was the only eight-year-old in my school who knew what a piloti was.

"He always carried a walking stick with a globe for a handle, so that he had the whole world in his hand. I knew he'd been an architect, but that didn't seem to have anything to do with what he was showing me. I didn't really know what architects did, partly because the way he talked, it sounded like that phase of his life had been a million years ago. I knew he was bitter about it. And then one day he got a call from the mayor's office: Meg Gunderson was a fan. They wanted to make the Telstar part of the city regeneration project, thought it would help to have the original architect on board. He was thrilled. It was a dream come true, to feel wanted again. He gave a few talks, addressed a bunch of committees, did some interviews, and then he disappeared."

"Disappeared how?"

She'd been talking quickly, but now she stopped to take a deep breath, then another.

"I don't know. He just went. One day he wasn't there anymore. I did the whole missing-person thing with the cops, they went through the motions, but they didn't do anything about finding him. And they were probably right. Why waste their time. We all assume he's dead. Somehow I *know* he's dead. And that's what I was doing that first night when I met you, walking through the city, trying to see it through his eyes, maybe looking for his ghost or something. I've done a lot of that, probably too much."

"That's terrible," he said, and he meant it. "Really terrible."

"It is," she said. "It's not the worst part."

She stood up now, took up a place at the center of the room, and a strange relaxation came over her. She let her arms and her body loosen, and she undressed completely. The clothes came off quickly and effortlessly. It wasn't an act of display, wasn't a striptease, but it was still quite a show. Before long she stood naked in front of him, her body smooth and delicate in the dim light of the globes, looking self-possessed yet defenseless. Then she turned around. There it was, the damage, a diagram of former pain.

Zak would never be sure whether he was surprised or not. The moment he saw the tattoo on her back, it seemed as though he'd always been expecting it, a kind of explanation but one that simply demanded other, more complex explanations.

"Take a good long look," Marilyn said. "You're the map expert."

He started at the top. High on her lean shoulder blades there was the beginning of the disorder, an ineptly drawn web of straight and curved lines, laid over the contours of her body. Some were reckless, some shaky, and yes, as he'd seen before elsewhere on other bodies, it was possible that they might be roads or rivers or railroad lines, but really they might be many other things too: cables, water mains, power lines. They paid no attention, no respect, to the flesh beneath. Then there was an overlay of misshapen squares and circles, buildings perhaps, and scattered among them things that could possibly be interpreted as bridges or underpasses, but some of the marks looked more like mere doodles, blots, and gouges, like the simple, cruel defilement of the soft skin. There were loose crosses, empty semicircles, and arrows that must be marking something or other, but their meanings remained utterly obscure. You wouldn't have wanted to read too much into any of that chaos.

Zak wondered for a moment if, possibly, there was really nothing to be read there at all, no code to be deciphered, no reference to any "real" world, if it was simply an attempt to obliterate the female body, to overlay it with mayhem and abuse. Maybe any reading of the map would be mere projection, seeing what you wanted to see, a futile exercise, like trying to use a set of Rorschach blots as a street plan.

As he'd already seen, things got worse as the tattoos descended the body. Below the taut nip of Marilyn's waist the scrawl became even more hurried, abstract, and bewildering as it careened across the curves of her buttocks, overlapping circles, swirls, scribbles, as if the tattooist was getting frantic, perhaps bored, wanting to get the task over and done with. It was a familiar incoherence, again incorporating, right on the tailbone, in the smooth softness at the top of the cheeks, an infinitely crude but quite unmistakable compass rose. Well, now Marilyn had two of the fucking things.

There was something else that he saw now, on the tight musculature of her lower back, something obscured by a welter of lines, as though the tattooist had made a design and then decided to cross it out with more tattooing. Under those lines of attempted concealment or erasure was a blob-like shape with a circle at one corner, like an amoeba and its nucleus, or perhaps like a fried egg. In the general illustrative mayhem it was impossible to be certain, but Zak thought it was neither an overactive imagination nor simple obsession that made him see those lines as the Telstar Hotel.

Marilyn began her story. She looked vulnerable but tough, and inured rather than tearful. Slowly and with difficulty she told Zak as much as she could bear to remember—the night, the walk, the attack, the smell of the leather hood, the ride in the back of the van, the basement ordeal, the various species of pain she experienced, then the relief of a strictly limited kind, and the damage that would never be wholly repaired. She talked until the point came when she couldn't tell him anymore, when she had nothing left in her.

"That's all I've got," she whispered.

She pulled on her clothes again, baggy pants, a T-shirt, a work shirt, a thick woolen jacket, putting on layers of protection.

"I have to leave," she said.

"No you don't," said Zak, "there's no reason in the world why you have to leave. I want you to stay the night. I want you to stay, period."

"I can't do that."

And she didn't. After she'd left, Zak was surprised to find that an ignoble part of him was relieved. There was already too much for him to take in. He felt hollow. He thought there must be some perfect words he was supposed to say, some magical action he should perform, that would make everything better: it might take him the rest of his life to work out what.

33. HUMAN

The city streets seemed abandoned. Marilyn Driscoll started to walk away from Zak, through the Arts and Crafts Zone, through the unraveling weft and warp of the city. She felt exposed but lightened. Zak would have found out sooner or later, why not now?

She was less than halfway home when she heard a car behind her, and she wasn't in the least surprised when she turned her head just a little, just enough to see that it was a battered metallic-blue Cadillac. Well, of course. It drove slowly past her and stopped a short way ahead. She kept walking until she'd caught up with the car, and then she stopped and looked in through the open passenger window to see Billy Moore at the wheel, miserable, shame-faced. Before he could say or do anything, she opened the door and got in beside him, like a grateful hitchhiker.

"I've been expecting you, Billy," Marilyn said. "What kept you so long?"

He had no answer, and neither of them said anything on the journey to Wrobleski's compound. He didn't even turn on the radio. As they were crossing the threshold, entering the courtyard through the metal gate, Billy Moore turned to Marilyn.

"I'm sorry. I'm really lost," he said.

Wrobleski was waiting for her in the courtyard. She had endlessly played and edited the scene in her mind, through all its possible fluffs, retakes, and alternate endings. And of course Wrobleski had always been the ogre in this scenario, the fiend. Now that she finally saw him, he appeared so much less monstrous than she expected, than she wanted him to be. Sure, he looked like a heavy, and was no doubt capable of any amount of malevolence, but he appeared, nevertheless, all too human. She found herself horribly disappointed. He gazed at her without much interest, then he turned, moved away, gestured to Akim that she was now his responsibility. She was having none of that.

"Wrobleski," she called, "talk to me. You owe me an explanation."

He gazed at her vacantly.

"You think?"

He said it quietly, with weariness but not with any great concern.

"Yes, I do."

"I really don't care what you think."

"No," Marilyn insisted. "That's not right, that's not good enough."

He stared at her as though she were a laboratory experiment that had gone awry and produced unexpected though not especially fascinating results.

"It'll have to do," said Wrobleski. "You want your big drama, your big scene. But I'm not playing."

She flew at him. He hardly moved, and did he really snap his fingers? In any case, before she was on him, Akim was standing between the two of them, and he was now thoroughly taking care of things. She felt a blow on the head, and then a jab from a needle. Akim's hands were on her, in all kinds of places they didn't need to be. And was she imagining it or did he say quietly in her ear, "Don't worry, it'll soon be over."

Then there was a new reworking of a familiar nightmare. For a while she could still scream and struggle, but then ropes were tightened around her, two thick layers of duct tape were stickered across her mouth, and then she couldn't see, though at least this time it wasn't because of a leather hood. She was dragged away, across the courtyard, deep into the compound, down a set of stairs, into a new basement room, the size and extent of which she couldn't fathom. It was hot and it smelled of weary bodies, and she thought she could hear voices, though it might only have been a TV. She would spend the rest of the short night on her back, on a mattress, bound, sightless, motionless, inert, and without feeling, but absolutely ready for whatever was coming next.

34. PELT

Billy Moore stood beside Wrobleski, shaking just a little. For reasons he couldn't fully understand he'd wanted to step in, to smack the stuffing out of that little jerk Akim. So why hadn't he? Because he was afraid of Wrobleski? Well sure, that might have been reason enough, but it was the symptom, not the disease. He knew that somewhere inside him, at his core, there was a growing, curdling reservoir of cowardice. That was perhaps worth knowing, but it didn't make him like himself any better.

Wrobleski put his hand on Billy's shoulder and squeezed it with what might very well have been his idea of affection.

"For you, old man, the war is over," he said. "You're free and clear. You're no longer in the Wrobleski business."

Billy couldn't yet allow himself to feel any relief.

"It's a shame," said Wrobleski. "I saw quite a future for you."

"Not sure it's quite the future I see for myself."

Wrobleski looked at him slyly. "Well, I'd never ask a man to do a job he didn't want to do."

Billy knew that wasn't true, but he still said, "Thanks."

"Nothing I can do to change your mind?"

"I don't believe so," Billy said solemnly.

"Don't look so worried," said Wrobleski. "I'll prove there's no hard feelings. You remember back at the beginning I said I'd show you the really good stuff?"

"The maps?" said Billy. He had no desire whatsoever to see Wrobleski's collection, but he knew he would have no choice, and he suspected it would not be a simple "showing."

"The maps, of course," said Wrobleski.

They began by following a route that Billy had walked before, past locked metal doors, as though again heading for that oddly cheerful waiting room and the elevator that led up to the roof. But before they got there, Wrobleski stopped at one of the other doors and, with more show and ceremony than Billy thought necessary, produced a bunch of keys on a globe-shaped fob, and painstakingly unlocked it.

"I can't show you everything," Wrobleski said. "That would take forever. I just want you to experience the broad scope of my interests."

And so Wrobleski walked Billy Moore through just a few rooms of his collection: large, cold spaces that must have been offices when the building was first used. There were maps thick on the walls, crammed together, edge to edge, and more stacked in piles on the floor. The light from fluorescent tubes overhead seemed deliberately harsh and ugly. The collection was not so much displayed as exposed.

The role of tour guide didn't suit Wrobleski. He preferred to let the maps speak for themselves. They were a wild and miscellaneous bunch: some gigantic, some miniature, a few ancient and crumbling in the frames, others very modern, very high tech, printed on Lucite or aluminum. A lot of them inhabited the disputed territory between cartography and art. Many were hand-drawn, intense, obsessive, massively detailed, perhaps drawn by madmen or disturbed children. Some showed mythical, invented, oddly formed countries, not from this planet or any other, one in the shape of a giraffe, one like a phallus, one like a slice through a human brain. There were plans of fantastical cities, the streets arranged in geometrical figures, some cruciform, some in the shape of pentagrams, some fashioned after crop circles or fractals. There were maps of cities in chaos or in ruin, after bombings or natural disasters. There were maps of the stars and planets, maps of the oceans, maps of the inside of the earth. There was far too much going on in most of them: the colors were eye-popping and unsettling, designed for show, not clarity; the cartouches were overelaborate; gods and mythical beasts, mermaids and angels ranged through the few otherwise empty spaces.

Despite Zak's brief attempt to educate him, Billy still didn't "get" maps, and perhaps he never would, but it did occur to him (and this was certainly a thought he'd never have had if he hadn't stepped inside Utopiates) that this collection was actually a map of Wrobleski's world, his psyche, a menacing, dangerous, and primitive territory, a place of lurid, angry colors, jagged edges, and dragons that were not quite imaginary. Billy tried to make the right noises, to show the appropriate degree of interest and quiet enthusiasm, but it wasn't easy, and unless Wrobleski was an idiot, and he quite conspicuously was not, he must have realized that Billy wasn't impressed.

"You know what would be a nice idea?" said Wrobleski. "You should bring that daughter of yours. She'd get a kick out of all this, wouldn't she?"

"I don't think she'd be interested," said Billy, making some nebulous attempt to protect Carla from Wrobleski, though, in fact, given what a weird little kid she was, he thought she probably would love to see this demented collection.

"I bet I could stimulate her interest," said Wrobleski. And then he had, or pretended to have, a new idea. "You know, there's a little something I really do want to show you. Maybe I shouldn't. Maybe you won't like it. But I'm going to show it to you anyway."

This ambivalence struck Billy as completely fake. It seemed

to him that Wrobleski had made up his mind some time back that he would definitely show Billy whatever it was, that this was perhaps the sole reason for giving him the tour.

Billy said, "It's your decision, Mr. Wrobleski."

"Yes, it is."

Billy knew there must be some reason, some meaning, perhaps some threat, in what Wrobleski was proposing, but what choice did he have? They came to yet another door, one that from the outside looked little different from the others, and Wrobleski duly unlocked and opened it. A wedge of light from the corridor pushed into the room and revealed a section of a deep, unlit, windowless space. Together they stepped inside, and Wrobleski closed the door behind them, so that for a few long, ominous moments they were in complete darkness; then his hand reached for a dimmer switch that slowly brought to life two overhead spotlights trained across an all but empty room. Here the walls were completely bare, there were no stacks of maps on the floor, and the spotlights were angled on a single item positioned in a far corner. It was a glass display case, not quite as tall as a man, and it contained what at first looked to Billy like a patterned shawl, or perhaps a shroud.

"What do you make of that?" Wrobleski asked.

"From here, not much," said Billy.

"Walk over there. Go take a good look," said Wrobleski. "Then you tell me what you think it is."

Billy moved toward the case. At first the thing inside appeared to be a pelt, a hide, a piece of unsuccessful taxidermy, but then he realized, with a twinge of delayed recognition, because somehow he'd known all along, that it was part of a bodysuit made from an actual body: a length of flayed human skin, mounted upright on a metal armature.

It wasn't the whole body—just the skin from the back and

buttocks, so that it looked like a stretched, painted canvas. It had a worn, yellowed, well-used look, and it was tattooed, intricately, skillfully: the style looked Oriental. And the tattoos did indeed form a map of a sort, although nothing remotely like the ones Billy had seen on any of the women. These tattoos showed a stylized but highly detailed rendition of a city: houses, roads, bridges, a river, a lake, a temple, a pagoda, and at the very center, in the very middle of the back, there was a volcano.

"Now who'd build a city around the base of a volcano?" Wrobleski said, as if addressing a dim child.

Billy's revulsion was instinctive, visceral, and although he tried telling himself there might be something fake about this skin, that it could be a horror-movie prop, a leftover from an elaborate Halloween party, he knew that was wishful thinking. The glass case also contained a photograph of the skin in situ, on its original owner, while she was still alive, a Japanese woman, small, dignified, serene, displaying her bare back and looking forlornly over her shoulder into the camera lens. The skin looked much better on her than off.

"You can see why it might resonate with me, can't you, Billy?"

Billy gave a little groan of consent.

"Now, I'm no scholar," said Wrobleski, "but I understand there was a time when it was common for people with tattoos to sell their skin. They made the deal while they were alive, got the money and spent it, and then when they died, the buyer went and picked up what he'd paid for. Sometimes I bet they had trouble finding the seller. Once in a while I bet they didn't wait till he or she was dead."

"I'll bet."

"Now, I know what you're thinking, Billy. You're thinking this would be the simple, elegant solution to all my problems. Get my women together, strip the skin off 'em—end of problem."

"I wasn't thinking that," said Billy. "I don't really know what your problem is."

"I don't suppose you do," said Wrobleski. "So maybe you were thinking, What's this fucking guy Wrobleski up to? Is he the one who did the tattoos? Why would he do that? And if he didn't, then who did? And what does he want to do now? What does he want from me? What did he ever want? That's pretty much what you're thinking, isn't it?"

"Pretty much," Billy agreed.

"Here's the thing, Billy. I've had enough of these women. In the beginning I thought it would be better to have them here rather than wandering the streets. I was wrong. Having a collection of drugged, kidnapped, tattooed women in your basement is quite a liability."

Billy had no problem believing that.

"But you know, I'm not some sicko, I'm not going to skin 'em alive, or bathe them in acid, or throw lye all over them. I just want somebody to dispose of them for me. And that's where you'd have come in, Billy. I thought you had potential. Killer instincts. I saw a promotion for you: better pay, better prospects. Wouldn't be such a big step."

"Yes, it would," said Billy. "For me that would be a very big step indeed."

"Oh, you might surprise yourself," said Wrobleski.

Billy wanted to protest, to insist that Wrobleski had got him all wrong, that he wasn't that kind of guy, that he didn't want to be surprised. But it wasn't an argument worth having.

"Why don't you kill them yourself?" Billy asked.

Wrobleski's face coalesced into a stiff frown, as if this was something he had been asking himself for a very long time.

"Professional ethics," he said, but it was only a suggestion, a theoretical possibility, not an answer he seemed especially to believe in. "Because I don't kill people unless I'm being paid. Is that a good enough answer?"

"Maybe," said Billy.

"And I don't kill women, period."

"But you think I do?" said Billy.

"Sure. I hold you to a lower standard."

It sounded like another of Wrobleski's jokes.

"I wasn't bullshitting when I said I liked the cut of your jib. You did remind me of me. An early version, an alternate version. But more than that, I saw something corruptible in you. And I wanted to corrupt it. I wanted you to be worse than me. Does that make me a bad person?"

"Yeah," said Billy. "I think it does."

"Anyway, it turns out I was wrong. I couldn't corrupt you. Good for you."

Wrobleski's face twisted into something that had the very slightest resemblance to a smile.

"And it's all academic anyway," he said. "You're in the parking business now. You're an ex-employee of mine. It's been nice working with you. Let me know if you change your mind about taking this new job I'm offering. Maybe you'll think of something I can do to persuade you. Or maybe I will."

35. ROAD RAGE

Driving: one of the lower functions, a task that can be accomplished when the mind is a very, very long way off, absorbed in its own static of words not said and actions not completed. Billy Moore's concentration was scattered like road salt.

He didn't consider himself a naïve man, but he did pride himself on never thinking he was smarter than he actually was. He was wise enough to realize he had no idea where he stood with Wrobleski. Could you really walk away from a man like that? Could you turn your back and say, "Thanks for giving me the opportunity to be a cold-blooded killer, but I think I'll pass, okay?" It seemed unlikely. He wanted to be on his own turf, with Carla. Turning down a job as a murderer might not be part of the standard definition of what it took to be a good father, but it was surely a start.

He wasn't driving fast, and he didn't think he was driving carelessly, but suddenly there was a sigh and a shudder from the car's front end. Jolted back to attention, Billy yawed the Cadillac to the side of the broad, desolate street and got out to inspect the damage. It was nothing more than a flat tire. He felt angry at first, and then inexplicably melancholy. The pancaked rubber suddenly seemed like the saddest thing he'd ever seen. Then again, a flat tire was encouraging somehow, suggesting that the night was going to peter out in trivial annoyance rather than high drama. That was to be welcomed. If the road gods had really been against him, wouldn't the car have burst into flames, wouldn't he have died in a ball of fire?

He was in the middle of nowhere, by the skeletons of some old silos and an abandoned greyhound track. He'd have to change the tire himself, which only confirmed his lowly status: he couldn't see Wrobleski doing something so banal. He opened the trunk to get at the spare and the jack. He found a woman's shoe jammed in the wheel well—Carol Fermor's, he supposed—and he tossed it into the gutter before manhandling the tire out of the car.

It was a long, awkward task: difficult to position the jack, and even harder to loosen the wheel lugs. As he examined the flattened tire, he noticed a small hole in the sidewall that looked suspiciously neat, as though somebody might have made it deliberately, to create a slow puncture that would ensure he'd be brought to a halt long before he got home. Did that make sense? Maybe he was being paranoid. And did it make any difference? He still had a tire to change. And only when the job was done did he realize he had oil, rubber streaks, and road gunk all over his new suit. Fuck it. You were so much better off wearing leather: the more you abused it, the better it looked.

For the rest of the drive home he tried to keep his mind on the road: that was a better place for it than any other he could think of. Sanjay would still be there, guarding the lot, keeping an eye on Carla. Poor guy, he didn't seem to have anywhere else to go. And yet as Billy approached the lot, there was no sign of him. There was a folding stool lying on its side by the front gate, and there was a book tossed on the ground some feet away. That didn't look right. But nothing else seemed amiss: the security lights were on, the gates, the subcontractors' trucks, the trailers appeared the way they always did.

"Sanjay?" he called, not too loud, not too insistently. He didn't want to wake Carla.

He thought he heard a groan, something feeble but close at

hand, and then as he moved toward it, in the direction of the trucks, he saw Sanjay lying on the ground, the pristine pink and black of his clothes now smeared brown and red. His body was twisted into a position no body could easily adopt, legs tangled at improbable angles under him, head sagging against the truck with the CAUTION: EXPLOSIVES sign. Sanjay had been mashed, pulped, beaten with his own baseball bat. He was scarcely conscious, but he was still able to look at Billy, twist his lips into a sad smile, half-raise a pointing hand, and say, "Carla."

Billy Moore looked toward Carla's trailer, and he saw that the door was open, and not simply open but broken wide, dangling from its buckled hinges. He ran across the lot, having just enough time to wonder which was the greater terror: that Carla would be there and in the same state as Sanjay, or that she'd simply be gone. He stepped inside the trailer. It was the latter: silence, stillness, disorder, emptiness. There was broken glass, a kicked-over chair, skewed carpet. Carla had not gone quietly. Well, Billy had never thought she would. He was searching around the interior, looking for something that would tell him what had happened, when he saw that Sanjay had dragged himself all the way across the lot to the trailer door.

It seemed he could barely speak, barely breathe, but he said, "I think, sir, they didn't kill me, sir, because they wanted me to give you a message."

"Who's they?" demanded Billy.

"Several men, one of them of African heritage, who did most of the talking."

"Akim."

"We didn't exchange names, sir."

"Keep it simple, Sanjay," Billy said, but simplicity wasn't Sanjay's way.

"This man told me to tell you that your daughter is temporarily in safe hands, being looked after by somebody named Laurel."

"My daughter's being looked after by a tattooed whore?"

"That I cannot say, sir. But the rest of the message is that 'Mr. Wrobleski would like to see you again when you've changed your mind about the job.' Does all that make sense, sir?"

His voice dribbled away with pain and exhaustion.

"Sense is one word for it."

"Now, sir," said Sanjay, "I wonder if you might be good enough to call an ambulance for me, sir?"

"I'll drive you there myself. We'll talk on the way."

Sanjay readied himself to do some more talking.

36. A BIGGER BANG

Zak Webster had never given much thought to dynamite, but if he *had* thought about it, he'd have assumed that today's mining and demolition engineers, such as those blasting the tunnels for the Platinum Line, the ones parking in Billy Moore's lot, would have something rather more sophisticated, more modern, in their trucks. Billy Moore, repeating what he'd very recently learned from Sanjay on the way to the hospital, was able to tell him he'd have been wrong about that.

Billy had gone from the emergency room back to the lot, and then to Zak's apartment, and even though it was the early hours of the morning, he found Zak all too awake, twanging with anxiety, debating if he should try to call or text Marilyn, wondering if he should go over to the Telstar Hotel, where he assumed she now was. Billy was able to tell him he was wrong about that too. He explained what needed explaining, that one way or another—and he knew it was wrong, and it was largely his fault, and he took full responsibility for his part in it, and yes, he was kind of ashamed of himself—both Marilyn and Carla were now inside Wrobleski's compound, but terrible though that was, he had a plan for getting them out.

"You see, Zak, there's no big mystery about dynamite," said Billy. "My man Sanjay just enlightened me; it's stuff geologists know, apparently. It turns out dynamite is just sawdust and nitroglycerin, stuffed into a tube, with a blasting cap and a fuse added."

"Why are you telling me this?" Zak asked.

Billy Moore pulled a single stick of dynamite from the inside pocket of his newly reinstated leather jacket and placed it gently in Zak's less than willing hand. Zak looked at it with some disbelief, amazed by the absurdity and what felt like the danger of the situation, even as Billy explained that the stick was harmless until the blasting cap and fuse were in place. As Zak held the stick, he felt a little like Wile E. Coyote, and the dynamite itself had an unreal quality about it. It looked so rudimentary, so provisional, wrapped in buff paper like a homemade firework, though the warnings printed on the side looked authentic enough.

"You place the stick," said Billy. "You walk away, you detonate the dynamite, and you're in business. I think we can do those things, can't we, Zak?"

"I can certainly walk away. I might even run."

"You actually don't have to walk all that fast. We're not talking about lighting the fuse, throwing it, and hoping for the best. See here."

He handed Zak a device that looked like a cross between a cell phone and an antiquated channel changer.

"It's a remote electronic trigger," said Billy. "Self-explanatory, yeah?"

"I guess so," said Zak.

"And really, you don't even have to get all that far away. Sanjay tells me that a single stick, put in the right place, is enough to move one cubic yard of rock, which weighs about a ton, depending on what kind of rock it is. When you're blasting a tunnel, like in the Platinum Line, you drill a hole and you put the stick in the hole, because that gives you maximum destruction: something to do with compression."

"Sounds reasonable," said Zak; then he wondered if he'd gone even further out of his mind than he realized. There was nothing even vaguely reasonable in what Billy was saying. Billy hadn't explained the details of his plan yet, but Zak suspected there would be little that was sensible or logical or even *recognizable* in what he was about to propose. Zak got the feeling that he was living somebody else's life.

"But we won't be in a tunnel," said Billy. "And in the wide-open spaces it's a whole different story, apparently. There's a lot of math involved, and I didn't really follow that part. But anyway, in the not quite so wide-open spaces, Sanjay tells me that one stick isn't that big a deal. It wouldn't be enough to completely destroy, say, a house, and definitely not Wrobleski's compound, but it would make one hell of a mess of a car, say, a big black SUV."

"You're going to blow up Wrobleski's SUV?"

"That's part of what I'm going to do, yes. There's more. That's where you come in, Zak."

37. THE BEST LAID

Marilyn Driscoll wouldn't have believed that she'd ever be able to fall asleep in that darkness, in that place, in that condition, but suddenly she was awake, the night was over, and she was rising, coming back from some gloomy, troubled, cloacal place in her dreams. She could feel somebody beside her, somebody touching her lightly, untying her.

"I'm Laurel," a woman's distant voice said: Laurel, a tattooed whore in Billy Moore's accounting. "It's okay, I'm on your side, more or less. It's been quite a night. I seem to be doing child care now."

Marilyn had no idea what she was talking about. Laurel busied herself undoing the ropes and pulling streamers of duct tape from Marilyn's body and face. Once her eyes were unpeeled, Marilyn saw she was in a long, low basement room, not quite a cell or dungeon, but claustrophobic, airless, and full of shadows, with one narrow, distant, barred window and a row of a dozen or so single beds. A cloud of tired female sweat hung low in the room, a TV played in the far corner, and on the wall she noticed a framed three-dimensional cartoon map of Hollywood, with a cartoon dinosaur rampaging over the sign.

She became aware of other people in the room, women, four more besides Laurel, and two of them she more or less recognized, though she didn't know their names: the homeless woman from outside Utopiates, the stripper from the club. There was also a blowsy, voluptuous woman, overdressed but shoeless, and a severe, professional-looking type with a gray bob that must once have looked pretty stylish. Quite a collection, mismatched you might think, but Marilyn knew precisely what they had in common: the maps that they weren't showing, and the violence that had created them. Besides that, they also shared a dejected, opiate-induced blankness. They stared vacantly in Marilyn's direction but hardly acknowledged her presence.

"I saw your little act last night," said Laurel.

"It wasn't an act," Marilyn insisted.

"Whatever," said Laurel. "What exactly did you think was going to happen when you got here? You thought you'd arrive and have some face time with Wrobleski and he'd say, 'This must all have been very puzzling for you, young lady. Now, allow me to explain.' Is that what you thought?"

Marilyn said, "No, I didn't expect that," but of course a part of her had imagined something precisely along those lines.

"It's okay, we're all allowed to have our fantasies," Laurel said, and she stripped away the last of the rope and tape, and then helped Marilyn straighten herself up. Marilyn stood, stretched, as if she were starting a warm-up session.

"Looking good," Laurel said. "We have food if you need it. It's not bad. The secret ingredient is drugs."

Marilyn shook her head. She stood up, walked a few paces, trying to get some sensation back in her legs. Her body felt all wrong inside her clothes, her bones and flesh pulled out of shape just as much as the fabric of her pants. In fact, there was something especially wrong with one of the pants pockets. There was something in there, something metallic and loose that didn't belong. It took her a moment to realize what: a set of keys. She pulled them out, a dozen or more keys held together with wire. She viewed them suspiciously, showed them to Laurel.

"I don't know how these got here," she said.

Laurel gazed at the keys with some puzzlement but considerable pleasure.

"I think I do," Laurel said. "I think Akim put them there."

"Who's Akim?"

"The specimen who tied you up."

"Planting the keys is kind of a weird thing to do, isn't it?"

"You want weird, stick around this place for a while," Laurel said.

She took the set of keys from Marilyn, then tossed them from hand to hand, so that they made a thin, insistent, metallic rattle that trickled through the room. It took a while before any of the others noticed. Finally a couple of them looked up, paid just the slightest attention, and slowly moved closer, like frightened animals drawn to the watering hole.

"What are those?" Chanterelle asked.

"A gift from Akim. Some of Mr. Wrobleski's keys," Laurel said. "Not his main bunch. Maybe Akim made copies."

"What do they open?"

"Only one way to find out."

"What's Akim up to?" said Carol Fermor.

"Your guess is as good as mine," said Laurel. "Maybe he lost his passion for the job. Or maybe he thought child abduction wasn't in his job description. In any case, I don't think we should turn down the opportunity."

"What opportunity?"

"To start opening doors."

"Why do we want to start opening doors?" Genevieve asked.

"Oh, I'm sure we'll think of a reason," said Laurel.

38. SHY

Wrobleski, Akim, and Carla Moore had been sitting together in the rooftop conservatory, in silence, for a good long time. The morning was becoming clear and pale, the sky slowly brightening through streaked glass. Carla was managing to keep it all together. Another kid might have cried or sulked or pleaded, but Carla looked beautifully, if studiedly, indifferent, and Wrobleski was impressed by that. Akim meanwhile looked like a man being quietly tortured, though he also managed to send barbed, peevish looks of disapproval in Wrobleski's direction.

"All right, Akim, your stink eye has been duly noted. Why don't you go away and prepare yourself for the impending arrival?"

Akim got up and slouched out of the conservatory door, his eyes now looking firmly ahead of him.

"There," said Wrobleski to Carla, "alone at last. I hate people who talk too much, don't you?"

Carla kept her silence.

"It's okay, I understand if you're shy."

She looked for a moment as if she might attack him. "I'm not shy," she said. "I'm pissed off."

"Well, of course you are," said Wrobleski smoothly. "You're just a kid. You expect your dad to protect you. But sometimes he can't."

Carla already suspected this might be true, but hearing it stated by this weird stranger, a man to whom she'd been delivered in the middle of the night, having been dragged from her trailer, a man from whom she needed protection, made it all the harder to bear. She looked as though she might, after all, start crying.

"Laurel looked after you all right, didn't she?"

Carla shrugged.

"I'm not good with kids," said Wrobleski. "Especially not girls. 'Specially not cute little numbers like you."

Carla had a feeling she was being complimented, but she wasn't sure.

"Have I been kidnapped?" she asked.

"No," said Wrobleski, feigning offense. "No way. If you'd been kidnapped, there'd be ransom notes and demands for money and I'd be slicing off your fingers and sending them through the mail. I'm not doing that, am I?"

"No," Carla admitted. "Not yet."

"Not ever. I just want your old man to see things my way."

Carla wondered if that really made any sense.

"How long am I going to be here?" she said.

"Just until he arrives."

"When's that?"

"That all depends on him, honey. He may have more important things on his mind than you."

"No, he doesn't," she said, and she very much hoped she was right about that.

She saw Wrobleski examining his own hand. Even at the very beginning, with everything else that was going on, she'd noticed the webbing on Wrobleski's hand was scarred with a set of teeth marks, some scabs, yellow staining.

"What's wrong with your hand?" she asked.

"Dog bite," said Wrobleski.

"Not good with kids *or* animals."

It was perfectly true, of course, but Wrobleski didn't care to admit it. He saw Carla staring vaguely at the relief map of Iwo Jima.

"It's not a model," he said to her helpfully, "it's actually a map in three dimensions, and the scale of the elevation, the height, that's exaggerated to bring out the features."

Carla sniffed.

"Come over here," said Wrobleski. "Come and look, I can tell you're interested. That father of yours said you wouldn't be, but I knew he was wrong."

Insulted, grudging, but not entirely unwilling, Carla got up and moved to the center of the conservatory, and stood a respectful distance from the case, looking down through the glass.

"Iwo Jima," said Wrobleski. "World War Two. An island belonging to the Japanese. But the Americans took it away from them. They landed here and here and here." As he spoke he used only his right hand to point at various places on the island: the left was hurting too much. "Here, this was an airfield. This was a dormant volcano. Here's an amphitheater. The Americans raised the flag here, but raising the flag didn't mean they'd won. The flag went up on day five: the battle went on for another thirty days.

"But here's the thing. The Japanese knew they were going to be attacked, so they'd already built a lot of bunkers and tunnels all through the island. When the battle ended, there were three thousand Japanese soldiers still in the tunnels. They'd lost the battle, but they didn't surrender. Some of them committed suicide, because that's what they were supposed to do, code of honor and all that shit. But some didn't. They decided to live. They stayed there in the tunnels underground, hiding, right till the end of the war. Here, the model even shows some of the tunnel openings."

Carla scrutinized the island.

"I thought you said it was a map, not a model."

"Very good, Carla, very good indeed."

Carla inhaled damply. She didn't want to be told she was good.

"Do they still have geography in school?" Wrobleski asked. "Or is it all earth science and environmental studies these days?"

"They still have geography," said Carla.

"So if I asked you what was the highest mountain in Africa, you could give me an answer?"

"Yes," said Carla, though she didn't offer one.

"Or the longest river in Europe. Or the capital of Mongolia."

"You can look all that stuff up online," said Carla. "We do more creative stuff."

"Do you?" said Wrobleski. "Creative stuff? You ever draw maps?"

"Sometimes," said Carla, feeling it was a confession.

"Why don't you draw one for me?"

"Why?"

"Something for my collection. You could draw me a map showing where you live, where you go to school, where you go on the weekend, things like that, so I'd know all about you."

"I don't want you to know all about me."

"Ah, a girl after my own heart," he said. "See. Aren't we getting on better now?"

"No," said Carla.

"Oh, I think we are, and tell me, Carla, what's wrong with your arm?"

"Nothing."

"Something must be wrong with it. You keep scratching."

"Want to see?"

Carla didn't give him the choice. She rolled up her sleeve to reveal her bare arm. While they talked, she'd been worrying at her skin with her fingernails. The message FUCK YOU now stood out on her forearm in a bold, ugly, embossed rash of letters. She showed it proudly to Wrobleski, and he was fascinated rather than insulted.

"All right," said Wrobleski, "dermatographia! Very interesting. I've never seen it before."

"But you've heard of it?"

"Don't sound so surprised. I know stuff. I'm not an idiot. And I know that 'fuck you' will disappear after a while, won't it?" said Wrobleski.

"Yeah, but I can make it come back any time I like."

"You're good," he said. "Obviously it doesn't run in the family."

Wrobleski's cell phone rang. It was Akim telling him that Billy Moore and his Cadillac were approaching the gate and that Charlie was about to let them in.

"I'll be right down," he said into the phone; then to Carla, "See, your father does care after all."

And then he hesitated. He wasn't quite sure what to do with the kid. Should he lock her in here while he went down to confront Billy, have Akim or Laurel guard her? No, that didn't seem right. He should probably take her with him, to show that she was unharmed. He turned away from her, knowing he should have worked this out earlier. And then something hit him on the back of the head, something hard, loose, and dry: a fucking potted cactus, small enough for a child to hold in her hand, and in this case throw with great accuracy. He was outraged. If you couldn't trust a twelve-year-old, who could you trust? As he turned back to glare at her, a second pot hit him, this time full in his left eye. He winced, blinked, rubbed away the dirt, drove a few cactus spikes into his cheek, and when he looked up, Carla was at the center of the conservatory, her hands on the top edge of the glass case with Iwo Jima inside.

She pushed against it with all her strength, and the supporting wooden legs slipped on the conservatory floor and the case keeled forward, and although Wrobleski moved to save it, the surprise, the pain in his hand, made him too slow, as the case carved a painfully precise course through the air, a simple 90-degree curve, and then hit the ground hard. The glass shattered, and the skill-fully molded plaster surface split open to reveal the innards, a rough construction of chicken wire and clumsily glued balsa wood struts. Involuntarily, pathetically, Wrobleski snatched at the fallen relief map, even as slivers of glass bounced across the floor. He succeeded only in catching a single shard that sliced into his left hand, agonizingly close to the throbbing dog bite.

"You know I've killed people for less than that," he said.

"Yeah?" said Carla. "But I'll bet none of them were such cute little numbers, were they?"

The Cadillac's horn sounded down in the courtyard. The man was impatient; well, he had reason to be. Wrobleski flung his arm around Carla's middle, hard enough to knock the wind out of her, and to lift her off the ground like a bundle of laundry so he could take her with him.

"I blame the fucking parents," he said as he strode out of the conservatory.

39. WROBLESKI DESCENDS

Billy Moore and Zak Webster sat in the Cadillac, in the court-yard, in the compound, waiting for Wrobleski to appear. The windows were up, and although Akim was visible through the windshield, he was keeping his distance, silent and sullen, look-ing as miserable as an emo teenager at a family Christmas.

"Is this too subtle?" Billy said to Zak. "Or is it not subtle enough?"

"It's not subtle at all," said Zak.

"Okay," said Billy. "That's the beauty of it, right?"

"Right," said Zak.

This was the first time Zak had ever ridden in a Cadillac: he wondered what the odds were that it might be his last. And then Wrobleski appeared, shambling down a set of metal stairs from an upper level, moving awkwardly, gun in one hand, Carla Moore tucked under the other arm.

Billy and Zak eased themselves out of the car, walked slowly, measuredly, toward Wrobleski. Billy Moore was aware that he was trying to behave "normally," though he had no idea what normal looked like when confronting a murderer who's holding your daughter like a rag doll.

"You all right, Carla?" he called out.

"What do you think?" Carla snarled back.

"Of course she's all right," said Wrobleski. "She's hurt me more than I've hurt her."

Billy looked at the damage on Wrobleski's face and said, "Well, good for her."

Wrobleski checked angles, casing his own joint. The place was surprisingly, unusually empty. Where were those guys he paid to be there when he needed them? At least Akim, resentful or not, was a reliable presence.

"Who's this scumbag you've brought with you?" Wrobleski demanded. "Your bodyguard? Your boyfriend?"

"This is my pal Zak," said Billy. "He knows a thing or two about maps."

"Well, good for him," Wrobleski said. "What's that he's got in his hand?"

Zak thought it best to speak for himself. "It's a cylindrical map case, leather, early twentieth-century . . ."

"I know what a fucking map case is," said Wrobleski.

"And there's a map inside," said Zak helpfully, nervously.

And then something clicked.

"Wait a fucking minute," said Wrobleski. "I know you, don't I? Akim, you know this guy?"

Nothing from Akim.

"No, you don't know me," said Zak, trying to sound as though he believed it.

"Yeah, you're the little fucker who climbed into my compound. You came back. You really are an imbecile. And this other imbecile brought you here. So what's this all about?"

"I'm a map dealer as well as an urban explorer," Zak said.

Wrobleski looked at him with mild, generic disgust.

"So? What has this got to do with you, Billy?" Wrobleski demanded. "What the fuck has this got to do with you and me?"

"I work for Ray," Zak said.

"Ray fucking McKinley?" said Wrobleski, becoming aware that this might actually be leading somewhere, though not anywhere he wanted to go.

"He's my boss. I work at Utopiates."

"What, that crappy little shop he owns?"

"That's my life you're talking about," said Zak.

"Zak has something we think you might like to see," said Billy.

"What's this 'we' all of a sudden?" Wrobleski said. "What the fuck are you two playing at?"

A vein danced in the flesh next to Wrobleski's eye. Billy could tell he was getting to him, confusing him: he liked that.

"Zak," Billy said, "show Mr. W. the goods."

Zak offered the map case to Wrobleski.

"Don't be a jerk. I've got a gun in one hand, a kid in the other. Hand it to Akim."

Zak held the case upright, pulled out the scrolled map, buckled up the case again, and gently placed it on the ground at his feet. He handed the map to Akim, who raised it to the height of his shoulders and let it unravel in front of him like a narrow length of wallpaper. It didn't look like much to hide behind.

"The Jack Torry rape map," said Zak.

"All right," said Wrobleski, not entirely unimpressed. "I've heard of it. Not bad. In another time and place we might be doing some business. But in the current circumstances . . . so fucking what?"

"We thought you might like to have it," said Billy. "For the collection. We're putting it on the table as part of the negotiation."

"We're not negotiating," said Wrobleski. "All you have to do is head down to the basement, do the job I've asked you to do, and you'll get your daughter back."

"Everything's negotiable," said Billy. "Everything's *renegotiable.*"

Akim continued to hold the map up, but he looked increasingly likely to screw it into a giant ball. Billy Moore took half a step forward, putting himself between Wrobleski and Zak, blocking the line of sight, so that Wrobleski couldn't see when Zak gently side-footed the map case under Wrobleski's SUV. If Akim saw it, he didn't care.

"Dad," Carla pleaded, "don't negotiate with the bastard!"

"The kid has a point," said Wrobleski. "You don't honestly think I'm going to take the map, give you your daughter, and say no hard feelings?"

"No," said Billy. "I don't think that."

"Then what do you think?"

"I think this. What if I do the killings like you ask, and let's say you even give me Carla, though there's no guarantee you will, well, that's not going to be the end of it, is it? What's to stop you turning me in for the murders?"

"Beats me," said Wrobleski.

"I think you want a fall guy. You want those maps gone, those women gone, and then you want me gone. You can see why I don't find that very appealing."

Out of the corner of his eye Wrobleski saw a movement up on a higher level of the compound, a flash of light. It was a distraction he didn't need.

"So where do we go from here?" said Wrobleski. "Akim's got the map, and I'm still the one with the gun and the girl."

Billy was not stupid enough to put his hand in his pocket, to appear to be reaching for anything. Instead, he placed his right palm against his chest, as though he was about to make a plea for mercy and decency, as though he was about to speak from the heart. He pressed harder, pressed through the leather onto the electronic trigger lodged inside his jacket.

The world around him, around all of them, seemed simultaneously to implode and explode. Sound waves, hard as rock, slammed against his ears. The SUV flipped up weightlessly in a violent cloud, ash gray and burnt orange, showering glass, steel, and automotive innards. Billy and Zak made a dive for the ground. The front end of the vehicle was hefted sideways, slamming against an internal wall of the compound, punching a hole as big as a double garage. Blue-black smoke and a film of shimmering gasoline fumes veiled the air.

Akim fell on his side, the map draping him like a scorched towel. Wrobleski staggered backward, crouching, choking, but he stayed on his feet. A weaker man would have let go of the girl, but he only held on tighter. He fired his gun impotently in the air, not at anything in particular. But with Zak and Billy still on the ground, he was able to dance away through the smoke, and as he went, he became aware that the explosion had caused small, localized fires in various places around the courtyard. He had people to deal with that, right?

He saw Akim crawling across the tarmac, dragging himself to his feet, finding his way to one of the fire extinguishers. It wasn't much: preventing your place of work from burning down seemed like the minimum requirement of any job, but it was more than he was getting from his other goons, now entirely absent. Akim brought the extinguisher to life, but then Wrobleski realized that he wasn't trying to put out the fires, he was simply clearing a path for himself as he headed for the gate. There was a brief, fierce argument between Akim and Charlie the gateman, but Charlie was no hero, and he didn't just let Akim out of the compound, he followed, letting the electronic gate shut itself behind him. And was Wrobleski imagining it, or did he hear an approaching siren, maybe more than one?

Then there was a new distraction, bright heavy things, swooping down on him like angular birds of prey, spinning from high across the other side of the compound. At first Wrobleski thought they were sheets of wood, pieces of metal and glass, maybe something pulled from the roof. But then came the sickening realization that they were frames, and not just empty frames, frames containing maps. His collection was taking flight, attacking him. He looked up and saw the women, their arms loaded with maps, launching them haphazardly into space. They'd got into his storage rooms. How the fuck was that even possible? The frames dive-bombed the ground, shattered as they hit. Splinters of wood and glass spiked around his legs.

The maps weren't aimed precisely at him—they weren't aimed with any precision whatsoever—but a random throw, one with an accidentally perfect trajectory, came heading right his way, and before he could sway or duck, a neat, stainless-steel corner gouged its way into the flesh above his cheekbone. His head jolted back, a piece of skin flapped open, and he felt blood on his face. He shuddered, tried to shake off the blow, but he couldn't, not quite, not immediately. Carla struggled to get free, flipped around like a baby shark: he tightened his grip.

Something loomed at him through the smoke. Billy Moore was on his feet and in action, and he grabbed hold of Wrobleski's gun arm. Wrobleski tried to shake him off, shoulder him away, aimed a venomous kick at him, even as Carla was biting him. The shark had teeth: he was fighting half a family here. He tried to turn his gun into Billy's face, but he felt the man's desperate, intractable strength. For a second he even thought of letting the kid go so he could deal solely with Billy, but no, he wasn't a guy who willingly let go of his assets: it was a matter of principle.

Then he got lucky. Another map sliced through the air above them. Wrobleski stepped back and he pulled Billy with him, into the path of the tumbling, curling, accelerating frame. It gashed Billy on the temple, hard, precisely: he sank to his knees. Wrobleski kicked him aside, so he could retreat deeper still into the compound.

Flames skipped around the doors up on the top level. The women were immolating his maps, his whole building. Wrobleski started toward the stairs that led upward. If he could get there, he knew he'd be able to handle half a dozen drugged, damaged bitches and save the rest of his collection. But then he stopped himself. Maybe there were other priorities. He hadn't imagined those sirens: they were real and they were getting louder and very close.

On the other side of the courtyard, Zak, shuddering, shaken, and astounded by the explosion, his sense of balance no longer reliable, looked up into the higher levels of the compound. He shouted, "Marilyn," but his voice seemed entirely within his own head. He could see bodies moving around up there, but there was no sign of her through the growing turmoil of smoke and flame. He couldn't pretend to know the feelings of Wrobleski's women; maybe if you'd been forcibly tattooed, kidnapped, brought here, you might feel differently about maps from the way he did. Even so, he couldn't help feeling that destroying maps simply because you despised their current owner was more than wrong, that it was a kind of blasphemy.

Wrobleski withdrew still farther as the world around him was thrown dangerously, giddily off-kilter. He was experiencing a brand-new sensation: panic. So this was what it felt like, what other people felt all the time. Not pleasant. Not good. His killings had always been placid, well-organized affairs, and he'd always been the one causing panic in others. He felt betrayed. He did the only thing he could think of. Clutching Carla like a security blanket, he hauled her into the deeper reaches of the compound, into a dark, untidy, familiar corner, where he lifted the flat, diamond plate hatch. It wasn't any version of escape, nor any version of safety. He hardly even knew his way around down there except for the one route that took him to the disused subway station, but he reckoned that was more than anybody else knew. A man with a gun and a little girl who could be used as a shield would surely find a way. Carla Moore might yet save him.

40. PENULTIMATE THINGS

Wrobleski and Carla Moore passed swiftly through damp, hanging, enclosed darkness. Wrobleski had crammed an oversized miner's helmet onto Carla's head, and one on his own. She looked almost adorable. Their feet were wet: dankness soaked into them. At some incalculable distance there was the vast sound of moving water.

Wrobleski told himself he'd been in tougher spots than this. Yes, he was in a sewer. Yes, he was in several kinds of pain, but in the end, pain was nothing, either it went away or you lived with it. And yes, sure, he assumed he would be pursued, and he didn't know exactly who by or how many there'd be, but in any case nobody he respected.

For now he was prepared to look upon the kid as an asset, although that could change, because looked at in most ways, she was a liability and a total pain in the ass. At least, now that they were down in the tunnels, she'd stopped kicking and biting. She seemed to have realized that, for better or worse, the two of them were in this together. Of course, she could find other ways of being irritating.

"Do you know where you're going?" she asked, as insolently as she knew how.

"Obviously," Wrobleski replied.

"Doesn't seem so obvious to me."

"That's because you're a kid. You don't know shit."

She let that hang for a while, as if it might be enough to shut her up, though of course it wasn't.

"Are we playing hide-and-seek?"

"I'm surprised you even know what hide-and-seek is," said Wrobleski. "I thought it was all computers and video games for you kids."

"Oh yeah, I'm very old-school. So how long do we hide for?"

"As long as it takes."

"We could be down here forever."

"Maybe *you* could, if you don't shut the fuck up."

"Boy, aren't we a grouch today?"

"Not only today," said Wrobleski.

Billy, Zak, and Marilyn stood in a corner of the compound, under a metal gantry, sheltering from smoke, flames, and cops. The good guys are always slow off the mark. They have to do the right thing, to make sure the victims are okay, which may also include finding out who the real victims are. They have to say something warm and supportive, or possibly cool and ironic. "You actually came to rescue me, Zak?" "Yes, Marilyn, I actually did. Don't sound so surprised." Then there's some explaining to do, to the cops, or the concerned citizens, and in this case also to the fire fighters. Which is to say that sometimes the good guys also have to prove they really are good guys. Establishing an "innocence" that involved blowing up a car with stolen dynamite in Zak and Billy's case, and in Marilyn's, opening locked doors, destroying property, and torching the place, might be a time-consuming business. By then Carla and Wrobleski could be anywhere. Maybe they didn't need to establish their good-guy credentials right there and then.

Billy Moore pulled open the steel trapdoor that led to the

world beneath the city, found a cluster of heavy-duty, rubber-sheathed flashlights hanging from hooks at the top of the stairs, and called urgently to Zak and Marilyn, "Are you coming down with me or not?"

"Of course I am," said Zak. "I'm an urban explorer."

"And," said Marilyn, "nobody descends into the underworld without me."

"The thing about hide-and-seek," said Carla, trudging on gamely beside Wrobleski, "is that in the end it's never much fun. You hide, and then nothing happens. So you get bored, and after a while you start wanting to be found. Is that what you want, Mr. Wrobleski?"

"Even if they find me, that doesn't mean they've caught me. That's when the fun really starts."

"Gosh, you sure are tough, Mr. Wrobleski. Tough and grouchy; I'll bet that makes you a lot of friends."

"Kid, shut up."

Then, out of nowhere, there was the sound of a deep, booming explosion, a sustained bass rumble, as though the earth around them was growling. Without thinking, Carla grabbed Wrobleski's hand, as if he were her protector, but then she immediately threw it aside, ashamed. Wrobleski was almost as surprised. In spite of everything, he actually felt somehow protective toward this infuriating little brat: he didn't completely hate the touch of her hand.

"It's all right," he said as gently as he knew how. "It's nothing. It happens all the time down here. It's the new subway line."

The sounds receded, the tremble diminished, though Carla continued to feel ashamed of herself.

•

In a tunnel not so far away, Billy Moore absorbed that same bass sound.

"Looks like the Platinum Line is getting by without that dynamite," Zak said.

"Quiet," said Billy. "I'm trying to listen. I'm trying to hear my daughter."

Zak Webster, Billy Moore, and Marilyn Driscoll moving through the underworld: brains, brawn, good looks, not necessarily in that order, and not evenly or discretely distributed. They plodded along a storm drain, the flashlights modeling yellow-gray cones through the darkness ahead of them. They were not exactly lost, but they had no clear notion of where they were heading. Sometimes they thought they heard voices and footsteps, but they knew it might be their own echoing back at them. Certain spaces and constrictions seemed more inviting than others, but to what were they an invitation? The darkness simultaneously beckoned and repelled, the air was thinner and colder than any surface air, and unidentifiable smells wafted through the tunnels, often foul, but sometimes surprisingly, incomprehensibly sweet.

"I suppose there must be maps of this place," said Marilyn.

"Sure," said Zak. "I know collectors who are only interested in maps of sewers, catacombs, subway systems."

"You hang with a really interesting crowd, don't you, Zak?" said Billy.

Zak didn't react to that one. Instead, he said, "Did you ever kill anybody, Billy?"

"No," Billy admitted, "but some people probably think I did, and that has its advantages."

"How about Wrobleski? Does he think that?"

"By now Wrobleski will have realized he knows absolutely nothing about me. Or about you either, Zak. That's good. He won't know what he's dealing with. We could have more dynamite.

We could have tear gas and stun grenades. We could be armed to the teeth."

"But we're not, are we?"

"No," said Billy. "But he doesn't know that."

"I think he might have a suspicion," said Zak.

Wrobleski was taking Carla to the one place he knew well belowground, the abandoned subway station. It was by no means a sanctuary, but it was where he had done some of his best work, where he had functioned with grim efficiency. He was familiar with its spaces and enclosures. He could lie in wait. He could face whatever he had to face.

They came to the low masonry of the arch that led through to the long, straight subway platform. Wrobleski shunted Carla inside, nodding his head, turning it, so that the light beam on his helmet moved steadily and with purpose, revealing the tilework, the benches, the rails, the darkness beyond.

"What is this?" Carla said. "Your own private train set?"

She wandered to the edge of the platform, and Wrobleski said, "Be careful, don't get too near."

She laughed at him. "What? You're scared something might happen to me?"

"Damn right," he said. "You're no good to me broken."

He stood beside her and looked down, so that his helmet light shone between the twisted rails, into the deep, shapeless cavity below them.

"What's that?" said Carla.

"It's a sinkhole."

"What's that?"

"A wonder of nature. Either that or a collapsed sewer. Good place for stashing things, just so long as you don't ever want them back."

Carla took a couple of slow steps away from the edge, her curiosity hardly satisfied.

"So how is this going to work out exactly?" she said. "We're just going to hide down here until they get bored and go away?"

"That's one way it might work."

"Not very likely, though, is it?" she said. "Or there's a big shoot-out? Or you say, 'Give me free passage, otherwise the kid dies'?"

"There are worse ideas."

"And then what?" said Carla. "They give you a helicopter and a suitcase full of money?"

"A suitcase full of money always comes in handy."

"Or," she said, "you could just turn yourself in. Say you're sorry. Make a confession. It would be good for your soul."

"I don't have a soul," said Wrobleski, "and neither do you."

Marilyn, Billy, and Zak pressed on ever more uncertainly. Zak thought he heard rats; at least he hoped it was rats. The tunnel diameter was narrow; the sides were caked in soft, loamy residue, a few inches of water slopped around their feet. Then the diameter reduced even farther, like a large intestine becoming smaller, with black fronds of what looked like half-digested seaweed hanging from the walls. Zak felt as though he were inside the city's gut. He wondered when and where he would be excreted.

They turned a corner and came to an abrupt dead end, a stretch of ragged tunnel blocked solid by debris. The roof had caved in, recently it appeared, a distant fallout from the subway line excavations. Concrete, earth, sections of ancient pipe, miscellaneous chunks of rock and ore had sunk down from above and were now filling the whole tunnel, side to side, top to bottom. Only a monstrous piece of machinery would be able to dig a way through. They would have to go back, pick a different route, start again.

"This is okay," Zak said, looking desperately, unconvincingly on the bright side. "At least we know they didn't come this way. We're narrowing the possibilities."

"No, we're not," said Billy. "The possibilities are pretty much endless. This is fucking hopeless. We don't know where we are, we don't know where we're going."

"Well," Zak hazarded, "getting lost is a form of mapping."

"Form of mapping, my ass," said Billy.

Carla Moore and Wrobleski sat together on a bench on the empty subway platform, backs resting against the curved tile wall behind them, commuters waiting for a ghost train that would never come. She was tired and scared, and she would have been tearful if she'd allowed herself to be, but she wasn't going to show any of that. Wrobleski kept watch along the length of the platform so he could see the entrance arch through which any new arrival would have to come, if they ever did. He told himself he was ready for anything they could throw at him, regardless of who "they" were, but there was no denying (much as he'd have liked to deny it) that he was feeling very weary; he realized he was also feeling very old.

"How's your hand?" Carla asked.

"It hurts," said Wrobleski.

"And how's that gouge in your face?"

"How do you think?"

"And the cactus spines?"

"Give it a rest, kid."

Something slithered and twitched down in the gloom at the platform's edge, something with too many legs, something the color of dust and shed skin. Wrobleski had to make quite an effort to stop himself from shooting into the darkness.

"Don't you have a first-aid kit down here?" asked Carla.

"Never needed one."

"Anything to eat or drink?"

"I didn't come down here for a picnic."

Carla turned and looked at him with what he couldn't quite believe was sympathy, but she didn't sound as though she was altogether mocking him when she said, "I'm sorry I broke your map. The one of Iwo Jima or whatever."

"Are you really? Well, that makes everything all right then, doesn't it?" he sneered.

"I wasn't the only one doing the breaking, was I? Why were those women so angry? Why did they want to smash everything?"

"I guess they just hate maps."

"That doesn't make sense," said Carla. "Nobody *hates* maps. I can see a lot of people don't care one way or another, but nobody really hates them."

Was she fucking with him? Or was she just being a kid? He held his silence.

"Why?" she insisted. "Tell me. Don't treat me like a child."

"Okay," said Wrobleski: he could see she had a point. "Those women hate maps because they have maps tattooed all across their backs."

"Why did they have them done if they hate them?"

"They didn't choose to have them done. Somebody did it to them."

"That's creepy. Did *you* do it?"

"No, I did not."

"Then who?"

"I don't know, but I have one or two ideas."

"Want to share?"

Wrobleski didn't answer. Carla had noticed that adults often behaved like this. They thought that if they didn't answer, then you'd forget you'd asked the question. Carla never forgot.

"So what kind of maps?" she persisted.

"You don't want to know."

"Yes, I do."

What did it matter? Maybe he could freak her out a little, scare her into silence, if not submission.

"Murder maps," he said. "Maps that show where certain murders took place, and where the bodies were stashed. *Are* stashed."

"But who did the murders?"

"That's something else you don't want to know."

"It was you, wasn't it, Mr. Wrobleski?" His silence told her what she needed to know. "Boy, you really are a bad guy."

He couldn't understand why he needed to defend himself, but he said, "There are worse than me. Far, far worse."

"That's it," said Zak. "That's it. You finally got it, Billy. You finally became a cartographer."

"You're out of your mind. I'm trying to save my daughter and you're fucking around talking about maps."

"No. The thing you just said about mapping and asses. That's what it's all about. Wrobleski only uses one route down here."

"How can you possibly say that?" said Billy.

"Because I've already seen the route he takes. And so have you."

"That explosion fried your brains," said Billy.

"And we have a version of the map with us. It's on you, Marilyn. It's in the tattoo. It's in all the tattoos. That's how the maps work. Above the waist they're all different. They show different parts of the city, and more than that, each one shows where Wrobleski committed a murder, then the route he followed through the city, and where he brought the bodies, which in every case was to his compound. Then he brought them down here. The parts of the maps below the waist show what he did with the bodies, which is why the tattoos all look kind of the same in that area. He was always taking the bodies to the same single location, belowground, somewhere down here. We were half right about the compass rose marking the spot, but it's not marking buried treasure, it's where the bodies are buried. And that's where he's going now."

Billy Moore said, mostly to himself, "And he's taken my daughter to the place where he dumps the bodies."

"Does this help us any?" Marilyn asked.

"Oh no," said Zak. "It doesn't help us in the least. I'd love to be able to look at your ass and work out the route . . . but you know, it's a lousy map by a lousy mapmaker."

"So you're saying Wrobleski did the map?"

"I don't know," said Zak. "I don't know if I'm saying that or not."

"I think you're kind of screwed, aren't you, Mr. Wrobleski?" said Carla. "You're sweating. I can't tell if it's a hot or a cold sweat, but you're soaked, Mr. Wrobleski."

"Shut up."

"You're just a big cowardly lion."

"Shut up."

She didn't shut up. She said, "Your collection's ruined. Your home's on fire. The cops are all over the place. And meanwhile you're hiding in a hole in the ground with a really annoying kid. And you can't kill me because I'm your little human shield."

"Don't be so sure. Get up. Turn your back to me."

"You're going to shoot me in the back?"

"If I feel like it. Loosen your shirt."

"Why?"

"You heard me."

"You want me to take it off?"

"Fuck no," he said. "What do you think I am, some kind of pervert? Just loosen your shirt and lift it up."

"All right," Carla said, frightened into compliance, and she gingerly turned her back to him, raised her shoulders a little, slowly untucked the rear of her shirt, hoisted it up as best she could. Goose bumps bubbled on her skin. A smell of rotting vegetables drifted along the platform. Wrobleski got to work. She could feel something pressing into her back, though she didn't know what.

"What are you doing?" she asked, though she thought she already knew.

He didn't reply. He was engrossed, serious. She could hear him breathing deeply, making a low, inarticulate humming sound. Her shirt kept rolling down her back, falling in the way of his handiwork. He pushed it up, got on with the job. And then he stopped, let the shirt fall back into place. It hadn't taken long. She didn't turn around: she didn't want to see his face.

She sensed him move away. There was silence, nothing, a lake of dead time, and then came the explosion, the slam, the gunshot. She only knew that's what it was because she'd heard Wrobleski fire his gun while they were up in the compound: more than a bang, more than a crack, very loud but brief and short-lived, like a radio being abruptly turned off. Here belowground the sound was louder still, but also more intimate, darker, more compressed by the narrowness of the station tunnel.

She felt something hot and wet running rapidly, thinly, down the insides of her thighs. She couldn't tell what it was at first, which part of her body it was coming from. But she did know that she wasn't in pain. She had no precise idea what it felt like to be shot, but not like this, surely. She was on her feet. Her body felt intact. And then she realized she'd peed herself with fright.

But that was okay, right? If Wrobleski had really shot her, then she wouldn't be able to feel herself pee, would she? Would she? Whatever Wrobleski had been shooting at, it wasn't her.

Well, who needs a map on flesh when you have the sound of a gunshot to guide the way? Actually, Zak could have said that "sound mapping" was a growing field among the edgier kind of cartographer, but he knew this was not the time. The noise reverberated wildly, came and went and came again, but there was no mistaking its direction. Billy, Marilyn, and Zak moved toward it as rapidly as they dared, though they didn't dare imagine what they might find when they got to the source. Billy called out, "Carla," but there was no reply, nothing except his own boomeranging voice. He shouted, "Wrobleski," and the absence of response seemed even more profound. They moved faster, dashing through the sodden dark, and at last came to the strange, low arch that looked like the improbable entrance to a station.

"What the hell is this?" said Billy.

"Oh man," said Zak, "it's the old subway line; this is the mother lode for urban explorers."

"Later," said Billy; and then he called, "Wrobleski," again, and once more there was only silence in reply. With infinite trepidation Billy led the way, taking the first determined yet dreaded half-step through the arch. He expected to be shot at; he expected worse, and then he heard his daughter's voice.

"It's okay, Dad, it's over. Come get me."

What could that mean? Still ready for the worst, Billy took a bold, reckless stride onto the subway platform and saw Carla standing just a few yards in front of him, her feet in a pool of liquid, her head drooping forward, the oversized miner's helmet still on her head, its lamp glowing weakly. She seemed not so much calm as inanimate. Her face was pale and still, and it conveyed absolutely nothing.

"It's all right now," said Billy, trying to console himself as much as her, moving in for a moment that was supremely natural and supremely awkward. "I'm here."

"Yes," Carla said, her voice drained of feeling and, despite herself, pulling away from him.

"Where is he?" said Billy. "Where's Wrobleski?"

"I don't know," said Carla. "I had my back to him."

Billy Moore shone his flashlight up and down the bare station platform. He saw nothing. It was still and empty. There was no trace of Wrobleski, and he surely wasn't a man to hide, to skulk in corners. Billy saw the tunnel entrances at either end of the platform. Yes, it was possible that Wrobleski had decided he could move more quickly without Carla, and had simply abandoned her and disappeared into one or another of those black mouths. If so, despite everything, Billy had no intention of pursuing him. Let the darkness swallow him.

Billy also saw the gaping sinkhole between the buckled rails. Was it conceivable that Wrobleski had decided to take the ultimate form of control and throw himself into the void? And the gunshot? Why that? A bullet in his own head before making the leap: the final anesthetic? Or something else, something that might almost be construed as compassionate—not so much a warning shot as a signal before he disappeared, the establishing of coordinates, a sound standing in for an x marking the spot.

"What did the bastard do to you?" said Billy.

With one long, skinny hand, Carla gestured over her shoulder to her own back.

Billy held her by the arms, tenderly turned her around, and raised her shirt again to reveal the bare skin of her back. It was blotched and inflamed. It wasn't immediately possible to make out what Wrobleski had been up to—the marks were so shaky and imprecise—but it was clear that he hadn't been drawing a map. Rather, Carla's back seemed to be written on, signed with a single word, though around it were various blots and rashes, signs of hesitation, false starts. Zak, Marilyn, and Billy peered at the marks. Some decoding was required, and it took a while before they realized what Wrobleski had written there, a name: AKIM.

Now the earth began to tremble again, another underground explosion, not so far away this time, a slow crescendo that seemed to come from all directions at once. The fabric around them pulsed, shivered, and trickles of pulverized dirt shimmered down from the tiled ceiling directly above their heads. As they froze, stood perfectly still and silent, a cracking sound echoed from the darkness. It sounded organic, less the noise of masonry than of a great tree tearing at its roots. They turned in the direction of the sound, looked at what was now a long, narrow fissure in the station roof, like a cartoon drawing of forked lightning, with brown ooze seeping from the crack.

"Are we going to be able to get out of here?" Billy said.

"Sure," said Marilyn, leading the way. "Just follow my butt."

41. THE REVOLVE

There is a psychological condition known as cartocacoethes, in which people see the whole world as nothing more than a series of maps. They look at clouds, rock formations, wallpaper patterns, the stains on a motel mattress, and they see examples of cartography. The puddle of blood looks like Africa, every high-heeled boot is Italy, a woman's pubic triangle becomes the Mekong Delta, before or after deforestation.

Some say this is a form of pareidolia, a condition in which arbitrary pieces of information suddenly take on unwarranted significance in the sufferer's mind. And this in itself may be considered a version of apophenia, seeing patterns and linkages in sets of essentially random data. Others say cartocacoethes is just a fancy word made up by map obsessives to glorify their own obsession. But perhaps we don't need to be suffering from any pathology in order to feel the need for orientation, to long for a method by which we can locate our position in a universe of uncertainties. We read the map, we read the world, we chart environments and faces and bodies. We hope to know where we are. We hope to read a message, a meaning, to work out a direction and a course. Is that so unreasonable? You could also argue that if the world is nothing but a series of maps, it's that much harder ever to be truly lost.

Zak Webster rearranged the items on his desk in Utopiates.

The computer mouse suddenly looked like an oversymmetrical island, an antique steel ruler looked like a man-made isthmus, while the swirling patterns in the fake wood of the desk's surface looked like contours, or isolines if you wanted to get technical. It was 6:30 on one of those shortening, restless, end of summer evenings, and he had no intention of closing the store. He was waiting for Ray McKinley to arrive. Zak had told Ray a few simple and plausible lies, chiefly that he'd found a new customer who was about ready to spend some serious money starting a collection, but the guy needed to be coaxed, to have his ego stroked by the boss. It happened often enough, and Ray McKinley was enough of a player to want to be involved in the game.

Ray arrived on time, wearing several layers of unmatched pastel linen and tasseled loafers without socks, looking like a man on a permanent vacation. If Zak had been trying to impress a new customer, he'd have worn something more formal, possibly tweedy, but maybe that was why Zak was just a shop assistant.

"What happened to your face this time?" said Ray. "Is that a rash or something?"

"Yeah, I'm kind of allergic to all kinds of things: cacti, dynamite, you name it."

Ray was prepared to take it as a joke, and he didn't need to understand his employees' jokes.

"You look like crap anyway," said Ray. "And this customer of yours is late."

"Barely," said Zak, looking at his watch. "Don't worry. He'll be here. He's very reliable."

There was already one customer in the store, in the back room, a woman in baggy pants and combat boots, a serious-looking camera slung over her shoulder, and her big dark eyes were looking out through ornate tortoiseshell glasses at an early map of

America, one that had California depicted as an island, its northernmost part designated New Albion.

There was a newly framed item propped up on the floor, its face toward the side of Zak's desk.

"What's that?" Ray asked.

"A little something I picked up," said Zak. "I thought you might like it. It's not really a map, it's more of a blueprint."

Zak picked up the frame and turned it around so McKinley could see its design, its muted colors, its simple, schematized lines, that might be thought to look like an amoeba and its nucleus, or perhaps a fried egg. Ray made a wet noise deep in his throat to convey disgust, anger, contempt: a whole legend of resentments.

"Why would I want that?" he said. "The Telstar's never been anything but trouble. Every day I own it I lose money."

"Well, you've done your best, Ray. You got rid of the original architect, you got rid of the mayor's right-hand man. What more could you do?"

McKinley's face suddenly looked rather less carefree. Harshly, but quietly enough that he hoped the customer in the back room wouldn't hear, he said, "I'm going to pretend I don't know what you're talking about. What's this buyer's name, anyway?"

"Moore," said Zak. There was no need to make up a false name. "I don't know him very well. But he means business."

"Maybe we can unload the Jack Torry map on him."

"I doubt it," said Zak.

"Get it out anyway. We'll have the map case on your desk; that'll pique his interest. Then you can roll it out with a big flourish. Go on."

Zak hesitated a long time before he said, "It's not here."

"Where is it?"

Zak could see no point in lying. "I took it to Wrobleski."

"I told you not to do that."

"Yes, you did, Ray."

"And what?" McKinley's face opened up with anger and disbelief. "You let him keep it?"

"No. Wrobleski's not in the market for maps anymore."

"Why not?"

"Well, he's in a hole in the ground, one way or another."

"What are you talking about?"

"Wrobleski's gone. Missing in action. His compound burned, his collection too."

Ray McKinley considered this. It wasn't the very worst bit of news he'd ever received. "But what happened to the fucking map?"

"Well, there was a lot of stuff going on in the compound. You know, women and tattoos."

"No, I don't know 'women and tattoos.' What are you talking about?"

"But you do, Ray. You know all about them."

"What's up with you, Zak? You come off your meds?"

Zak ignored that. He said, "At one time I thought it was Wrobleski who'd done the tattooing, but I don't believe that anymore. And Wrobleski assumed it had to be Akim doing it, which was a reasonable assumption, because Akim was there when Wrobleski did the murders, and he helped him dispose of the bodies, so he had all the information he needed to make a map. So Akim *could* have done it, but he didn't. Wrobleski was wrong. Akim was only the messenger, right?"

Ray flicked a glance toward the customer in the back room. Was she hearing all this? He said, "This isn't the time or the place."

Zak continued, "Well, it'll have to do. Since Akim knew the details of Wrobleski's murders, he was always in a position to rat him out. And I guess he ratted to you first. He told you all the dirty details so you could make use of them, didn't he? You seen Akim lately, Ray? I think he's another one who won't be around much anymore."

McKinley folded his hands extravagantly in front of him. He now looked like a man whose vacation had been irredeemably ruined. He said, "You know, I think it might be much better for your future health if you just shut the fuck up now."

On cue, Marilyn, all feigned casualness, strolled through from the back room of Utopiates. Ray McKinley directed a professional smile in her direction, though it was less than full strength.

"I'm sorry," he said. "We have to close up the store now. My employee here is having a breakdown or something."

"Too late for apologies, Ray," said Marilyn.

He hesitated, looked at her guardedly.

"Do I know you?"

"Well, you put a leather hood over my head, so I can see why you might not remember my face. And you brought me here, didn't you? You brought me to Utopiates, took me down to the basement, did the inking down there. This place gave me the creeps the first time I saw it. Instinct, I guess."

"I don't know what you two are playing at," said Ray, "but it's very dangerous."

Ignoring this, Marilyn continued, "You paid Wrobleski to kill the architect of the Telstar, and then you marked his granddaughter with a map of the murder. That was pretty ugly of you, Ray."

"Ah," said Ray, "I think I'm beginning to see." It took him a moment or two to grasp the full implications, but it sank in before too long. "Yes," he said, "that was pretty sick of me, wasn't it?" He did not mean it as an apology.

A car pulled up outside. It was a cheap, clean rental. Billy Moore got out quickly, to distance himself from this piece of junk he was forced to drive while his Cadillac was out of action, having sustained a little fire damage. He was inside the store before Ray had decided what his next move was, before he'd calculated how many moves he might have left.

"Ray," said Zak, "let me introduce you to Mr. Moore."

Another customer, another interruption. Ray had no idea if this was good or bad, and then he knew it was the latter. Billy's right fist made dry, brittle, solemn contact with Ray's chin. His head seemed to pull him backward, sprawling on his back across Zak's desk. Then he was viciously scooped up, dragged into the back room, and tossed into a corner, where he landed brokenly, beneath the map of Greenland. Between them Billy and Zak tied Ray's hands and feet with cord, but left his mouth free, to do some talking, no doubt to try to talk his way out of it.

"Come on, Ray," said Zak, "we've worked out most of the story. Fill us in on the fine print."

"I can do that," Ray said. He showed a fine, glib pride as he started to explain. "This tattooing thing, it's always been an interest of mine. I'd been doing it for years in an amateurish way, you know, just a leisure-time activity, cheap thrills, if I could find a more or less willing girl who'd let me work on her. I'm not saying I was any good. I knew I wasn't. And I always had trouble knowing what design to use, but it was no big deal. I had no ambitions.

"And of course I knew Wrobleski—we go back a long way— and I knew what he did, and once in a while he did it for me. When you're in real estate, there's always somebody who needs killing. And in the beginning I thought I was better off not knowing the details, but then along comes Akim, who's got one or two grievances against Wrobleski, and he wants to share, to give me all the chapter and verse about what his boss does. He gets quite a kick out of describing it. You know, I'm not the only sick puppy in this story.

"And then, right, I have my brilliant idea. I like tattoos, I like maps, I especially like coded maps: I've found my subject. Akim describes events and I illustrate them, by putting a lousy tattooed map on the back of some random girl I pull in off the street, though okay, not so random in your case, Marilyn darling. Akim helped sometimes. Akim likes to watch. And that's all it was, no big deal, no different from a couple of guys going out, having a beer, shooting some pool.

"And then I start having problems with Wrobleski. I ask him to do a simple job. And he won't. I don't like it when people say no to me. It's the principle of the thing. I want to fuck with him. And I suppose I could have threatened to give an 'anonymous tip-off' to the cops, but I didn't need to do that, did I? All I had to do was make sure Wrobleski knew the tattoos existed. And as fate would have it, my little sick friend Akim had been keeping an eye on the women. He knew where they were, knew where to find them again."

Ray McKinley was not entirely surprised when Billy Moore kicked him a couple of times, once in each kidney.

"How did Wrobleski even find out?" Zak asked.

"Our Mr. Wrobleski had an occasional taste for prostitutes. Akim made the arrangements. Akim and I made sure he got a girl with a map of one of the murders on her back; I think her name was Laurel. He looked: he saw the map. Okay, it was a shitty map, and it was coded. But Wrobleski could decode it better than anybody else on earth. He could read the signs because he already knew what they meant. He realized that somebody knew his business, but he didn't know who or how or why. And that bothered him. I liked it that way."

"And how was this supposed to end?" said Zak.

"Wrobleski was supposed to kill the fucking mayor. If he'd done that in the beginning, we wouldn't be having this conversation."

Billy Moore kicked Ray again, in the stomach, just to keep up his own morale. Ray McKinley seemed to be coughing up blood.

"So now you know," said Ray thickly. "You can all sleep easier now. And where do we go from here? You want to call a cop? No. Why would you? Wrobleski's gone. Akim's gone. Old man Driscoll ain't coming back. You don't want a court case with a missing murderer and no bodies, do you? The real question is, and this is always the *real* question: what exactly *do* you want?"

It was not a question any of them had expected Ray to ask. They had expected denials, threats, perhaps pleading, but not this.

"I'm not unreasonable," Ray said. "You know that, Zak. You want me to set you up in your own little shop, 'Zak Webster: Map Seller to the Gentry'? Tell me what the price is. Tell me what these other two clowns want." He turned to Billy: "Property, cars, drugs?"; and then to Marilyn: "Tattoo removal?"

"We want you to take a little trip," said Marilyn. "Downstairs into the basement. We've got some women who are dying to meet you face-to-face."

Ray McKinley started to say something, but Billy Moore grabbed him by the scruff of the neck, pulled him to his feet, and dragged him across to the other side of the room, tearing open the pale lime-green linen of his jacket in the process. Zak had opened the door that led to the basement, to another, different kind of underworld. Ray looked down the flight of steps, but could see only darkness at the bottom. Then he heard women's voices, though he couldn't make out any words. He could also hear a mechanical noise, an intermittent drone, a buzzing, the sound of a tattoo machine being brought to life.

"So much can go wrong when amateurs start tattooing," said Marilyn. "They get carried away, scrawl obscenities all over your body, or your face, or your dick. And you know, a lot of beginners don't care much about hygiene. There's a lot of risk: blood poisoning, tetanus, hepatitis, toxic shock. You can imagine. But you won't have to imagine."

Billy Moore picked Ray up for the last time, one hand on his collar, one on his waistband, the weight evenly distributed, then tossed him forward, hard and fast, through the doorway, so he would have no chance of gaining a foothold as gravity pulled him down the steep decline of stairs. His legs and arms flailed, he grunted some indecipherable words, and then there was the sound of him hitting the bottom like a sack of root vegetables. A low, pale light flicked on, revealing female silhouettes, circling, homing in.

Zak closed the door to the basement. Then he closed and locked the store. He and Marilyn and Billy walked away. He felt no guilt. It was already well past closing time.